STRANGELY FUNNY II

Edited By
Sarah E. Glenn

Mystery and Horror, LLC
Tarpon Springs, FL

STRANGELY FUNNY II
Edited by Sarah E. Glenn
Copyright © 2014 by Mystery and Horror, LLC
Published by Mystery and Horror, LLC

All stories in this anthology have been printed with
the permission of the authors.

"Dirty Dybbuk", by Anna Taborska, first appeared in *For Those
Who Dream Monsters* (2013), pub. Mortbury Press

This is a work of fiction. Any resemblance to any actual person
living or dead, or to any known location is the coincidental invention
of the author's creative mind. This includes historical events and
persons who may have been recreated in a fictional work.

ISBN-13: 978-0-9915825-0-1
(Mystery and Horror, LLC)
ISBN-10: 0991582500

Library of Congress Control Number: 2014945039

Printed in USA by Mystery and Horror, LLC
(www.mysteryandhorrorllc.com)

STRANGELY FUNNY II

Edited By
Sarah E. Glenn

Mystery and Horror, LLC
Tarpon Springs, FL

TABLE OF CONTENTS

TABLE OF CONTENTS CONTINUED

ACKNOWLEDGEMENT

We would like to thank David Goudsward for his invaluable research into the plural version of Bigfoot.

GOLDY LUKE AND THE THREE GATORS

By David Bernard

Once upon a time, we found out the world had ended. And like electricity, telephones and county water, Sanders Grove was completely overlooked again. Joe Quinoa, who ran his airboat up to Lockhaven every month for the mail and supplies (mostly of the 90 proof variety), came back with the news that Lockhaven was nothing but empty ruins and zombies in tacky tourist shirts. From what Joe could figure out from the last few issues of the Miami Herald blowing around the streets, a giant meteorite had hit the Pacific Ocean and caused a tidal wave that wiped out most of California. That was bad. What made it really bad was when all the drowned Californians started getting up and eating the survivors. Apparently there was something in the meteor – spores or radiation or something. Joe didn't cotton much to all that scientific mumbo jumbo. The zombies followed the refugees east, and that was the end of civilization. Luckily, Sanders Grove is a godforsaken speck of dry land out in the Everglades; like most things, we completely missed it. However, since we are talking about the end of the world, folks couldn't get too upset about missing that particular party. Of course, zombie apocalypse or not, Joe did manage to load up his airboat with as much inventory of the Lockhaven Package Store as he could carry. He explained that it wasn't like the zombies would be looking for a cold brew and a good cigar.

All things considered, life went on pretty much same as

usual in Sanders Grove. Joe Quinoa made a trip back to Lockhaven and brought back most of the remaining inventory of the Package Store, enough ammo to start a small war, and a couple of books from the Lockhaven Branch of the Broward County Library System on home brewing (Joe had his priorities).

As time passed, the walking dead did occasionally wander into town, mostly by sheer dumb luck since the local alligators never had been real particular about whether lunch was fresh. After a while, it almost seemed like the gators developed a taste for easy-to-catch zombie. This was good news for Sanders Grove, since we only had the supply of ammo that Joe had brought back from Lockhaven and wasting it on shooting something we couldn't eat just seemed wrong. And the library apparently didn't have any books on making your own bullets.

So to save ammo, we just fenced in a section of swamp on the west side of town and trapped a few gators in it like a pen. After that, we just rounded up the walking dead when they staggered into town and let the gators handle the problem. Alligators are faster than zombies, so they rarely lose the battle and it's not like we don't have plenty of replacement gators available. Once the well-fed gators get too big to manage, we slaughter them and replace them with fresh ones. We cure the meat and tan the skin. We may be the last folks on earth, but we all have genuine gator-skin boots.

Joe Quinoa made another trip to Lockhaven, but never came back. He wanted to get some gas for the airboat and maybe find a portable radio to see if there were any other breathing people out there. More than likely, he also tried to make one last trip to the Package Store too, and found out three times was not a charm. We expect he'll show up sooner or later, but by then, he'll just be walking gator chow. We will miss that airboat though.

Down on the south side of Sanders Grove was a crazy old hermit named Lucas, who lived in a two-room shack down by the big cypress grove. His real name was Lucas McKenny, but we already had a Lucas Smith, a Luke Espallo, a Lukey MacDougall and a Luke-Mack Winnemack (Lucas was a very popular name in the 70s in Florida Cracker circles). We already had too many Lukes and since he was crazy, we felt obligated to give him a mildly spiteful nickname. The old hermit was convinced there was gold in the Everglades and he had spent years trying to figure out to get gold out of the swamp bottom. He kept up coming up with these crackpot schemes that were crazy, even by crazy people standards. So, we started calling him Goldy Luke, which got shortened over the years to Goldy.

After an unfortunate incident involving a lightning rod, the coil from a 1925 Studebaker, and an electrical cable feeding power into the water to attract the gold, we briefly discussed calling him Smokey instead. But Studebaker parts were hard to find, so Goldy learned his lesson. As his eyebrows grew back, he convinced himself that cypress trees were the answer. They had the roots obviously designed to filter out the gold and collect it at their bases. All he had to do was get the cypress grove to cooperate. He talked to the trees. He bribed them with fertilizer. He threatened them with an axe. He crossbred cypress stock. Eventually, crazy or not, Goldy finally started to get the impression the trees were just not going to help him get rich. So he switched to catfish, and started trying to train them like hunting dogs. But either catfish don't take well to training, or they couldn't smell gold. Plus, Goldy was crazy, which probably didn't help. After Armageddon, watching Goldy quickly became more entertaining than watching gators eat zombies.

With no luck with gold extraction plans to date, Goldy got to thinking about his failures (apparently the fact there's no gold in the Everglades was not a consideration). He came to the brilliant conclusion that the gators must know about the gold and they were there to protect it, by messing with the cypress tree roots and eating the catfish. He decided that the

—

3

gators must have some sort of gold magnet in their brains that worked the same way the birds had something in their brains that let them follow the earth's magnetic field. (I believe crazy has been mentioned).

So, Goldy set out to trapping some gators to dissect their brains. To create a fair cross sample of brains, he shot a baby gator, a momma gator and a big old bull gator. Technically, I suppose it was poaching, but the only game warden we had seen lately was more interested in ripping your skull open and eating your brains than stopping out-of-season hunting.

Not having a laboratory in his shack, Goldy butchered them on the porch, cut out the brains and put them in soup bowls on his kitchen table. Then he went out to collect kindling so he could fire up his oven and dry out the brains. It wasn't exactly a high point in the history of science, but then again, I suspect there aren't a lot of PhDs still alive to critique Goldy's scientific method.

While he was out collecting dry kindling (not the easiest thing in a swamp), a zombie apparently got wind of all the gator blood on the porch and brains sitting out on the table. Zombies have a keen sense of smell, at least until their nose falls off. When ol' Goldy got back, his door was smashed in and the room was in shambles. He knew it had to be a zombie because the heat tends to make zombies decompose fast, and based on the bits of blue meat everywhere, this dead guy must have been a particularly ripe specimen.

Goldy looked at the table and sure enough, some damned zombie had been into his fresh gator brain experiment. The big male's brain was barely touched. Based on the shattered teeth stuck in the medulla oblongata, the dead guy must have found it too tough to chew. The momma gator's bowl was covered with streaks of gore, meaning the skin on the zombie's hands was rotting off and he couldn't get a grip on the smooth bowl. But he got to that baby gator's brain just fine and ate it all up. Goldy had a temper and he was starting to simmer.

—

4

He looked around the room and found his big old beanbag couch had been ripped up. So had the old rocking chair he inherited from his mother. But the worst damage was the old high chair that his kids had sat in so many years ago. Apparently it still smelled of baby after all that time, because the chair was gnawed up pretty bad. That was the final straw. Goldy was a sixth generation cracker, and crackers are not noted for their even disposition. He was fit to be tied. He grabbed his rifle and was ready to charge out into the swamps and kill the first brain-stealing, house-wrecking piece of dead meat he found.

Then he noticed the door to his bedroom was open. Goldy always kept that door closed - he learned that the hard way during a very brief attempt to train possums to search for gold. He quietly crept in and sure enough, there was the zombie, lying on the bed. It wasn't sleeping; apparently it tripped on the rug, fell on the bed and just forgot to get back up. Goldy pointed his rifle and blew that zombie clean back to hell with one shot.

Of course, it took him three full days to clean up the mess, but as he did, he noticed something. The zombie was full of bits and pieces of metal. Gold teeth, brass buttons, rings, earrings, zippers, buckles – if someone was wearing metal when they were eaten, the valuables got eaten too. And suddenly ol' Goldy wasn't quite as pissed off at that old zombie any more.

Goldy may have been crazy, but he wasn't stupid (although the lightning rod incident still makes that statement debatable). He went out and set up a snare trap, looking for another zombie. Sure enough, a few days later, he had a fresh one dangling from a tree. Goldy took his hunting knife and filleted the dead guy, which annoyed the zombie to no end, but of course, didn't kill him. He cut out the stomach and sure enough, there was an antique wedding ring that, once the finger was removed, looked expensive. You could hear the crazy laughing cry of triumph all the way through town, with the emphasis on the crazy part.

Next thing we know, Goldy is skulking around the edges of town with a lasso and his hunting knife. This was more than the townsfolk were willing to tolerate. It wasn't the skulking; it was Goldy's enthusiasm. Although he was doing great work trapping zombies, more than once, he came close to filleting some of the live residents. You have not heard cussing until you've heard a swamp rat hanging upside down while a crazy neighbor tries to gut him. Of course, Goldy was cussing right back him for pretending to be a zombie and wasting his time. It was entertaining, but sooner or later, Goldy was going be too fast and we couldn't afford to lose anybody, especially since we didn't know if there were anyone else was still out there.

So, a few of us sat Goldy down and we had a nice long talk about personal boundaries, good civic behavior and not cutting up non-zombified folks. We came to an agreement that made Goldy happy and made the town happy, especially Lukey MacDougall, who Goldy had already snared three times. Although in all fairness to Goldy, Lukey MacDougall does have a really bad complexion and does kind of shamble when he walks.

Nowadays, when a zombie comes wandering into Sanders Grove, we ring a big bell and Goldy comes running. He's accumulated a barrelful of slightly chewed gold jewelry. Of course, there's no use for all that gold, since there are no banks or commerce, but it keeps the zombies off the streets without wasting bullets. And if it makes the old guy happy to wrangle zombies, gut them and remove the stomachs before feeding them to the gators, who am I to say otherwise? After all he's crazy, and if there's one sure thing in this world (or what's left of it), it's that the townsfolk of Sanders Grove never argue with crazy. After all, it took the end of the world to accomplish it, but Goldy had finally figured out how to get gold out of the Everglades.

David Bernard is the pen name of Dave Goudsward, a native New Englander who now lives (albeit under protest) in South Florida, a paradoxical place where, when temperatures drops below 60°, locals break out parkas to wear over their shorts and sandals. His most recent works include short stories in anthologies such as Once upon an Apocalypse *and* Mortis Operandi. *His next book is* A Horror Guide to Massachusetts *from Post Mortem Press. This is his second appearance in the* Strangely Funny *series, proving you can fool some of the editors all of the time.*

—

BEDROOM BUREAU

By Gwendolyn Kiste

In the midst of a search and rescue mission to locate wayward laundry, I noticed my six-foot bureau skip off the floor. It landed back in place on the flaking tile and then soared into the air again. I waited. Nothing else moved.

Setting the basket of unpaired socks and strawberry-stained blue jeans on the bed, I crept toward the pseudo-sentient furnishing as it jumped for a third time.

My eyes scanned its close-to-rusted hinges and weathered corners but found nothing noteworthy on the outside. With a single movement, I heaved open the doors. Sulfurous smoke poured from the shelves. I coughed, protecting my mouth with one hand while waving the other to disperse the billows of black.

An enormous figure, all grey and translucent, burst toward me. The creature filled more than half my master bedroom, and its screams sent the entire house wobbling in trepidation.

"You, girl, will do my bidding!" The behemoth extended a handful of butcher knife fingers. "You will do as I instruct or the storms of hell will arrive at your threshold!"

I slammed the bureau shut and marched downstairs in protest.

"I told you before, Chelzebub. If you want me to sign off on your passport, bullying isn't the way to do it." I shook my head. "Cheap smoke and mirrors. Perfectly shameful. I hope you can hear me! Makes your whole kind look bad."

I was still battling annoyance when I heard the patter at the front door. At first, I mistook it for another of Chelzebub's tricks, but the knock transformed into a full throttle, demanding a response. I trudged out of the kitchen, sad to abandon my plate of fresh pie.

On the porch, a man in an ill-fitting suit stood as tall as he could rally.

"What wonderful timing," I said and bid him inside. "I just took a pie out of the oven. Used apples from my own trees out back. Would you like a slice?" I smiled until my face ached. Although I baked daily, I never got to share my confections, at least not with humans, so the prospect excited me.

"Ma'am, my name is Horatio Miller. I'm here with Advocate Gas and Drilling. We need to discuss my company's future development plans."

"Sure, but will your immediate plans involve pie?" It seemed rude of him not to answer my initial question before launching into his formal business.

"I apologize, but no," he said without inflection. "I'm on a diet. Need to lose these last ten pounds."

I shrugged and returned to my fork.

"Do you own this property?" He removed a thick manila folder from a well-oiled briefcase and placed it next to me on the kitchen table.

"Of course." Concerned his rigmarole might ruin my appetite, I flicked the documents away, careful to use only quick strokes and the tips of my fingers.

"Really? You seem a bit young." The way he struck the last word made me think he meant immature instead.

My gaze remained fixated on the paperwork mussing up the hand-me-down table. "I inherited the place from my parents. They passed away a few years ago." I sighed. "Demonic tragedy."

He hesitated, suspending another folder midair. "Do you

10

mean like a possession?"

"Heavens, no!" I giggled. "Not a possession. A demon picnic. Everyone was real sorry it happened too. Turns out demons play this game called 'Escape the Angry Mob'. My mom and dad lost."

The second folder assumed a position so close it touched my plate. "Demon picnic? Is that slang?"

I tilted my head. "I don't think so."

With his documents flanking my pie on all sides, he examined me with an apologetic look. "They told me this would be a difficult process for you, seeing that you make your livelihood here."

"Your company knows about my livelihood?"

"The orchard," he said and pointed through the wall. "The sign's right out front."

"Oh, no. The orchard's how I make money. It's not my livelihood."

"Good. Hopefully you'll be more amenable to our proposal."

He explained that the gas company had deemed my property ideal for their latest pipeline project. Now all they needed to bring the scheme to fruition was a bulldozer. No more trees. No more house. No more bureau. And in his bloated pomposity, he seemed more concerned with me signing in six places than listening to any counterarguments. So I refused to sign anywhere. And even if he wanted it now, I wouldn't have given him any apple pie. Not even a crumb.

"If I'd known you were coming," I said, though he didn't listen, "I might have included a certain almond flavor." That was a bluff. I didn't have any cyanide. But a couple of street savvy demons could remedy that void anytime.

"I don't think you understand," he kept repeating. "They have right of way. They'll do it anyways."

The last morsel of caramelized perfection vanished from my beige saucer. "Then they'll spend the rest of their lives regretting it."

Horatio slammed his fruitless pen onto the lacy placemat. "Are you threatening me?"

"No, of course not," I said. "I'm not threatening you. But the demon dimension won't be happy about rerouting their transportation system. They'll probably threaten you. And most people don't like demonic forms of intimidation." I drew up my nose. "Nasty business."

"I see." Horatio squinted at me and began to collect the documents he'd worked so hard to arrange just moments prior. "In that case, we'll have to talk to my boss's boss. He's the one who handles these unique cases."

He didn't believe me. He was going to return to his supervisors, and together, they'd concoct some hare-brained plan to steal my land from me, claiming I was crazy or some other nonsense. I'd simply have to offer him hard evidence to convince the gas company to leave me and my demons alone.

"Before you go--"

He turned from his briefcase antics.

"I need your help moving something."

"What?"

"A bureau."

He scowled.

"I won't bite. They might. But I won't."

In my bedroom, I motioned to the wooden giant.

"There's a heavy suitcase in there you'll need to remove first." I leaned against the doorframe, knowing I'd get the best view of the show from there.

He watched me, eyes cast over his shoulder, but advanced toward the bureau nonetheless. As he readied himself to move the cumbersome creation, an infinitesimal streak of smoke flitted out of the mahogany doors, so thin and languid it looked like nothing but the aftermath of my earlier encounter. I worried for a moment that Chelzebub might have evacuated the area.

So like that trickster demon, I thought. Not being around when I need him.

But my concerns proved unfounded as Mr. Horatio Miller unfastened the bureau and out popped Chelzebub in all his otherworldly grandeur. Not settling for his usual phoned-in frolics, the banshee even evoked his patented light show, the one so admiringly dreadful it was registered with the demon copyright office. I tasted brimstone for the next hour.

As ethereal gatekeepers, my family long ago promised never to advertise our job titles. But when I had no other option, I sure had fun watching mere mortals panic in the face of demons. As the bureaucrat cowered in the nearest corner, I detected new lines etch into his brow and fresh gray hairs sprout atop his head. My hand fluttered across my lips to assuage a laugh.

"Such a small world they live in," my mother used to say.

While Horatio recoiled, I decided to use his silence to issue a didactic lesson.

"As you can see, if you flatten my house for whatever asinine project you people have invented, demons like Chelzebub will have to spirit themselves into our realm some other way. They can't use their passports if there's no agent to validate them."

Horatio wasn't listening. He was too busy quivering.

I scoffed. "No reason to be so scared. That just gives Chelzebub more to feed off. Our fear's like petrified spinach to them."

After another minute or so of pointless lecture, I retreated to the first floor and cleaned the kitchen of white flour and apple peels. At around four in the afternoon, a couple more men came to the door inquiring about the whereabouts of Mr. Miller.

"He's in my bedroom," I said. After they expressed phony shock, I added with a glower, "It's not like that."

We trekked upstairs where Horatio the Brave hadn't moved from his position in the corner or stopped with the trembles.

The other men rushed to him. "What's wrong? What happened?"

I wasn't sure if they were asking me or their hapless coworker, but I decided to answer anyhow. "He looked in the bureau there and freaked out. Been like this ever since."

"Well," they said, "what's in there?"

I went over and opened it. It was just a bureau again.

"Nothing," I said, a little disappointed I'd see no encore. But Chelzebub probably gorged on all the human fear he could muster for one day and headed home to nap. That much terror is like tryptophan on Thanksgiving for the demon set.

"The devil. It was the devil. It was hell." Horatio clung to the men's collars and thrust a finger toward me. "She saw it."

I struck my tongue to the palate. "I've never seen any hell dimension in my life." I hate when people use demons and devils interchangeably. It's the epitome of paranormal ignorance.

They gathered their friend to his feet and dragged him out the door.

"Are you sure you can't stay for pie? I baked it fresh today."

But nobody seemed interested. Apples were out of season, after all.

Tuesdays proved my busiest days. I don't know what it was about that portion of the week in the demon realm, but something special must have designated it an ideal time to emigrate. Maybe there were mandatory floggings.

The Tuesday after my meeting with Horatio, I scheduled an interview with a delightful family of imps.

"So what business do you have on Earth?" I donned my interviewer hat. It was one of those 1960s stewardess types, but with a little Mad Hatter-esque note that read, "Official Demon Immigration Agent" pinned to the front. Demons took the passport process a bit more seriously if I looked dignified. Granted, some might still try to harangue me, but I'd point to the sign on the hat, and they'd stop.

Zebily, the patriarch or at least the one that pretended to be patriarch — gender distinction is a purely earthbound paradigm — spoke first. "My partner and I want to start a new life. We've heard there are millions of people to frighten here."

"That's the kind of place we want to raise our children," his spouse Sallifay overlapped, leaning forward in her chair, but almost toppling forward with the momentum of her engorged tummy. Pregnant demons sort of resemble full-bellied ticks, and I always bet if you put one on its back, it wouldn't be able to stand up again. I never tried it of course. That would be an abuse of power.

Their firstborn stood next to the bureau, pulling at her pigtails and gnawing her bottom lip. Her parents had dressed their progeny in the best human clothes demon money could buy, right down to the polished saddle shoes.

I turned through their crisp bundle of paperwork, all inscribed with small block letters. Proper penmanship announced the demons most eager to gain admittance to the human world. The accomplishment was especially impressive considering English wasn't the native language of any demon species. I once heard French was though, so I'd sometimes greet demons with a hearty 'Bonjour'. They never looked impressed.

I inhaled and then recited my spiel. "You understand if any humans are scared to death, your passports and that of your current and yet-to-be-born children will be revoked. No member of a humancidal family is permitted to stay." Imitating my best stern expression, I glanced at them to ensure they understood.

"Of course," said Sallifay. "We're more nightmare demons than anything."

"That can occasionally induce death, so keep it in mind," I said and removed my regulatory stamp from its metal container.

———

As I authorized the first passport, I reveled in the tiny streams of smoke emanating from the inky seal. Though it couldn't compare to Chelzebub's displays, it was my favorite part of the process. I used to watch my mother conduct interviews just so I could see the validation stamp perform its magic. Way more ceremonious than my hat.

But before I reached for the second passport, the doorbell rang and spoiled the moment. People should act with enough politeness not to interrupt such an important occasion in a demon family's life.

I set the stamp on my makeshift immigration desk. "Give me a moment."

It was another one of those drilling representatives.

"Yes?" I stared at him, feigning ignorance as to who he was or what he wanted.

"Hello, ma'am. I'm here from Advocate Gas and Drilling."

"Are you an advocate?"

He stammered out something resembling a no but pretending to be a yes.

"What do you need?" I asked. "I'm in the middle of an interview."

"I'm sorry. Should I come back later?" A frown squashed into his face, he appeared unconvinced by my hat but kept reading and rereading its sign anyhow.

"No, don't come back either." I hesitated. "How about you come upstairs instead and sit in on my interview? Then you'll see why your people can't raze my home."

"Is this another agent?" Sallifay nodded in misplaced reverence as I introduced the man with the sewn-in Jack nametag.

"No," I said. "He and his company want to demolish my house."

Zebily growled, the demonic equivalent to a gasp, which set the company advocate back several steps. "What will happen to the immigration station?"

I shrugged. "I don't know. And they don't care."

We glared in unison at this so-called Jack who, for his part, inspected each of us with deliberate confusion. Other than their red-tinged eyes, the three-and-a-half demons resembled any typical nuclear family. That is, until the little girl clenched both fists, opened her mouth, and flicked a seven-foot tongue at the invader. Two high-pitched screams accompanied the motion, one wraithlike and one childish. Either could have belonged to the pintsize demon but only one did.

Jack flailed a path along the hallway and down the stairs. I listened for the door. He slammed it behind him. Good thing or I would have had to return to the first floor and close it. I couldn't risk a stranger waltzing into my abode. There are maniacs out there.

My shoulders drooped. "And I didn't even get a chance to offer him a slice of blueberry cobbler."

"That was a delightful scare, young lady." Zebily patted his daughter's head. "Plus, it should keep you satisfied until dinnertime."

"Even the baby got a good snack." Sallifay placed a hand on her stomach and then turned toward me. "That wasn't against the rules, was it? Dining before we're officially admitted?"

"No." I smiled at the pigtailed beast who scowled and smacked her lips but otherwise resumed her little girl façade. "I think she's adorable."

My stamp performed the rest of its work, happily smoking away, and I handed the validated passports to Zebily and Sallifay.

"Would either of you like a plate of cobbler before you go? I promise it's the best you'll find in the human empire."

"Oh, no," said the husband. "We're stuffed."

Tuesdays were apparently flog-heavy at Advocate Gas and Drilling too because the very next week at the same time,

—

a third representative knocked on my door.

"Hello, Ms. Gardner?" He was the youngest of three, right around my age.

"Come on in." Fortunately, I'd finished with my interviews for the day or else the rep would have faced off with Illanis, the pain demon who received a permit that morning to start an S & M club in Pittsburgh. I just can't say no to plucky entrepreneurs.

He followed me into the living room where we stood without speaking for several minutes. I refused to be the one to initiate conversation. I hadn't invaded someone's house in an effort to destroy the demon equivalent of the Chunnel. This would-be evildoer could open the dialogue.

When I showed no signs of breaking, he fumbled to locate a clipboard in his bag and pointed at the first thing he saw on it. "It seems other representatives have been here, but I can't find any discernible paperwork about their visits."

"But you found indiscernible paperwork?" I grinned and imagined the last two envoys scrawling across official forms with finger paints and crayons.

"That's classified internal information." Judging from his labored sigh and deflated posture, I guessed I was close to right.

"Did they use Crayola or an off-brand?"

"What?" He stared at me, and I noticed he too had a permanent nametag. Robert.

Poor Robert, I thought. You'll soon join those wacky coworkers.

"Would you like some peach pie?" It was the least I could offer before he descended into madness. "And if you were wondering, it's almond-free. I just had a slice myself."

"Thanks but I'm not hungry." With a slight scowl, he added, "And I don't have a nut allergy or anything."

"Everyone's allergic to the flavor I'm talking about." I started upstairs. "But if you change your mind, I promise the pie's nontoxic. I thought after the previous two debacles, your people would surrender, so I didn't plan anything subversive."

"I guess that's good?" He sounded plagued with confusion already, and the feature presentation had yet to commence. "Where are we going?"

"To show you why you can't tear down my house."

With rote resignation, I trudged to the bureau and flipped it open. As usual, Chelzebub waited there, loaded with empty threats.

"Filthy mortals!" The declaration shook my jewelry box from a nearby nightstand.

"Silly beast," I muttered and scooped my trinkets from the floor as Robert gawked at the scene.

The demon ignored the newcomer and focused his ire at me. "You, girl, will sign my passport! I command it!"

I rolled my eyes. "I've told you before, Chelzebub. Schedule an appointment. Anytime Monday through Friday, normal business hours apply."

Mouth agape, Robert moved closer to the bureau and waved his hand at Chelzebub, striking the demon square on the nose. I threw my head back and chortled. Chelzebub tossed fireballs at us, but only the sort that disintegrate before they burn the skin. The wraith couldn't risk losing all human dimensional privileges over a minor slight.

"That's no illusion!" Robert charged toward the opposite wall. "That's real!"

"Of course it's real." I sneered, shocked someone would accuse me of common charlatan gags. "I don't know anything about special effects and whatnot. Though Chelzebub here is a whiz at it."

"Oh, I wouldn't say a whiz." Despite his ashen pallor, I could discern a decisive blush bloom across Chelzebub's cheeks. I think those were cheeks. Demon anatomy is an ever-changing puzzle.

"Don't be modest," I said to Chelzebub and patted what I was certain was his crown. "You're a demon for the ages."

—

"How'd... how'd it get in there?" Robert swung from side to side and examined every crevice of the bureau but maintained a respectable distance as Chelzebub derided him with flames.

"Convenience," I said. "Could have been a broom closet or a hamper. The demon transportation system prefers something with large doors. Otherwise, the likes of Chelzebub might get stuck."

The demon snuffed in agreement.

Robert melded into the paneling. "So it's supernatural?"

"Not the bureau. It's a regular old thing. I even store some extra blankets in there." I reached toward a drawer. "Excuse me, Chelzebub."

The demon shifted to one side as I removed an old comforter and handed it to Robert. He turned it over and over again, stunned at its existence as much as the misanthropic monstrosity still leering over us.

"They don't usually touch my stuff," I said. "But given the sulfur situation, I'm careful about what I keep in there. And no clothes. You can never get the smell of demon dimension out of casual wear. Believe me, I've tried."

Robert kept staring at the blanket, possessed by its high thread content. I decided to leave Chelzebub to his meal.

As I wiped the kitchen counter, I thought about calling Advocate Gas and Drilling and asking them to peel another administrator off my bedroom floor. But before I could locate the phone number, Robert plodded into the kitchen.

"I can get you a historical exemption," he said. "Like what they do for places of significance. Battlefields and those establishments with the 'George Washington Slept Here' markers." A moment of meditation. "Though I doubt Washington hung around with demons, so we might need to doctor some of the sections."

"Chelzebub told me he once scared Thomas Jefferson almost to death, so who knows?" I rinsed a crust-covered bowl with hot water. "Maybe Washington was in on the gag."

"In any event, I should be able to manage," Robert said, his voice struggling to find an even cadence. "You can keep your house and your… bureau."

"Great!" I chirped. "Do you have some paperwork I need to fill out for that? I understand these things always have lots of paperwork."

"Yes, paperwork," he said, diverting his gaze to me. "But first, I was wondering if I could have some of that peach pie you mentioned."

I smiled and cut him a more than charitable slice.

With parents who married on Halloween and read her Bradbury stories long before she started kindergarten, Gwendolyn Kiste considers horror, fantasy, and all things strange to be her birthright. Her genre editorials appear regularly on sites such as Horror-Movies.ca *and* Micro-Shock, *and she is the resident "weird wanderer" for the travel-centric* Wanderlust and Lipstick. *With a background in cinema and theatre, she has written and directed several feature-length and short horror films, and her plays have been produced as part of the Big Read, a program of the National Endowment for the Arts. An Ohio native, she currently resides in the wilds of Pennsylvania with her husband, Bill, and cat, McQueen.*

CARYARD JACK

By Omar J. Sakr

On the 30th of November, 2012, I woke up.

I know, hardly the most dramatic opening ever. Aside from the fact I'd been asleep for the better part of 1200 years, give or take a month or so. "Asleep" or "totally dead", I mean, the terms are basically interchangeable when you're a necromantic sorcerer.

"What the fuck is necromantic?" I hear you say, "Are you really quibbling on this? You either are or you aren't."

It's a valid point. All I mean is, I'm not only a necromancer, you know? I have other skills, other powers. People like to pigeon-hole you, they like to say, you're this or you're that - it's like being more than one thing blows their tiny little minds. You can't even imagine what happens when I tell them I'm a half-caste bisexual, too.

Brains, man. Splattered everywhere. Granted, that's often because their next moronic comment sends me into an apoplectic rage, but still, you get my point. So anyway, back to what I was saying: I woke up.

Why did you wake up then, how, who killed you the first time, what was being dead like?

Whoa, whoa, slow down. Your questions are numerous and boring. See, I know what you're thinking. You're thinking, I bet some dumb young kids read about your various legendary exploits, your battle with the Warlock King Nilroshi, that time you head-butted the Devil, or lost a bet with Odin, or any of the wars and tragedies that cloak your

---

past, and decided it would be fun, heck just a lark, to resurrect you on Samhain's Eve.

Well, you'd be wrong. Know how I know? Because that's what I thought. Hell, I'd been thinking that since I died. But no, turns out it was a total accident - besides which, they missed Samhain by a good month. As it happens, there I was, little more than a speck of consciousness in a hole full of dust and bits of bone, when some punk kid had the temerity to die above my grave. His soul rushed screaming down my metaphorical throat and I woke, gagging on his panic. Which sounds awful, but actually, was the best feeling ever: the sweet rush of power, the tingling sensation of life returning, of bone and blood and muscle blooming. Which sounds poetic but actually hurt like a motherfucker. For a time, I was agony incarnate.

An eternity later, I crawled up out of the ground and into the 21st Century.

I prodded the dead boy with a foot; most of his head was gone, simply torn away somehow. I examined the remains carefully, neither afraid nor disgusted – it was just a husk now. I'd consumed his soul in its entirety, poor thing - unthinking, unknowing at that point. I'd existed as nothing but need, a desperate thirst. Now, he was useless to me, even as I sat here on this hill and chatted idly with his corpse. It was the only thing that seemed normal, the only way I could deal with the torrent of information I'd scanned from his still-cooling flesh. It was mostly garbled nonsense, but the images, they needed no translation. And they terrified me.

Here's the thing about the 21st Century: there are So. Many. Fucking. People. I never would have imagined there could be so many - how are they all fed and clothed? That is a magic beyond my ken, truly. I never could have imagined it because I assumed you'd all be dead by now, or well and truly conquered by demons or Hell-spawn or someone with my skill-set who is far more proactive and ambitious.

And yet, you have thrived, you poor dumb beasts. To be honest, as admirable as that is, it's frankly incredibly depressing. What happened to all the God-Kings? What happened to Mount Olympus? To the sundry gods and demons and sorcerers? Hell, even the milquetoast humans back then had ambition enough to match us, to want to conquer the planet and make it their own. Meanwhile, my kind are dead and gone, and you addle-minded children sit in front of your flickering boxes and do what? Nothing.

Something wet and warm tickled my desiccated toes and I looked down to see the boy's blood gleaming wickedly. It began to sink into my bones, and I sighed with pleasure. I put my hand on the boy's shoulder - Joey was his name - and sent a gentle request into the ether. Gentle because I had no power to speak of right now and because asking is always better than forcing. It might surprise you to hear from a sometime-necromancer but in my experience, the dead are usually willing to give what unthinking brutes will always try to steal. So much unpleasantness could be avoided if only people thought to ask.

While his soul was gone, Joey's body still retained a shadow of his consciousness, a thin memory that would soon fade. It acquiesced with barely a murmur of protest and just like that, his flesh melted off his body and began to flow over mine in a red wave. Sensation returned in a rush and I could feel wind against my skin once more, and the hardness of the dirt beneath me, and the light of the stars bathing down. It was absolutely fucking glorious: I was home again. Slowly, unsteadily, I rose from the ground, a living man once more, and cast my eye at what would soon be my kingdom.

As kingdoms went, it wasn't much.

"Fuck, what's it doing?" Gary said, his voice a hiss in the gathering gloom. He and Sam were crouched in some shrubbery at the foot of the hill. At the top, beneath a tree, a figure from nightmare leaned over their dead friend.

"I don't know, dude," Sam said. "I - I think it's talking to Joey."

"Shit." Sweat trickled down Gary's flushed cheeks. "Shit, shit, shit. I still can't believe you didn't check his body."

"Hey fuck you. You didn't just kill somebody. *I did.*" Sam's jaw was thrust out in challenge, but his watery eyes gave away his fear.

"So? You ran."

"Fuck yeah I ran. Still got his blood on my shirt, don't I?" That put a stopper in both their mouths. Crickets chirped, and wind whistled in the dark. Neither of them wanted to confront what was happening, or what they'd seen. It kept flashing behind Gary's eyes. The gunshot. Joey's bubbling breaths. The horrible half-crumbling skeleton seeping out of the tree's roots.

After a moment, Sam continued. "I didn't think he'd be dumb enough to have it on him, shit. And what the fuck is this thing anyway? What do we do now?"

"I – " The words died in Gary's mouth. The hill was empty, and night had fallen in swift silence.

"Do you know what a heartbeat sounds like to the recently dead?" a voice asked from behind them. They froze, and the overpowering stink of death wafted over them. The next words were an ugly whisper. "Like a fucking thunderstorm. And oh, how I do love a good, wet, storm."

They didn't even have time to scream.

"Sammy, Sammy, Sammy," I said, looking down at the bloody mess of bodies. "Am I saying that right? I'm speaking English now, I believe. Can't imagine what I must've sounded like to you just now, in the dark – that must've been scary as hell. Probably like a sword on a whetstone, yes? Or the screech of the Krakatow bird. Do you know them? No? Ah, well. Nasty little buggers."

Sam didn't reply; his gaping mess of a throat wouldn't let him. I tutted. "My dear, traitorous, deadly little boy, it's rude not to reply, don't you know? Do they teach you nothing in this misbegotten century? Wake!" Power thrummed through the word, and Sam gasped, and spasmed back to life.

I smiled. I was feeling much more myself now. "Your soul reeks," I said. "Did you know?"

He just stared at me. His eyes were as black as his friend's skin, and he blinked. Once, twice, his gaze heavy and dull.

"What," he said. "The fuck."

I nodded. "Indeed," I said. "An apt summation. You'll be feeling all sorts of things right now, I know. Confusion, fear, pain. Oh, so much pain. That's one of the great misconceptions about death, you know. That it stops hurting. On the contrary, you are free from all the distractions, all the physical sensations stopping you from fully immersing yourself in your soul's wounds." I sucked in a breath, enjoying the feel of words on my tongue once again, of my chest rising and falling. Rising and falling. Sam just looked on.

"So, I'll try and be quick here. Let's sum up: I woke from a 1200-year sleep when you and your idiot friend killed someone above my unmarked grave. I ate his soul, quite by accident, and then you two delightful little meat-sacks actually came back! So I killed you. And ate your friend Gary's soul, this time quite purposefully. Honestly, there wasn't much to it – it was a stringy, ugly little thing. Normally, I'd be above such mean fare but times are what they are, you know? All clear so far?"

Sam blinked, a red bubble forming on his lips.

"Great!" I said, and paused, overcome by dizziness for a moment. All the information I'd taken from Gary and Joey was taking some time to settle; I couldn't even be sure I wasn't slipping into any of a dozen languages right now. I looked to the enclosure behind us, the one lone building I could see for miles around. Clearly, the owner must be the ruler of this domain. Even his name was writ large for all to see, from earth or sky.

"Who is this Caryard Jack?" I said. "I must speak with him."

Sam's lips trembled, fat and red.

"Perhaps it's time to be a bit more direct," I muttered and placed my hand on his skull. His mind was a blue quagmire, a turgid swamp but I bore up with it.

- *Caryard Jack?* I demanded, saying it as one.

- *Car. Yard. Jack.*

Thoughts and ideas flowed instantaneously with Sam's mind voice. A quick history of automobiles flashed behind my eyes, and I saw the titular figure himself, a fat, balding man, as Sam had last seen him: tied up and gagged in the bathroom, his face red from screaming. I grunted.

- *Why did you kill your friend?* I asked.

- *Money.* Sam's voice was flat, ugly.

- Ah, so in this at least, nothing has changed. *Did you know this was my resting place?*

- *No.*

I couldn't help but feel a small flare of disappointment.

- *What of my kind?* I said. *What of magic? Do you know it?*

I'd expected an immediate no, but instead, he hesitated.

- *Speak, slave!*

I poured power into the command, and his body jerked beneath my hand, his eyes boiling in their sockets.

- *Joey! It was Joey, man! He was into the occult, into spooky shit. We thought he was fucked but... but it actually worked. He could do things.*

And so, the petty little tale played out. Joey proved to have a small talent for low-level magicks, parlour tricks to my like, but unbelievable to one from this dead age. And so, what did three wayward boys in a dead-end town do with this newfound power? Why, rob a bank, naturally. Steal from people. It wasn't long before Gary and Sam realised they'd be nowhere without Joey, began to fear his power. What would happen when it grew, they thought? He would leave them far behind, and take the money with him. So they ganged up on him, waited until he'd spent himself on one last steal, his meagre little energy supply tapped out – but he'd surprised them one last time and managed to get away.

He led them on a merry chase out into this desert, to this last pit stop outside the town, and here he died. I took my hand off Sam's skull, and chunks of melted flesh came off with it. "Ugh." I may have been a little too rough on him, it seemed. I wiped my hand clean on his shirt, feeling soiled from his pathetic little mind, though it had answered some pressing questions. No wonder Joey's soul had been able to revitalise me to such a degree – he was a practitioner, despite being a beginner.

It seemed he'd had some idea of where he was going too, I thought, else this would be too great a coincidence. Moving quickly, I fetched the weapon from his pants, a "gun" of some kind and slipped it into my new ill-fitting coat – Gary had kindly loaned his clothes to me, what with him being murdered and all – handling it gingerly, lest it go off somehow. It had fearsome power, this thing, for all its small size; Joey's torn skull was proof enough. That done, I stretched, stomach gurgling. *Hunger.*

"Great gods," I said. "But it's good to be alive." I turned and faced the sprawling enormity of the junkyard behind me, twisted heaps of metal piled high into the sky. Above it all towered the sign with miniature stars lit around it: Caryard Jack.

"Well, there's no time like the present," I said, still thrilled with the power of speech. And when you're as old as I am, you can get away with being a little crazy, I figured. "Let's go see what Jack's got to offer."

I left Sam there, with some tiny vestige of consciousness left, for when the crows came.

It turns out Caryard Jack had little to offer, having choked and died around the oily rag shoved in his mouth. Vomit encrusted it, and the little cubicle stank so much I didn't bother going near it. What more could he tell me? Nothing of value. Already, alien thoughts were racing around my skull. Ipods. MTV. WWF Wrestling, a pantomime not unlike the Greeks of old, which I could at least appreciate. Who doesn't love a bit of buff near-naked men thrashing around? However, that didn't seem to be what Gary had got out of it, at least not consciously.

This world, I thought, had grown smaller and uglier with every year. It seemed loving men was frowned upon, and unlike the Greeks, it was feared and repressed. Well, tough, I thought. These people have become as children – let them try to tell me who to love, let them see my answer. Hint: it involves death, and oh-so-much pain. As much as the notion amused me, however, I couldn't help feeling a little lost in this place. Nothing is as it was, and I... I am very much an aberration, a disturbance in the weave of reality. Already, I could feel it tugging at me, as though life itself saw me as a plague in its body, and was trying to rid itself of me.

I wandered around the front of the building, to the car the boys had arrived in. Using all the information I could understand from my mind-communication with Sam, I can tell you it was brown and square-shaped. I got in; the keys were, thankfully, still in the ignition. I started it, and the beast coughed into life, roaring. "Aha!" I said, slapping the wheel. "Now this is something." I stared dubiously at the controls, pushing on the pedals experimentally.

"Hm. How hard could this be? Those barely-functioning worms seemed to have managed it." I nodded to myself, lifting the handbrake and slammed my foot down. The car leapt forward with a heavy grumble and smashed into the building ahead; glass shattered, metal screamed, and everything went black.

I stood atop a hill in a sea of flames, untouched by heat or pain. My cloak was less impervious, tattered and smoky. I had both staff and sword held up to the sky, which, along with the various accoutrements of power secreted around my body, hummed with force – and I was using it all to keep the dragon at bay.

Something about this moment, this hill, seemed very familiar to me. The forest was mostly ash now, the landscape a charred heap of slag, the sky a mess of black. Hot, gusting winds blew my hair back from my face, and, more irritatingly, left my lips painfully dry.

"Come now, Damon," I said, projecting my words above. "This is a little too much, don't you think?"

The dragon screamed, and the air itself seemed to tear. It was a huge scarred beast, all of white, with red eyes. In short, it was beautiful and ugly all at once. "Okay, so you're taking the break-up a little harder than I am. You'll find someone else!"

Still bugling its rage, it dove at me, power cresting from it in a wave. I kept my will focused to a diamond point, the air around me taking on a blue-gold tinge, until our sorceries collided.

The dragon's screech hurled me awake again; no, that was the godsawful car horn my cheek was pressed against. I sat up blearily, and groaned. My mouth was flooded with the iron taste of blood, and I'd broken at least one rib, judging from the splitting pain in my chest. *Pain. Fuck.* I'd forgotten what physical pain was like, and honestly, could do with forgetting again. This was the sucky part of being alive, I thought.

The dragon screeched again, and I finally took stock of the situation. The hill and surrounding land around Caryard Jack's once fine establishment was on fire, and blue and red lights flashed everywhere. There were half a dozen cars with lights atop them – *police*, the word came to me – and several military jeeps. Men scrambled behind their vehicles and gunfire sprayed the air with an endless *thunka-thunka-thunk*. For all that this was a different age, the sounds of war, I found, were little changed.

Men screamed, men died, and flames crackled merrily. I watched in a daze as the dragon, ratty and mostly made of bone, swooped from the sky, body shuddering from bullet-blows, and breathed white fire. I blinked, trying to shake the fog from my mind; that was new. And this, this was no dream, no mere remembrance. Somehow, Damon had followed me back to life. My own death was shrouded in darkness, but from his presence here, I assumed we both died in our last encounter.

That would have pleased his prissy little heart, I thought, stepping out of the car. I stumbled, and fell to the ground, stomach rebelling. I spewed what little acids were in my gut onto the hot sand. It seems I'd done more damage than previously estimated. I took a calming breath, or tried to – it sounded more like a wet, heaving gulp but I assure you, I was in control. I tried to calm myself, but my heart was raging in my chest, blood pumping so hard my pulse thudded in my neck. It took some doing, but I managed to carefully stand up. As I did, I oriented myself and sent my senses abroad; this place was drenched in death and pain. Excellent.

A tragic, unholy mess for some – fuel for me. I sucked it in, feeling one or two souls wrapped in the pull, bringing them inexorably forward. They bucked in my mind, full of fury and the memory of life – these were no teenage souls, no mere mists, these were men and women who had lived.

Strong souls, souls dedicated to fighting.

I didn't have time to struggle with them, so instead – with the dragon's shrill dead screams in my ears all the while – I opened myself up to them. In that moment, they could see all of me, all of who I am, and what I wanted to do. *I need you,* I said, *to join me in this fight. I am too weak to stop him now. With you, I can. Let me put an end to this once and for all.*

The two souls stilled, like miniature ocean squalls suddenly becalmed and resolved into images: a man, and a woman. They looked at each other for a moment, and something passed between them. As one, they turned back to me and nodded.

"Thank you," I said.

And ate them.

The situation was, all in all, less dire than I'd thought. For all their puniness, humanity's new weapons were devastating and Damon was not as he was. He must've taken Sam's leftover spirit, a shocking oversight on my part, but in fairness, I'd had other things on my mind – a million of them, really. An eternity of information racing through my brain and a shitty little murderer who deserved some punishment. So sue me for not remembering the danger of a long-dead, past flame. Heh. Flame. Get it, cause – oh, forget it.

As spirit dragons went, he was far smaller than when I'd faced him more than a millennia ago, and riddled with holes besides. I walked forward, past the haphazard line of cars, and out into the firestorm.

"Hey!" A man shouted. "The fuck – who is that?"

"It's a fuckin' civie!"

"Sir! Sir, the fuck?! Get down! Get – "

Their shouting was drowned out by gunfire, and I left them to it. I didn't have my staff, or any of my usual trinkets; all burned, all dust now. My memories were gradually returning. In bits and pieces at first, then a flood. Our fight had been titanic, and far too long. Had we both not recently fed on a battlefield of dead, it would have been nothing, but we were full cups, brimming with power.

And so we fought.

Supernatural fights usually attract all sorts of scavengers, spiritual parasites and lowlifes seeking any advantage, but this one had none of that. Even the Gods left us alone as we fought. At some point in that endless battle, I'd hacked part of a leg off, and forgotten it. Foolish, really, against a shape-shifter like Damon – especially a dead one, I mean, he'd surprised me, truth be told, coming back like that. Wouldn't have thought he had it in him, but he had so much more than I ever gave him credit for.

The limb morphed behind me into a pointed spear of bone and rammed into my side. And so my reign of not-

---

really-terror ended, buried not beneath a mass of Godlings or buxom wenches and lanky fellas (the only two acceptable deaths, I'd long ago decided) but on some shitty hill in the middle of nowhere. Shafted by a jealous ex-lover, and not in a good way.

Of course, he couldn't resist coming close to gloat, and I couldn't resist blowing that smug look off his face – literally, not the other way – by detonating the power I'd been keeping in check. Now, the same scene looked destined to play out again.

"Damon," I called, projecting my voice into the maelstrom of heat and flame. I used some measure of power to keep myself from burning but I couldn't keep it all at bay. Sweat poured down my skin and I had to shield my eyes from the light. The fires were not insurmountable, but still had more than enough to kill me. I made my quickly through it, keeping a tight bubble of compressed air around me, unconsciously going to where I knew he'd be. Sounds faded behind the force-field.

Above, distantly, the sound of leathery wings beat the air.

Gunfire echoed intermittently, and then didn't.

Maybe they were all dead. Maybe I've been in this flame, this endless fire, forever – and this whole thing has been a dream, a façade played out over and over as punishment for my sins. I snorted. What nonsense – I knew life and death all too well. No necromancer worth their salt would be confused by the two. I was just feeling morbid and dramatic, which, to be fair, these circumstances totally warranted.

I stumbled up onto the hill, coughing, my lungs scraped to shit. There was some room to stand up here, some freedom from the flame. Damon waited by the foot of the blackened tree, his torn-up wings curled around his small, withered body. He had the form of an adolescent boy now, albeit with the wings. It was a deliberate ploy, a call-back to the shape I liked best: we used to fuck like this, and pretend he was an angel indulging in sin. He looked the part now, fallen in truth.

"Damon," I said, and stumbled to his side. I cradled his head in my lap, and his eyes fluttered open, as blue as I remembered.

"Oh," he said, and half-smiled, his teeth covered in blood. "You – you're here after all."

"Of course I am. Where else would I be?" I said, crooning to him, letting what remained of my power seep over his body. He was broken in more ways than I could hope to repair.

"I – I don't know," he said, chattering with cold. "I woke up and you weren't here, and, and, everything was… wrong."

I closed my eyes, heart thudding in my chest. Why had I ever thought it was great to be alive again? At least after a millennia of death, everything had faded into a sort of peaceful oblivion. To go through this twice seemed hideously unfair.

"I thought they'd taken you. Knew you were gone, see. W-we've been here for so long, lying beneath this tree. Thought they took you from me."

"They could never take me, sweet one. You know this."

His voice was tremulous, childish. "Wanted to hurt them."

"I know," I said. "I know."

I knew he was dead when the fires winked out, knew I was crying when I tasted salt on my lips, but otherwise, otherwise I sat there rocking for the longest time, and let everything go.

I was walking dully toward the Caryard when I felt it, a shiver in the air, a note of grace. Someone good, someone pure was nearby. A practitioner. It was nearly sundown now, and crows and vultures circled the bodies and melted cars, but aside from that, it was eerily empty. A few steps more brought him into view, a shortish man, rather young, nervously clutching a wooden staff. Wearing a big, dumb cowboy hat.

"Welcome, sir!" I called, voice hoarse and full of ash. "To my broken empire. I'm afraid my vehicles are rather under the weather, but you won't get a fairer price anywhere, that's the Caryard Jack guarantee."

"Come no further," he said, and he did not stutter. Did not falter. He had more grit than his appearance suggested, then. "You are done here, creature. Your time has long past."

"So it has, so it has," I said agreeably, stopping only a metre or two from him. "I don't much find this time to my liking anyhow, you know."

"Ah," the man said, and tried not to visibly sag in relief. Tried, and failed. "Then we have no quarrel. It will all be over soon."

"Ah, but there you're wrong, I'm afraid," I said. "As much as it fucking sucks to be alive, as it much as it hurts every goddamn minute, and a good part of me wants to curl up and cry, or else drink myself to sleep, as much as all that… I still don't want to die. I never have. 'Fraid that's where the whole necromancy thing began, you know?"

The man's face hardened. "I can't allow that," he said. "And you are nearly finished already, I can sense that."

He levelled his staff at me and a gentle pulse of power knocked me to the ground. I stared up at the sky, wondering if he'd meant to be kind or if that's all he had. Wondering if I'd meant to go along with it, or if I was really done. Probably the latter. After a moment, his face took over the sky.

"Go to rest, creature," he said, which was nice, and held his staff over me, which was not.

Why is it these suckers always have to stand so close? It's just plain foolish. Because he was right, I was done, I was finished.

Except for Sam's gun, which I'd drawn then.
And fired.

The sheer stinking mass of humanity is overwhelming, I

mean, godsdamn, it's just not healthy. I've spent the past two years surveying you, watching you, loathing you. Listen, humanity, you've let yourself go. You've lost sight of what you once were, grown fat beyond reason. In my day, compassion and brotherhood were the norm, people felt a kinship to one another because they knew at any given moment a demon could rip their fucking souls from their body. You had to value what you had, had to value each other. All that is gone. You're sheep, little humans, and you've forgotten the wolf.

Well, no matter. I'm here to remind you. I'm here to be the flashing teeth in the dark, the primal fear that dogs your step. I'm here to wake you up. Oh, and to screw often and eat burritos (food of the heavens!), because the gods only know, I'm not all about work. I gotta have my priorities straight. So rest up, people. Enjoy your last breath of excess, because before you know it...

I'll be coming for you.

At least, that's what I want to say. My past self would say that, theatrics and all, because much as I teased Damon for it, my own heart tended to melodrama as well. But I can't say it now, can't because my soul has been irrevocably changed. Oh, not from any moral lesson learned, no. Please. Because of the two brave souls that merged with mine, shining white mixing with my murky rainbow. I didn't really eat them, so much as join with them: fully accepting of them and they of me, we became one. The rarest of occurrences facilitated by utter necessity to be sure, yet here I am, still breathing, still kicking, and despairingly human.

Yes, I shot the shaman – Harold was his name, nice guy – but only in the hand. Told him I could have killed him but didn't, that I was done with death for now. He'd examined my spirit, said something about consulting some Elders, and taken off. As though he were still in command. It was cute, I won't lie. But I like my men tall, so he's got no chance.

———

So, what's next for me? What's next for Caryard Jack? Relax, I haven't decided yet – except that this is my home now, my resting place, and that of the poor sweet, psychotically violent Damon.

And I will defend it until the end.

That's the Caryard Jack guarantee.

Omar J. Sakr is an Australian writer and poet with a Masters in Creative Writing from the University of Sydney. His short story 'Aftertweet' was selected as part of the Twitter Fiction Festival, *and his poetry has featured on* Cordite Poetry Review, *as well as the* ABC. *He has poetry forthcoming in* Meanjin *and* Carve Magazine. *You can follow him on Twitter @OmarjSakr or on his website http://omarsakr.wordpress.com*

THE MONSTER BY THE LAKE

By Paul Gleed

Some like to talk of an intuition or sense that can detect something strange nearby, even if that something lingers still out of sight. Clearly, however, no one in this group possessed such a gift; or, if they did, they possessed an even greater gift for masking fear and uncomfortable thoughts.

He watched the four hikers moving along a thin, half-cleared path, dust clouding low in their wake like exhaust fumes. Talking happily amongst themselves, their mood reflected the sudden emergence of sunshine through the gathering dullness of autumn. Following their chatter through the woods as if it were bird song, he tracked them until evening shadows blocked the path and the group made camp for the night. He nestled silently in the foliage alongside their temporary base, taking in their conversation, the smells of their cooking, and the vicarious warmth of their glowing fire. He was too far removed to feel its actual heat. But not by much.

The hikers, two men and two women, finally fell asleep after midnight, the cool of the night forcing them at last into their tents. He waited for the snoring to begin, possessing an ear that could discern four distinct patterns of breathing as they slowed into sleep. Once the fourth and final sleeper was detected, he moved cautiously, almost gracefully, from his hiding spot and into the clearing where his newly acquired companions rested.

If any of the four had awoken, they would have seen something unforgettable, something they would have told stories about until they had no more words left in them. Not until much later, long after the more blatant elements of shock had been experienced, might they have pondered how something so big could move so quietly, even gracefully. But they did not wake. His large fingers unlatched a backpack and his hand gently circled through its contents like a spoon stirring tea in a delicate china cup. He found what he wanted, what he had seen earlier in the day, the reason he had followed these four strangers across miles of thick Oregon forest. With no more celebration than a smile, he carefully latched the backpack up again, turned on his big but nimble feet, and mingled into the night while his benefactors slept on.

This Bigfoot, known to his kind as Walter Davis, was a bibliophile in the traditional sense. He loved the feel of pages, firmly soft and leaping form thumb to thumb as he read; the first welcoming crack of a book's spine; and, more than anything else, that universal smell that books exuded, regardless of where they had been purchased, kept, or last read, a smell so precisely uniform from book to book that Walter imagined it was nothing less than a genetic characteristic traceable to the odor of a single library in some long forgotten medieval monastery. And, years ago, he had prized nothing more than to steal a book or two from unsuspecting backpackers. In this way he had learned the majesty of Stephen King and Ellery Queen, witnessed the universe as sketched by Stephen Hawking and Richard Dawkins, and been given restless nights from the divergent evils recalled by Rachel Carson and Erik Larson.

But books, much as he loved them, were a rare delicacy in these parts, and like a good meal, they seemed to be consumed fully in just a few exquisite moments. But then came the e-readers. While he once made do with the occasional truffle underfoot, now he had access to a ranging supermarket of film, literature, and music. And, thanks to the solar charger he relieved one well-equipped walker of, the only limit to his acculturation was the regrettable need for sleep. And tonight he had acquired another Kindle, another little tablet that was nothing less than the Library of Alexandria to him. He had also acquired a purpose.

"It's just unfair, though," said Walter. "I mean, don't you agree?"

"Well," said his good friend Dudley Capers, a Bigfoot whose literary appetites were satiated mostly in the pleasure palaces of erotica from Scandinavia and South West Asia, "I see your point, but I just don't much care. I'm not going to get agitated about it anyway."

"Don't you have any pride?" pushed Walter.

"Now don't start—"

"No," continued Walter, "I'm going to start and finish. Hear me out. Zombies, vampires, aliens, ghosts, demons, and they're all making a killing. Book deals, movie franchises, television series, millions of screaming fans around the world. You can't change the channel nowadays without witnessing a bleak apocalyptic vision of man at war with supernatural or extraterrestrial evil. But what does the Bigfoot get?"

"*Harry and the Hendersons*," sighed Dudley, familiar with the direction this conversation was taking.

"Right," snapped Walter, "Harry and the Fucking Hendersons."

"I've warned you about this before, Walter, and I advise you don't go down that path again."

Dudley put down the rotting squirrel carcass he was sucking on, wiped his hairy lips clean of coagulating slime, and cleared his throat.

"You know my line on *Harry and the Hendersons*, Walter, but if you wish to hear it again, I'm only too happy to oblige. In 1987, as you will recall, William Dear crafted the great masterpiece of post-Hitchcockian cinema. The film was ahead of its time thematically, visually, technically; one might call it visionary, if one was prone to understatement. As you well know, the film touched me personally, as it did for all of our kind, Walter, even you! I remember when I first saw it. Dear's film spoke to me, it sang of my world, my experiences. Innovative and brave, the material required a cast of human performers capable of materializing the great director's dream, and in a young John Lithgow, Dear had found the man for—"

"But it was almost thirty years ago, Dudley! Three decades!"

An awkward silence followed in which Dudley removed several ticks from his upper body and flicked them away. The second, by apparent misfire, struck Walter in the head. Dudley looked pleased with himself, as though the gesture sealed his victory. Walter, sensing his friend's smugness, decided to strike back with explosive force.

"I'm writing a book." Walter offered no more detail, letting the drama of his statement burrow into his friend like the ticks he'd just plucked out.

"Are you now?" said Dudley with affected indifference.

"Well, three to be precise," continued Walter, as if unaware of Dudley's posturing, "A trilogy of Young Adult novels. An epic romance of forbidden love between a sullen young woman and a handsome, mysterious Bigfoot who begins attending her high school."

Dudley paused, and then emptied his bowels with exaggerated relief. Flies instantly swarmed from all directions, as if they had been hungrily waiting hours for the event. Dudley scooped the waste up in his cupped hands, the shining mound darkly frosted with flies, and hurled it over the tree tops. More flies, late arrivals, looked lost and confused, wondering where the party had gone, weakly buzzing away in disappointment.

"You don't say," muttered Dudley as he licked his hands clean. "I suppose you have an agent and publisher lined up for this sure-fire hit?"

"Not *yet*," replied Walter, with his back and shoulders forced tall.

Dudley looked at his friend and remembered how Walter had always been a dreamer of the tragic kind, one whose talents never matched his ambition. It would be easy to ridicule Walter's idea, but, as Dudley looked over the nobly imperfect features of Walter's face, scarred deeply by the desire to be someone in a world that literally didn't know he existed, Dudley knew that a more compassionate line was needed. He dropped the ennui routine, placing his now clean hand on Walter's shoulder.

"I would read it," said Dudley, "but I wonder if there's a market out there for it. I mean zombies embody deep-seated fears of self-effacement and societal breakdown. Vampires… well, vampires are just sexy. I'm just not sure we're quite made of the right stuff, my old friend."

"Exactly! That's exactly my point. It's time we reinvented ourselves. It's time to make Bigfoot contemporary, modern, cool…scary-sexy."

"Now let's be realistic, Walter—"

"I say sexy and I mean it. Everyone knows about men with big feet. Well, what about fellows named after the very enormity of their feet? That should have them swooning, don't you think?"

Without transition of any kind, Dudley turned the conversation to Poison Ivy remedies, pulled a squirrel from the tree, opened it, and handed it to his friend with fraternal warmth. Walter allowed the diversion and, as he used the dead squirrel's tail to brush his teeth after the snack, he knew he couldn't win the argument with Dudley until his friend could see it all for himself.

Fortunately, Walter was further along with the first novel than Dudley supposed, having only a final round of copy-editing to go before the work was ready for its first reader. But that first reader would not be Dudley. Dudley, thought Walter, was something of a follower, someone not to get on a bandwagon until there was standing room only. He wouldn't be able to get behind the project until the publishing establishment gave its seal of approval, and he didn't want his friend to make a fool of himself by dismissing the work out of hand. No, Walter reckoned, he had to pitch it and have a contract in hand before he could show a word of it to his kind. They had all been conditioned by anonymity for so long, too accustomed to being the overlooked parochial cousins of the cool freaks and monsters. They couldn't see beyond their own limited imaginations and stunted self-worth. But Walter could. *The Forest for the Trees* would change all that, stick it to the vampires like a stake through their cool, sexy hearts, and completely decapitate the cultural capital of zombies (he vaguely imagined this as copy from the *New York Times* review of his book). It was a masterpiece of Young Adult fiction, Walter sincerely believed, and the merchandizing would be of a scale to match. In his mind, the big, furry novelty slippers that would soon be all the rage danced happily in pairs off the shelves at Target. And he knew how to make it all happen. A wealthy publisher from New York summered in a cabin a hundred miles north from where Walter and Dudley now talked. It was almost time.

That night, half asleep, half awake, he imagined himself edgily quipping to a TMZ reporter: "There's more buzz around this franchise than when I stepped in a fucking beehive last week." He chuckled himself to sleep, snoring contently until morning sunlight parted the trees.

The publisher's cabin was remote, accessible only by boat on the lake or an uneven trail slipping down a steep drop of trees and stone. A rough road ended a mile shy of the building, the last place where civilization on wheels could reach. The rest would have to be dragged or carried, but that was how Arthur Rinkin liked it. Rinkin, whose career was so advanced, and his skills of delegation so honed, that he could spend a portion of his summer away from the fetid polish of New York City, loved to exist sparsely here in the forest for August and September each year.

The old man sat on a small jetty, its wooden pillars greasy and green after years dipped in the lake. Like the jetty, Rinkin had long ago lost the smoothness of youth but remained strong, steady, and full of splinters. He was the kind of man who, on his eventual death, would be eulogized as someone who "did not suffer fools gladly," but, in life, was simply recognized as a mean-spirited bastard.

Walter Davis watched the old man dangle his feet in the lake, the surface of which burst with a thousand explosions of reflected light in the early morning sun. He was just sitting there, looking out on the flat plane of the lake, and Walter wondered what to do next. In his hands he clutched the laptop on which he had written *The Forest for the Trees*; he even had the screen opened up and the document ready at a particularly good page of first-rate prose. The passage was selected carefully: not over-written, economical but still stylish, all showcasing a nice mix of description and dialogue sparking like the lake below. He went over the elevator pitch for his novel several more times in his head, recognizing this as a delaying tactic even while he savored the phrase "mysterious, bigfooted, brooding stranger." He began to walk down the slope, unintentionally gaining speed as he went due the path's slant. He was almost jogging now, clutching his open laptop tight, the first words of his pitch bouncing up and down in his mouth like loose teeth.

As Walter noisily reached the jetty, Rinkin turned to face him, eyes squeezed almost shut because of the lake's glare turned red in his eyes and the absence of his glasses.

"There's something about the new kid at Glendale High, something that no one can quite put their finger on," began Walter. His heart bounced around in its own deep vibrations while his skin was heating and reddening unseen beneath the fur covering his body. "Not even Jessica Jacobs, whose absent father drives a big rig while her mother passes the days drinking in nearby woods. Is Jessica the only one who has noticed how the stranger's feet have been in those casts all semester, and that he visits the barber daily? Certainly no one—"

"Are you pitching me a fucking book?" hollered Rinkin. "Are you actually here, on my property, in my silence and my solitude, pitching me a fucking book?"

Walter stammered as Rinkin's anger grew.

"Get the hell out of here, you fucking hippie, before I go back to the cabin and get my rifle. Believe me, son, I'm at the age now where I'm taking care of the things on my bucket list, and, frankly, I've always wanted to shoot someone right through the heart. You'll be giving me the chance if you haven't fucked off by the time I count ten."

Walter felt tears gathering in both eyes as he turned away, moving swiftly back into the trees. Rinkin was already heading back to the cabin for his glasses and, no doubt, the rifle, too. It was not until Walter made it over the slope and back onto flat ground that he realized his laptop was back at the jetty. Turning back, he saw Rinkin emerging from the cabin holding his rifle like a lover, close and passionately. For a moment Walter considered a dash for the laptop, clearly visible to him a hundred yards away, but reconsidered as the now bespectacled Rinkin scanned the forest.

While Walter was familiar with the writer's creed of "kill your darlings," abandoning them in the grounds of a malicious mad man seemed a far colder fate.

As he reflected on this cruelty, a shot vibrated through the air, coming to rest in a tree no more than twenty yards to Walter's right. The bullet motivated him into action; turning once again to face the forest he started running, his large, dexterous feet gripping the ground hard to give each stride greater distance.

Nine months later, having given up on his dreams of writing a novel (Dudley had worked tirelessly to stress how Young Adult was trending away from the paranormal and more towards realism, and that Walter's novel had simply

—

46

arrived at the wrong time, a moment when the literary tide was turning), Walter had moved his attention to woodworking, especially the production of fine, ornate trays on which the Bigfoot now fondly served each other breakfast in turns. He did, however, follow from time to time the vagaries of the publishing world, just in case he detected the wind blowing there in his favor.

And so the headline on one trade website heralding "The Return of Monsters in Love" made Walter sit up, alert with excitement. Reading on through the article, his mood sank those big feet of his in soft, rain-soaked mud. The book behind this storm of anticipation - and, yes, the film rights had been snatched up before the work was even released - was an exciting new novel entitled *The Woods and the Trees*. Its author, whose handsome, symmetrical and privileged face would soon be adorning the book pages of many fine news sites, was one Chad Rinkin, nephew of the famed publishing mogul, Arthur Rinkin. Chad, freshly graduated from an Ivy League school where he had majored in casual sex and the decadent spending of money he had not earned, was instantly the darling of the literary set. In particular, the highbrow publications celebrated young Rinkin's use of "irony and pastiche" to "revitalize the spent genre of paranormal romance."

"The figure of the Bigfoot," Chad Rinkin was quoted as saying, "was ripe for reappraisal, and I found in it the perfect emblem of how the simple and honest things in life are under attack by the invasive malice of corporate America." Walter simply stopped reading when he reached Chad's declaration that "the book came to me all in one go. The writing process was exceptionally easy, I would say."

With a calmness that surprised him, Walter looked up and away from the article on his Kindle. Dudley approached with a finely made tray laden with dead birds and squirrels, flies appearing like garnish around open wounds that marked each animal.

"Rotting to perfection, my good Sir," smiled Dudley.

Walter took the tray, inhaling the fine stench with relish and emptying his bowels to signal appreciation for the meal he had been given.

"Thank you, my friend. Thank you."

Paul Gleed was born and raised in Portsmouth, England, but currently lives in the Northeastern U.S with his wife and two children. He holds a First Class degree in English from Lancaster University, England, and writes fiction in a number of genres. He can be found on Twitter @PaulGleedWrites.

LABOR ECO-NOM-NOM-ICS

By John Lemut

The office was small and too hot. He was left alone, sitting in one of the two visitors' chairs, for going on five minutes. He had time to slowly look around the office. It wasn't meant to be an office, he decided as his knees became sore from pressing against the desk, because it was just too small. There was room for a desk and a chair, but not for the two visitors' chairs positioned facing the desk and two filing cabinets. *How could two visitors hope to civilly get in and out of this office?* he wondered.

The radiator, one of those old cast iron jobs with rusty water running through it, really pumped out the heat. It made him regret wearing a long-sleeve collared shirt and a sweater.

He had already counted the ceiling tiles and had taken more than enough time to read the inspirational and/or witty musings push-pinned to the bulletin board on the wall: *Complaint Department 500 miles* with a big red arrow pointing left; *Hear the meaning within the word*; *If men be good, government cannot be bad…*

He turned his attention toward the desk and spotted a stack of about fifty tri-folded flyers on the edge closest to him. He leaned slightly forward and spun one around with a single fingertip so he could read it. The flyer proclaimed: *Milton Welcomes Its First-Ever Zombie! Coming In April!*

Every Word Capitalized, he mused sing-songy in his head.

It was March 15th.

He held the flyer and just as he opened the first fold, footsteps echoed in the hallway. He stuffed the flyer in a front pocket of his dress pants. He glanced at the desk hoping nothing was out of place, though he touched only the flyer. The name plate on the desk said JEANINE JOHNSON in a fun yet businesslike font. The footsteps continued into the office and a woman in her mid-forties stopped just inside the door. He turned in his chair to look and recognized her as the same woman who warmly greeted him and brought him into the office before receiving a phone call and hastily excusing herself.

He stood as he was taught to do when a lady entered or left a room and she smiled, either at his chivalrous showing or just because she smiled a lot. JEANINE JOHNSON spoke as she squeezed between a filing cabinet and a side of her desk to reach her office chair. "I apologize for the delay in getting started; things have just been absolutely maddening around here. I hope if we go longer than our scheduled appointment I won't be keeping you from anything."

"It won't be a problem at all," he assured her.

"Wonderful." She smiled again and arranged a few papers and manila folders on her desk before grabbing a single manila folder from a stack of a couple dozen. She placed it in front of her and opened it. She held up a piece of paper and skimmed it. He recognized it as his resume, even from the other side of the translucent paper. He felt the dampness that had formed on his forehead gather and threaten to make a run into his eye. He wiped it away in a motion that, to the layperson, would appear to be a hair adjustment, he hoped.

He took a daring, extended look at her breasts which were harnessed behind a tight flesh-colored sweater and, most likely, a soft cup bra. If not for her dumpy ass and '80s hair, JEANINE JOHNSON would be pretty okay.

She set his resume down and placed her hands over one another. "So..." She glanced down. "...Ken, can you tell me what brings you to Milton?"

Ken's eyes darted uncontrollably from her face to her breasts. Twice. "Uh, I was raised in Oakton, just across the river, and lived there pretty much all my life. I always liked coming to Milton, especially your downtown, so I guess when I had the chance to pick up and start over, I couldn't think of anywhere else I'd rather do that."

If she caught him checking her out she didn't show it. "And what, if may I ask, is the cause of your relocation?"

Ken didn't want to go into it, so he gave her the truth, but just the barest of details: "I had a relationship end and, coincidentally, my job with the city was eliminated at roughly the same time." He regretted using the word "job" right away. JEANINE JOHNSON would have more respect for the word "position" or possibly "posting." Even Ken liked "posting" better.

Ken kept track of how frequently he glanced at her chest. He told himself if he made it out of the room and was able to count the number of times on two hands, he'd stop for tacos.

"I'd like to switch gears and talk a little bit about what the job will entail," she told Ken after numerous additional questions about his education, hobbies, strengths, weaknesses, and a challenge to list ten uses for a pencil other than writing (he could only come up with seven—eight if you counted "stabbing someone," which he did not say out loud).

Ken nodded. His light perspiration turned into a full-on flop sweat and his internal debate about whether or not to take off his sweater took his undivided attention from the interview.

"Wonderful," she smiled with very white teeth. "Well, we are all very excited about the new attraction coming to our town. We'll be the only city within 500 miles with our own zombie!"

A stray thought entered Ken's mind about the potential of seeing an erect nipple through the material of her bra and sweater.

—

"Rather than using shock collars and invisible perimeter fencing like some...*other* cities, we've decided to do the humane thing and hire three shifts so we can provide around the clock service to watch after the zombie and return it to its designated areas should it venture too far from them. The official title for these positions is 'Post-Mortem Achiever Logistics Specialist,' but we've all just been saying 'Zombie Wrangler' around here. It's kind of cute, don't you think?"

Ken nodded.

JEANINE JOHNSON continued to talk about the position. Neither of her nipples made an appearance.

At the end of the interview she handed him one of the flyers from her desk, thanked him for his time and assured him they would be in touch soon. Ken's breast-glance tally totaled eleven, but he still went for tacos afterwards.

The hard corn shell stuffed with seasoned ground beef, lettuce, cheese and sour cream broke apart as he bit into it. The taco contents dropped onto the tray in front of him. Also, a sharp taco shell edge cut his inner cheek.

He read over the flyer as he ate and found himself engrossed in the bullet points of zombie facts:

-Zombies are rarer than pandas!

-Less than 1% of those who have the very uncommon "zombie gene" actually become zombies after they die.

-Nothing of the living human survives in the zombie.

-You can *not* become a zombie by getting bitten or scratched.

-Zombies rarely attack humans. They are mostly harmless.*

Did JEANINE JOHNSON *cover this in the interview?* Ken asked himself. He could not remember. Much of what they talked about was a blur. Ken finished his tacos and thought about JEANINE JOHNSON in the shower for the next three mornings.

Ken was called back to the hot little office exactly two weeks after his interview and was formally offered the third-shift (11 p.m. to 7 a.m.) position of Post-Mortem Achiever Logistics Specialist.

The Zombie Wrangler.

It gave Ken thoughts of wearing leather chaps and a Stetson hat. Six-guns on his hips and ammo belts slung diagonally over each shoulder. Showdowns in the middle of Main Street. Taking the whorehouse madam to a creaky bed even though she didn't let customers have turns with her anymore.

He was being told that the job was an eight-month gig. "The zombie will be taken off display for the winter months, just like the bears at the zoo," JEANINE JOHNSON told him cheerfully. "From November 15th until March 15th the zombie will be stored. We're doing this to, first of all, keep it from freezing solid and, secondly, to fully capitalize on the tourist months."

"The Ides of March," Ken said wistfully.

"Pardon me?"

He had thrown her off-track with his comment.

Ken stammered, "No, excuse me. It's nothing, please continue."

"Might I suggest that you take the initiative and become a certified snow plow driver? That way, you could have year-round work with the city."

Ken nodded. Their discourse seemed to go better when he mostly nodded. He felt that was how he got the job.

For the rest of the day Ken signed lots of forms after having the gist of them explained to him. He underwent a full medical checkup, including tests to determine if he carried the "zombie gene." He was given a crash HR course and told the ins and outs of his new job. "Check in on the zombie frequently, but keep your distance. We're trying to preserve

—

the appearance that it's just there." "Tidy it up a little, but not too much. We want it to have that natural look of decay. That's what people want to see." "Try to keep it within the confines of greater downtown where all our marquee shops and restaurants are. We want tourists to have to search for the zombie, but not too hard." Ken was handed a map with a pale-green zone denoting the zombie's official stomping grounds.

JEANINE JOHNSON gave him a tour of the municipal building where he would not need to come very often. He followed along behind her and stared at her. It was casual Friday and she wore jeans that molded her dumpy ass into some nice curves.

Ken met the other two Zombie Wranglers, a couple of real losers. One of the guys, Jimmy, had previously worked at a fish market for six or eight months at a crack, just long enough to save money to let him live out the rest of the year without having to work. Jimmy was well over six feet tall and sickly-thin. His eyes were sunken with dark rings under them. The other Wrangler was an obese, foul-smelling pig named Warren who didn't seem to have a job history. Ken wondered how on earth he had been given the third shift. To appease his own ego, he decided it was randomly chosen.

At the end of the day, Ken was issued a smart phone and a beat-up Chevy S-10 pickup that had CITY OF MILTON sloppily stenciled on the doors and tailgate. It was Ken's first company car.

He started that coming Saturday, when the zombie was to be unveiled to the public.

Two blocks of Main Street were shut down for the official unveiling. The high school marching band played a variety of lively songs that all sounded the same. Multi-colored flag garland festooned the street and a stage with red, white and blue bunting stood in the middle of the crowd. Upon the stage were the mayor, several other local dignitaries

---

and business owners, JEANINE JOHNSON, the trio of Zombie Wranglers and a wooden crate stood up on its end.

Ken stood between Warren and Jimmy. He tried to stand apart from them, but one of the anal-retentive coordinators wearing a headset moved him by his shoulders between the fat one and the skinny one and then gave a satisfied, one-sided smile to herself as if she had just solved a James Patterson mystery before the final chapter.

Several people spoke about how wonderful Milton was and how the new attraction would do the local economy and the residents wonders. Even though they kept their remarks to less than five minutes each, with the introductions, handshakes all around, polite applause and marching band fanfare, it was over an hour before the mayor stepped behind the podium.

He was greeted with minor applause from the minority of residents who either did not care about or were unaware of the YouTube video of their mayor drunk in a bar and hitting on a woman half his wife's age. Undeterred, he thanked the crowd and smiled. "What a beautiful day, Milton! And a momentous day, as well. Our new attraction is sure to provide a much-needed boon to our economy by way of new jobs..." The mayor lazily waved to the team of Post-Mortem Achiever Logistics Specialists. Ken's face flushed. "...and tourism dollars. This is an exciting time and we're all pleased so many people have come out to witness this history-making event."

The mayor continued for several more minutes and called for a drum roll as he stepped away from the podium to unlatch the crate's hinged lid. The mayor shoved the lid open and absent-mindedly jerked his arm away from the crate's opening. He smiled and laughed self-consciously, eyes darting between the crowd and the box.

The drum roll ended when the crate was opened, but nothing emerged. The crowd waited silently. The sun was just behind the crate so only a motionless human shape was visible inside. The mayor snapped his fingers to get the

—

attention of the Zombie Wranglers and waved them over. Warren hustled across the stage, hitching his pants up as he went and Jimmy followed a step behind.

They decided to tip the crate forward and let gravity take over. A few people in the audience laughed nervously as the opposite body types struggled to tip the crate together, but the plan worked well and the zombie shakily stepped onto the stage and into daylight.

It had been a man, a middle-aged man of average height and average build. Then, after he died, he became a zombie and was shipped far from where he lived so he could provide an economic edge for a city with no industry and cheap fun for tourists. Parents in the crowd were relieved to see the zombie had no obvious, hideous, gruesome damage. Many youths were clearly disappointed because of this.

Someone had dressed it in a two-piece suit that hung oddly off slumped shoulders. The zombie's skin was beyond pale and pallid; it was grey and looked like it would be chalky to the touch. Its mouth hung open slightly, eyes focused on nothing. Its arms hung limply like a forlorn child's.

The zombie took another step away from the crate, closer to the edge of the stage. Many in the front of the crowd resisted the urge to take a step back. The zombie took another step and turned on the stage. It let out a soft moan: "Uuuunngggh."

The crowd cheered and applauded like they had at last year's divisional championship football game. The zombie lifted its head higher and faced the crowd again and moaned louder and longer.

Ken had stepped off the stage when the fat one and the skinny one were fiddling around with the crate and was almost home when he heard the noise of the crowd.

It didn't take Ken very long to find ways to do his job with minimal effort. The city put a location monitoring anklet on the zombie that sent a text alert to the Zombie Wrangler on duty when it ventured beyond the designated "Zombie Zone." That was what everyone called downtown now: the Zombie Zone. All Ken needed to do was pull up the phone's GPS app and drive to wherever the zombie was, put it in the bed of the truck and drive it back to downtown.

Ken's biggest problem turned out to be the drunken college kids who accosted the zombie after last call, but unless someone was going to stick a screwdriver into its head, Ken didn't have to worry about the zombie too much.

Someone cut a finger off the zombie after about a month, but it only served to enhance its mystique. That occurred on one of the day shifts.

Some days, Ken stayed home until his phone informed him the zombie wandered too far.

Normally there wasn't too much trouble, but one busy week Ken had received a text every day that the zombie was outside the Zombie Zone. By the time he caught up to the zombie, it was several miles outside of town wandering in a cabbage patch. Ken knew that someone was playing a trick on him, probably sticking the zombie in the bed of their own pickup and having a good laugh at his expense.

It also didn't take Ken long to grow to hate the zombie. Ken mostly couldn't understand why people would come to see a dead guy walking around. Was it the same morbid curiosity that makes people look at car accidents or stand around outside a house fire? Ken didn't have to interact with tourists; they came out during the day. He had to deal with locals, ignorant drunks who couldn't care less about a zombie. They had to give the slow shambler the right of way when it walked into the street. If it wandered into a building, people had to call for a Zombie Wrangler to remove it. The locals essentially gave the zombie the same treatment a stray cow gets in Delhi: tolerated but often neglected.

In spite of its negatives, Ken preferred the night shift. He didn't have to hear children scream or witness yokels from a neighboring state scramble to get a good picture with an

—

uncooperative, moving target. The streets were mostly quiet and the zombie was mostly docile at night.

Ken's handling of the zombie became rough, and nobody was around to witness that so late. When the zombie wandered outside of its zone, if it was in the road, Ken would drop the tailgate and back the truck up into the zombie. The racket it made as it flopped into the bed of the truck was quite loud and satisfying to Ken in the cab. He would then leisurely drive back to the Zombie Zone and unceremoniously drag it from the bed onto one of the historic, brick-lined intersections.

An alert text came in just before one in the morning on a Saturday. Unlike the automated texts when the zombie passed out of its zone, this one came from the main office. The zombie had gotten inside a bar called Shebangers. Ken thought the whole situation odd as he pulled on some clothes because he knew bar patrons just handled the zombie by themselves, the city ordinances be damned. Ken's apartment was less than five minutes away, but he still expected the situation to be resolved before he arrived on scene.

It had not.

Shebangers was a long and narrow bar where the bartenders unbuttoned their tops to the base of their cleavage so you could see the bit that held the bra cups together. As soon as Ken entered the moody tavern, he could tell right where the zombie was. It had a buffer zone of about three feet surrounding it.

Before Ken made his way deeper inside the pub, someone put their hand on his upper arm gently. He spun around and came face to face with weekend JEANINE JOHNSON. Her hair was even more '80s: her bangs came out and down over her forehead more dramatically and the rest of her hair was extremely teased up. She wore a low-cut top and Ken could not stop staring at her pale, most assuredly soft flesh in the dim bar light. She wore her casual Friday jeans, as well...or a pair just like them.

—

"Ken!" she yelled a little too loudly even for a bar. "They wanted to kick him out but I told them, 'You have to do it by the book. Call the city.'"

Ken didn't know how to respond so he just nodded. JEANINE JOHNSON smiled and slid her hand off Ken's arm instead of just removing it. Ken pulled his eyes away from the dark, shadowy chasm between her breasts and shouldered his way through the crowded bar.

The zombie did not turn to greet him, but Ken preferred to accost it from its blind side anyway. He grabbed hold of its waistband and put his other hand on its shoulder. The zombie responded to Ken's puppeteering and they began working toward to door. The din in the bar started rising as the zombie got closer to the exit. Ken could hear some of the drunker patrons make general threats at the thing he escorted. Someone said, "Get that fucking dead thing out of here." Another man yelled, "And take the zombie outside, too!" Lots of people laughed at that. JEANINE JOHNSON, who had been right behind Ken the entire time, stopped to warn one of the drunks about the hefty fines and potential jail time involved for those who participated in the destruction or defacement of city property. She was getting pretty worked up, standing inches from the random bar-goer. Ken decided to escort her out as well, and grabbed her arm and gently pulled. She came along willingly enough, but continued her harangue until after they were outside.

The night air was cold enough where they could see their breath. She exhaled furiously a couple times looking a bit like a dragon and then said, "What a dick, right?"

Ken piled the zombie into the back of the truck and slammed the tailgate up. "I'm going to drop it off a couple blocks away, then I think I should drive you home. Why don't you hop in?"

She nodded and walked over to the passenger's side of the truck and climbed inside. As they bounded down the road, Ken was sure he could see her nipples poking through

—

her top when they passed under street lights.

After he pulled the zombie out of the truck and left it in the road he hopped back in the truck, careful to not mash his erection. JEANINE JOHNSON had other ideas and groped at his crotch as soon as he closed his door. After a very quick period of dumbfounded inertness, Ken grasped a breast in one hand - pinching her nipple through her clothing - and her denim-covered ass in the other.

They noisily and sloppily kissed and dug under each other's clothing for skin. Ken pulled her on top of him. Her back bumped into the steering wheel with each thrust, eliciting a series of brief horn honks.

Afterwards they pulled their clothes on and she told him her address while adjusting her hair in the sun visor's tiny mirror. She had to bob her head around to see the outer limits of her hairstyle. When she finished with the mirror, her hair looked no different. She flipped the visor back up to the headliner with a snap and said, "I bet you've been waiting to do that for a long time."

Ken couldn't determine how she meant that. Was she being sultry or condescending or were there hints of threat and regret in that statement? He suddenly thought of a quote he read on an aged piece of paper stuck to her bulletin board: *The state has no business in the bedrooms of the nation.* He thought it was an odd choice to pin up on an office wall. Seconds had already passed and still he couldn't think of how to answer her. Looking straight ahead he pursed his lips and nodded.

His response must have satisfied her because she said nothing more and looked out her window for the rest of the ride to her house. When he pulled into her driveway, she leaned over and kissed his cheek before hopping out of the cab. He stayed until she made it inside safely and also to watch the way her butt moved when she walked.

For the next couple weeks Ken drove past Shebangers Bar several times each night, hoping to see JEANINE JOHNSON coming out, but she never did. He resisted the urge to drive past her home, far away from the Zombie Zone. He thought about her constantly, imagined having sex in a bed or on a rug, fantasized about fooling around in a mostly empty movie theater. He would teach her how to make a perfect three-egg omelette. He had conversations with her in his head and felt empty when he realized they had never really spoken to each other.

His phone beeped and snapped him from his delusions. He put the truck in gear and drove to pick up the zombie. Things had been quiet since that night at the bar. The zombie still ventured outside of its designated area, but no one had driven off with it or accosted it during Ken's shift.

The GPS app indicated the zombie was only a block outside of the Zombie Zone. Ken parked against the curb and got out of the truck. The nights were getting longer and colder. He hadn't done anything about the snow plow driver posting. *Maybe I can get work as a barista*, he thought.

The GPS said the zombie was nearby. As Ken approached the alley between his favorite *taquería* and a vacant building, he heard laughing. When he turned the corner he observed five people, two women and three men, standing in a circle around the zombie.

One of the men pushed the zombie into the girl standing opposite him in the circle. She squealed when it brushed against her and said, "Stop it, Jeff! That's so gross."

Another man pulled his penis out, walked like a penguin up to the zombie and urinated on it. He danced and peed all around it. The other girl laughed and kissed the last of the three men.

The kissing man was holding a bottle of liquor that he passed to the next person once he took a drink from the bottle. They were all drunk.

Ken walked to within a few feet of the group. "Hey, what's going on here?" he asked in an attempt at an authoritative voice.

61

Everyone stopped and turned to look at Ken. Then the women cackled and the men squared their shoulders to Ken. The one who pushed the zombie said, "Well...if it isn't the zombie babysitter."

Zombie Wrangler, Ken thought and imagined firing some rounds off into the air. "You guys should take off and there won't be any problem."

The pisser walked partway around Ken and sneered, "Maybe you should *fuck off*!"

Ken was watching the pisser and did not see the kisser move behind him; they formed a triangle around Ken. The pusher said, "Hey, man, let me ask you something." Ken looked away from the pisser. "Did you have to apply for this horseshit job?"

Ken nodded and the kisser punched him in the back of the head. Ken lost his balance and fell to his knees. The three men kicked him in his ribs and head. Ken curled up on his side and covered his head with his arms.

The attack came to an end as quickly as it began. Ken was only semi-conscious when the group walked out of the alley. Their laughter bounced off the brick walls back at him. Rage boiled over into frustration and Ken began to cry. He rolled onto his back. Every part of him hurt. He could feel blood seeping out of a head wound. He wondered if JEANINE JOHNSON liked scars.

Ken tried to move his arms and legs but couldn't. He didn't think he had been paralyzed, rather he assumed he was too bruised to move without significant pain. *Maybe I'll just sleep here*, he thought.

The sound of something dragging on pavement close to him gave Ken a moment of fear that pusher, kisser and pisser had come back for seconds. He opened his eyes and looked up at the zombie.

It stood over Ken's head, its head hung low. It was staring at him with the same slightly open mouth it always had, but it was staring at him. Gone was the vacant stare at nothing it always had. Ken remembered the bullet point with the asterisk from the brochure.

-Zombies rarely attack humans. They are mostly harmless.*

Way at the bottom of the page, in fine print, it had said:

* *Those with fresh abrasions, lacerations, menstruating women, and people prone to nose bleeds are advised to avoid direct contact with zombies. Like sharks, it is believed zombies become aggressive when they smell blood.*

The zombie groaned with an energy Ken had not heard before. It fell upon him and sank its teeth into Ken's throat.

He had no choice but to listen to the sounds the zombie made as it sloppily fed. It didn't hurt. If he closed his eyes, the sound almost reminded him of kissing JEANINE JOHNSON. As the darkness pushed its way in from his peripheral vision, Ken had two distinct thoughts: he relived the feel of JEANINE JOHNSON's soft breasts and considered that his test for the zombie gene had come back positive.

John Lemut is this dude who lives in Wisconsin. He spends his time watching too much TV, brewing and drinking beer, writing, editing, and marrying people. No, really. He has officiated two weddings (both marriages are still going – yay!). Relax, anyone can get ordained online, and it's way legit. You're probably more concerned with his writing chops though, as you should be. Well, he actually went to school for it (also yay!), and it shows (eh...). It's not his full time job though – that doesn't take too much in the way of writing skills – but he writes when he likes, and is published when he gets lucky.

In addition to defining the occasional word on UrbanDictionary.com, his short stories appear in the anthologies First Time Dead, Say Goodnight to the Bad Guy, Vampires

Aren't Pretty, *and* Night Gypsy: Journey into Darkness. *Someday he might write a novel. We'll just see. His website is johnrambles.com* .

NEW HUNTING GROUNDS

By Gustavo Bondoni

The day could have been perfect. The sun, directly overhead, shone down through a cloudless sky and the breeze held a whisper of the sea, even this high in the mountains, even this deep in the desert.

Of course, it would never be perfect as long as the fat human kept blowing smoke into Tarnetisney's nose. That tended to put a damper on even the most pleasant of days. And the other man, the man speaking to the smoker was, if anything, even worse. To the dragon's sensitive ears, his nasal tones sounded like two cats having violent sex while raking their claws down a blackboard.

He seriously considered eating them, but thought better of it. Every time he ate a human, it seemed like the rest of the species would appear in the mountains to try to find what had happened. There was no danger of discovery, of course, but the peace would be broken for a few days, and that was anathema to a dragon of regular habits.

And besides, the fat one would give him gas– and didn't smell all that fresh, anyway.

So Tarnetisney listened.

"Anyway," the companion was saying, "she's twenty-one and lives in South Korea. I spent all night chatting between observations. You should see her profile pics." He made another sound, one that, against all odds, made the cats sound pleasant.

The fat one took a long drag on his cigarette. "Too bad,"

he said.

"What?"

"Well, it's a pity when you consider the problems."

"Problems?"

"I suppose you didn't tell her you were a middle-aged astronomer who lives with his mother."

"I don't live with my mother!"

"Well, you do whenever you're not out in the middle of a desert in Chile." Another puff, straight into the dragon's face. Tarnetisney knew that the humans couldn't tell his well-camouflaged features from the surrounding desert rocks, but were they truly clueless enough that they never noticed that large rocks in the area had a tendency to move around from one day to the next? "And am I right in assuming that you used a fake photo for your avatar?"

"Of course I did. I prefer to establish a mental connection without distractions."

"And to establish the correct mental connection, did you let her think that an 'astrophysicist' is just like an astronaut?"

A pause. "Well, yes, but can I help it if people are a bit vague on language details? I still think it's important to keep the physical side in check until we realize how compatible our minds are."

"And the fact that your face looks like the 'before' picture in a leaflet for hemorrhoids surgery has nothing to do with it?"

"I resent that."

"I would, too, if I looked like that." The fat man chuckled. "Anyway, isn't our bandwidth a little limited to be using it to pick up women half your age in chat rooms?"

"Not anymore. They upgraded our service since the last time you were here. We can download anything we want."

"Oh, great, lonely astronomers with lots of porn. I bet the local sheep are going to be really happy."

"The local sheep disappeared completely. Haven't seen one in weeks."

"They've probably heard about you."

"Very funny. But I wonder what happened to them all."

"How should I know? Do sheep migrate?"

They went on in this vein for a few moments more, but Tarnetisney wasn't listening. He was concentrating on staying very, very still and trying to force the two men to stop thinking about sheep, or more precisely, the lack thereof. Even these two would eventually realize that hundreds of semi-feral desert sheep wouldn't disappear overnight from the vicinity of the only watering hole for a hundred miles except under enormously unusual circumstances.

He also resolved to do a better job in hiding the big pile of bones he'd left just on the other side of the mountain.

But when the humans left, Tarnetisney surprised himself by not rushing off to see to the bones. There was something else the humans had said that was bouncing around inside his skull, snowballing into an idea, then a plan, and finally, an obsession.

Dr. Ferdinand Shelley popped another can of Coke. He knew the sugar wouldn't help his waistline all that much, but he was beyond caring. His wife was long gone, having run off with the yoga guru, or whatever they called them now, so there was no real reason to stay in shape. He knew he wasn't a prize catch, but an eighty year-old bald dude who looked like Yoda? Really? He took another drink, and wished they had donuts.

Life in the observatory wasn't all that bad. Even though the old optical telescope had been surpassed by more glamorous options – radio telescopes, microwave observatories and, of course, space-based optical telescopes – there was enough sky for everyone, and there would be for the foreseeable future. However, the budget only stretched to two operators, and that meant things could get lonely, especially if your only companion was a very strange fellow from Croatia, obsessed with finding a girlfriend despite geographic obstacles, age differences and, to be brutally honest, unfortunate physical limitations.

The clickety-clack of keystrokes echoed through the image-analysis room. Dr. Bajuk was trying to convince a girl in Guam that the photo of a young Ernest Hemingway he'd pulled off the net somewhere was actually him. Judging by the way he was perspiring, he wasn't having much luck.

"Damn," he said, finally shutting down the chat window. "Why are people always so shallow about these things?"

"Look Marko, maybe you're just trying too hard. Have you tried telling the truth? You're a smart guy, and some girls like that," Ferdinand said. *Of course it seemed to be the same type of woman who would then run off with a guy whose head looked like a wrinkled egg.* He didn't say this, though, since he realized it might weaken his argument.

Besides, Bajuk wasn't buying it. "You're kidding, right?"

"No. I mean it. You've just been having a bad run. There are people out there who don't judge us by the way we look."

"Good-looking people?"

Of course not. "Of course. And, even more important, people who are beautiful on the inside. Now come on. Let's go outside. I'm dying for a cigarette."

They turned towards the single exit and stopped.

"Er... That's new," Marko observed. "Why did you bring it?"

"I didn't. What would I want with a rock that size?"

"I think they're called boulders when they get that big."

"All right, a boulder that size, then. And do you really think I'd be able to drag it in here? Up the steps?"

"Well, maybe if you rolled it," Marko said. His expression made it clear that he was unhappy with the fact that Ferdinand had chosen to redecorate without consulting him, and, furthermore, had serious doubts about the choice of styles.

"No, I didn't. Besides, look at the thing. That is a very

big rock. The door is a regular-sized door, maybe a bit on the small side. There's no way it could have fit through the opening without a whole lot of modifications to either rock or door. And if you look closely, you'll notice that both are unscathed."

"True. But then how do you explain it? I was on duty all night, so I certainly didn't bring it here. Do you think the boys at CERN are trying for a few cheap laughs?"

"You mean teleporting rocks here? I doubt it. We don't rate an exotic-physics practical joke. Besides, I'm sure I've seen that rock before, somewhere."

"Of course you have," the rock replied in a deep, rumbling bass. "You stood next to me just yesterday, spewing both inanities and noxious fumes." It paused before going on. "I've always wondered how humans ever managed to survive with such tiny brains."

"I'll have you know," Marko replied indignantly, "that I have a PhD in astrophysics and my post-doctoral work is published in *Science* with some regularity. I am one of the most intelligent people on this planet."

"You mean everyone else is even worse off than you are?"

Marko took a deep breath, ready to deliver a suitably scornful retort.

"Er, Marko?" Shelley said, before the man could speak.

"What now?" the Croatian replied testily.

"You're arguing with a rock."

"So?"

"I just can't see how that can be healthy."

The two men stood in silence for a second, a silence which Ferdinand broke reluctantly. "Maybe we should find out what it wants."

Marko shrugged. "It's a rock. It probably just wanted some shade. That desert out there can get warm."

"I have trouble believing you two are for real," the rock said, exasperation evident in its voice. "I see some explanations are in order, to compensate for your lack of anything remotely resembling intelligence, or we'll all go mad." Now it was the rock's turn to pause. "To save time, I'll assume you aren't already mad."

As Ferdinand watched, the rock suddenly began to shift in ways that most rocks don't. A brown extrusion seemed to unfold from one side, followed in short order by three more, all pushing down against the floor. And suddenly, it became clear that the rock had grown legs, and was standing there looking a bit embarrassed. "Er, you might want to move back a little for this next bit," it rumbled.

Both astronomers complied as quickly as the limited space and their less than ideal physical conditions allowed. Just as they finished flattening themselves against the opposite wall, a small pop sounded and the rock expanded, tripling its length.

For some reason, Ferdinand heard his stomach rumbling, and tried to understand why – it took him only a moment to realize that the newly expanded thing in their analysis room reminded him of a giant hot dog with legs.

This illusion lasted only for a second, however, as yet more changes took place. Knobs appeared where only smooth rock had been before, a pair of leathery wings seemed to materialize and expand deep into the corners of the room, where they damaged expensive scientific equipment that had been gathering dust for decades, and what seemed to be a nose pushed itself out of the side nearest the scientists.

Just as Ferdinand was telling himself not to be ridiculous, that it couldn't be a nose, two large golden eyes appeared above the protuberance, and a mouth filled with teeth of distressing size opened below. Shelley, in a bid for sanity, decided to ignore the mouth and concentrate on the eyes for the time being. He had a sinking feeling that he was going to get his chance to think about those teeth soon enough.

"It's a dragon!" Marko exclaimed.

"Don't be ridiculous, dragons don't exist."

The golden orbs, each the size of a softball, focused on Marko. "It seems I owe you an apology. Perhaps you are smarter than most humans," the voice rumbled. "At least you were able to identify a dragon when faced with one."

Marko turned to face his colleague. "How cool is this? We have our own dragon. No more problems getting girls for us."

The dragon's head dropped. "Perhaps I spoke to soon. I assumed that a supposedly gifted member of an intelligent species would be able to comprehend the fact that you don't have me. You see, the reality is that I have you."

It was true. The dragon – or whatever it was, Ferdinand thought mutinously – was standing between the scientists and the door. The only place they could go to escape it was up into the telescope room, but even that was an iffy proposition: the spiral staircase leading to the observation floor was on the other side of the room, and the chances of making it there without those teeth catching at least one of them were slim. And while Shelley was more than willing to sacrifice Marko in order to get there, there was no guarantee that the dragon would choose the correct astronomer. Furthermore, even if he reached the second level, there really wasn't much he could do other than to wait for the dragon to get bored and leave.

Ferdinand stood still. "So, what do you want from us?" he said.

"Well," the dragon began. "I have a bit of a problem. It sort of comes with the territory of being a dragon, but it's still not ideal. And I was wondering whether you would be able to help me with it." It turned those huge eyes on each of them in turn. "Of course, I won't force you to do it – you can refuse, and then I'll just eat you. No hard feelings."

Ferdinand swallowed.

"This is ridiculous," Marko said for the millionth time.

Shelley was inclined to agree, but he wasn't sure

whether his companion was referring to the fact that they were being held hostage by a dragon, which would have been a reasonable motive for complaint, or whether the man was upset that the dragon was hogging the bandwidth. Knowing the Croatian, it was probably the latter.

"Perhaps, but what can we do about it, actually?" Ferdinand said with a shrug. "It's not as if we can run away." The bruises from the last time they'd tried to escape the dragon's vigilance were still fresh – as was the dragon's promise that any further attempts would be met with considerably less leniency.

"Maybe if we disconnect the router, it will give the whole thing up."

"I'm not so sure. After all, when a large reptile that doesn't sleep tells you that it's only keeping you alive for tech support, it might not be the best idea to have the system fail, don't you think?"

"I think we have to do something. We can't stay here while it gets over its Internet addiction. Those things only get worse with time."

"What's it doing, anyway?"

"From what I saw, it's spending all day in chat rooms. Then he looked over at me and said that I was invading his privacy, and could I please go away. I went."

"I'm going to try to talk to it."

"Good luck."

Ferdinand walked out of the room before the weakness he felt in the vicinity of his knees managed to change his mind for him. The dragon was precisely where they'd left it: hunched over a computer that had been dragged to the main foyer – the one place where its body had enough room to be comfortable in and where it could watch the door at all times. The two scientists were free to roam the facility just as long as they stayed far from the entrance – the dragon, as they'd discovered much to their chagrin, was a very light sleeper.

"So," Ferdinand said before he could stop himself,

"what's up?"

The dragon looked away from the screen and cocked its head to one side in a surprisingly human gesture, as if trying to ascertain what, exactly, Shelley was up to. Then it slapped its tail on the ground in frustration. "Not a lot. I'm trying to open a Facebook account, but it won't let me enter my age. And these stupid interfaces are anything but claw-friendly, let me tell you!"

That's because they were designed with humans in mind, not some demonic abomination, Ferdinand didn't say aloud. His experience in dealing with dangerous creatures was limited to the time he'd been married, so he fell back on that. One thing that always worked was to get them to talk about themselves. "So, why are you trying to get onto Facebook?"

For a second, Shelley was certain he'd miscalculated and that the dragon would simply chomp him in half. But then it sighed. "You have no idea how lonely it can get out there. Nothing to do all day but hunt sheep and hide from humans. And since dragons are territorial, you can't get close enough to talk to another one without violating all kinds of treaties."

"But if you're so lonely, why don't you talk to people instead of running from them?"

Ferdinand could swear that the expression that crossed the dragon's face this time was the pained look one gets when dealing with a particularly slow child. He told himself to stop anthropomorphizing it.

"I have found," it said evenly, "that there are two types of humans wandering out in the desert: those that, upon encountering a dragon, run away as fast as their legs can take them until, eventually, they either die of dehydration or fall off a cliff, and those that are too stoned to put together a coherent sentence. Neither type make for scintillating conversation, although the druggies do raise some interesting points about the nature of the universe."

Ferdinand considered it. If he encountered a twenty-foot reptile out on the plains – or anywhere else, for that matter –

running like hell would probably be his answer as well.

Then inspiration hit. "But why don't you just stay in your stone shape and talk? No one would be scared of a rock."

The tail slapped to the ground again. "Would you really want to spend your whole time talking to the kind of people who'd have conversations with a rock?" The dragon glared at him, all expression of companionship gone. "Now, are you going to help me get this thing set up or not?"

"All right," Ferdinand replied, bending over the keyboard to look at the screen. "There should be a pull-down menu of years to choose from. Here it is. Now what year were you born?"

"Well, that's the problem, of course. I was born in northern Africa just as Hannibal was sailing for Italy. Of course, I've moved since then. But there's no choice for years before 1900, and besides, I happen to know for a fact that you humans are so dumb that you lost count of the actual years a couple of times in the Middle Ages, so it's all bunk anyway. What can we do?"

Ferdinand's mouth fell open in shock; his salvation came from an unexpected source.

"The first thing you're going to do," Marko said, appearing from behind the bank of mainframes that had concealed his eavesdropping. "Is to lie about your age. You won't get any friends at all if you tell them that you're a dragon old enough to be their grandfather."

"Technically, I'm much—"

"We won't get anywhere unless you listen to me," Marko interrupted. "I can make you popular in a day, famous in three. Now, do you want to bumble through this on your own, or do you want to learn at the knee of the master?"

The dragon looked at Ferdinand, who shrugged. "It's not what I'd call orthodox, but he does get results – at least online."

Dubiously, the reptile nodded.

"Good," Marko said. "Now let's start with the name."

———

"My name is ancient and respected."

"Are you kidding me? No one is called Tarnetisney. No one. Anywhere. This is the twenty-first century – you'd get beat up for having that kind of name even if you grew up in a yurt in Mongolia. You look like a Jack." Saying this, he typed 'Jack Draco' in the name field, and pressed Enter. "And don't even get me started on your hobbies. Classifying rocks? Unless you want to be catalogued as the biggest loser on the net, you need to get rid of that pronto. Let's see..." his eyes lit up and he chuckled to himself. "Skydiving. Yeah, and we wouldn't even be lying."

Ferdinand left them to it and went to see if he could find something to eat that hadn't been in a can for more than a year. Marko's evil laughter drifted through the once-productive scientific outpost. Ferdinand almost felt sorry for the dragon.

The days dragged on. Pretty soon, the station's stores had run out of alcohol and the remaining food consisted entirely of canned beans. The running water was purified by a perfectly good filter and there were sufficient stores of the indestructible beans to last them a few hundred years, so there seemed to be little chance of their starving to death, sadly.

Ferdinand split the endless time on his hands between making random observations on the telescope – true science meant logging the parameters, something he couldn't do while the dragon kept all the computers occupied with his forums, social networks and chat windows – and wondering why in the world the accountants at ESO had, in their infinite wisdom, decided that beans were the way to go. He'd been at Paranal, just a few hundred miles to the south, and the team there had had a much more varied menu. Of course, only the stars went to Paranal.

Marko's attitude, on the other hand, seemed inexplicably upbeat. He spent most of his time teaching the dragon how to get women – mainly underage women, Ferdinand noted with distaste – to talk to him online. And yet, when confronted, the Croatian would just say 'trust me' and change the subject, a twinkle in his eye.

At that moment, the two were discussing the merits of some poor victim in Santiago.

"The young of your species aren't really that good at making conversation," the dragon rumbled.

"She won't be fifteen forever," Marko insisted.

"But what will I do until then?"

"Patience. You've waited millennia to be able to communicate with humanity, a few more years shouldn't worry you overmuch. And you'll have molded this one to be the perfect friend by then."

"In the meantime, though, can't I talk to adults?"

"Not worth it. They'll just grow old on you, they have more responsibilities. Kids, mortgages, spouses. My way is much better."

"But five hundred girls between the ages of twelve and sixteen? Can't we replace at least a few of them with someone a little older?"

"Are you going to listen to me or not? You've built up a persona now. These people like you. They believe you're a twenty-eight year-old American scientist stationed in Chile for a few years. Now some of these girls are local, all you have to do is keep trying to convince one of them to come up to the station for a visit."

"I doubt their parents would look too kindly on that."

Marko chuckled. "That's the beauty of it. They're at an age in which they'll do anything their parents are against. Once here, you can show yourself to them as you really are, and their flexible young minds, seduced by the way you've already charmed them online, will open up to you and accept that a dragon can be a friend."

The dragon nodded and went back to looking at the screen, and Ferdinand decided he'd heard enough. Trying to stop the progress was likely to get him eaten – he didn't like the fact that the dragon, having been seated in front of the computer for nearly a month without food, was beginning to look lean and hungry. He didn't like it at all.

Trying to give the 'you're addicted to this' speech would only result in the same response it always did: 'I can quit any time I want', and then descend to bickering and name-calling, so Ferdinand did the only thing worth doing. He went up to the telescope room and went to sleep.

But in an installation infested by dragons, one cannot bet on getting much shut-eye, and correspondingly, his rest was immediately cut short. At around three o'clock in the morning, piercing sirens and whuffing chopper blades interrupted Ferdinand's rest. A man with a megaphone began to spew incomprehensible inanities at them. He didn't sound at all happy.

Ferdinand's Spanish was pretty limited, but he thought he caught the words 'storm the building' after they'd been repeated a few times.

This should be good, he thought, as some kind of battering ram began to shake the building. *Dragons versus SWAT. Brilliant.*

But he was doomed to disappointment even in this. About five seconds after the door splintered, two black-clad officers charged into the room, screamed at him in Spanish and secured his arms behind his back with cable ties. Where were the sounds of bullets striking dragonhide? Of claws tearing Kevlar? None of that was in evidence as they dragged him down the spiral staircase and tossed him roughly onto the floor beside the prone form of Marko.

"What the hell's going on?" Ferdinand hissed.

"We got busted for being sexual predators on the Internet. Chile's famous for not having much of a sense of humor about that kind of thing."

"But how'd they find us?"

"Oh, the dragon went way over the line with his invitations, eventually. They just backtracked the IP address and came down to arrest us."

"Why didn't the dragon fight back?"

"Look at it."

Ferdinand did. In front of the computer, where the scaled monstrosity had made its home for the past weeks, there was nothing but a nondescript brown boulder which seemed to be causing the policemen a certain amount of consternation.

"Now," Marko continued, "Chilean law contemplates a couple of months of effective jail time if we're convicted, but we can probably convince them we're nuts. Just tell them the truth about everything that happened here since the dragon arrived, and we'll get off on insanity. They'll assume the desert air and the loneliness finally got to us. Plus, it's much better to label us insane and deport us than jail a pair of foreign nationals. No international incident that way, you see."

Realization suddenly dawned. "You did this on purpose! And now our careers are gone for good."

Marko shrugged, unrepentant. "It was either that or end up as a dragon's lunch. Not much of a choice, was it?"

"But how did you know the police would show up? How did you know which buttons to push?"

This time Marko did blush. "Let's just say this isn't my first arrest for this kind of thing." Immediately changing the subject, he began to explain, in broken Spanish, that the large rock behind them was actually a prehistoric creature of a species thus far undiscovered by humanity.

Ferdinand rolled his eyes and agreed with everything the Croatian said. With any luck, one of the cops would shoot the thing just to prove them wrong.

Gustavo Bondoni is an Argentine writer with over a hundred stories published in ten countries, in four languages, and a winner in the National Space Society's "Return to Luna" Contest and the Marooned Award for Flash Fiction in 2008. His fiction has

---

appeared in a Pearson High-school Test Cycle in the US, *a Bundoran Press anthology,* The Rose & Thorn, Albedo One, The Best of Every Day Fiction *and others.*

His latest book, an ebook novella entitled Branch *was published by Wolfsinger Press in March 2014. He has also published two reprint collections,* Tenth Orbit and Other Faraway Places *(2010) and* Virtuoso and Other Stories *(2011, Dark Quest Books).* The Curse of El Bastardo *(2010) is a short fantasy novel. His website is at www.gustavobondoni.com.ar.*

THE TROUBLE WITH DECORATIONS

By Marc Sorondo

Jason threw another motion-activated skeleton decoration on the pile that was growing by the pull-down stairs. This skeleton screamed, whereas the other one, the glow-in-the-dark one, wailed.

"How much do we need?" Sarah asked from the other side of the attic.

"All of it," Jason said. "Of course we need all of it." He opened a cardboard box and found it full of glass Christmas ornaments. "When we put them away, let's keep all the Halloween stuff together."

Sarah came over, her back hunched beneath the low attic ceiling, and dropped a family of rubber bats onto the pile.

Jason opened another box. "Whoa. What the hell." He reached in and pulled out a doll. It was an elf carved of small pieces of wood. Its body was covered with green and red cloth. An oversized grin was painted on its face, and its eyes were glossy black and just a bit too big. "Now this thing is creepy. I don't remember this one."

"Oh, that's my elf," Sarah said. She reached out for it with a nostalgic smile.

"It's hideous," Jason said as he handed it over.

"No...I loved this guy. You've never heard me talk about it?" She smoothed out the cloth over the front of the doll's torso. "I thought I'd lost it."

"Can we put it out?"

"For Halloween? Hell, no." Sarah wiped dust from the

elf's face with the palm of her hand. "He goes out at Christmastime. You sit him on the mantel and he watches the way everyone behaves. Then, at night, he sneaks off and reports it to Santa."

Jason let out a boisterous laugh. "Holy shit. That's the freakiest thing I've ever heard. That's one way to scar a child for life."

"It's only scary if you're naughty," Sarah said. She turned the doll to face Jason and shook it at him.

He snatched it away from her. "This thing is horrific." He tossed it back into the box. "I guess this is enough stuff. Let's go put it up."

Jason and Sarah surveyed the yard. Sarah held their infant son, Matthew, who reached out for the glossy black wings of a low hanging, rubber bat dangling from a tree branch. The decoration spun slowly in the late October breeze.

Their daughter, Katelyn, ran from place to place, setting off all the motion-activated traps and examining each of the more basic decorations. She skidded to a stop as a plastic gargoyle growled, its clawed hand jabbing out at the movement that had triggered it.

Katelyn giggled and moved on. She stopped beneath a noose, her neck craned to stare up at the oval loop of rope that hung from a small dogwood tree at the center of the front yard.

"Daddy," Katelyn called. She pointed up at the noose. "What's that?"

Jason came over and crouched beside the eight-year-old. He put his hand on her shoulder. "That..." He sought some cute explanation before opting for the truth. "That's a noose. When someone is really, really bad, you hang them from that rope as punishment."

"Jason," Sarah snapped, "don't tell her that kind of stuff."

He shrugged and flashed her an apologetic look.

——

The kids were asleep, the dishes were done, and Jason and Sarah finally crawled into bed at 11:15. Sarah rolled over, pulled the comforter up to her shoulders, and laid with her face nestled into the pillow.

Jason sat against the headboard. He reached over, turned on the bedside lamp, and took a beaten-up paperback from the nightstand.

"Are you really going to read now?" Sarah whined.

Jason sighed. "I guess not." He returned the book to the nightstand and turned the light back off. He slid down, still lying over the covers.

He was surprised to find that his eyes felt heavy almost immediately, that he was comfortable without having to roll around and test a handful of positions first.

He only realized he'd dozed when a sound woke him and he checked the digital clock on his nightstand. It read 12:45 in electric blue light.

He wasn't sure, at first, what had woken him. Then he heard it again: a scrabbling, scraping noise from overhead. He sat up and cursed.

"What's the matter?" Sarah asked groggily.

"Something's in the attic."

"In the attic?" She turned on her bedside lamp. Her eyes were now wide.

The scratching noise came from above them again, the sound of it distinctly moving across the plywood floor of the attic, traveling away from the area over their bedroom.

Sarah sprang up. "Oh my god. Do you think it's mice?"

Jason rubbed his eyes. "I don't know. I guess I'll take a look."

"Maybe wait, and we'll call an exterminator tomorrow," she said. "I don't want you to get bitten by anything."

"I'll be careful. I'll take a quick look to make sure that's even what it is."

"What else would it be?"

———

"I don't know. Don't worry. I'll be right back." Jason got out of bed, stopped at his dresser to get a flashlight from its top drawer, and headed out into the hall.

He passed Katelyn's bedroom and then the nursery on his way to the end of the hall just before the kitchen. He hesitated beneath the piece of rope that dangled from the end of the pull-down stairs.

He envisioned himself climbing up the stairs and finding himself face-to-face with an angry rat or a rabid raccoon. He imagined how his face would look by the time he got away from its claws and teeth. Worse yet, he imagined all that could go wrong if it got out of the attic and into the main part of the house.

He thought about taking Sarah's advice and waiting until morning to deal with it, but he didn't hear anything anymore. He figured maybe whatever it had been was asleep or curled up in some corner where it wouldn't be a danger to him.

Jason reached up and tugged at the rope, pulling the stairs down with a high-pitched squeak that made him wince.

He turned on the flashlight, took a deep breath, and headed up the stairs. He paused halfway up and listened, but the only sounds he heard were the low creaks of the attic stairs as he adjusted his weight on a step and his own breathing.

He climbed further, stopping once his head and chest were above floor level. He lifted the flashlight and shone it towards the area over his bedroom. The beam illuminated only the normal clutter: cardboard boxes filled with decorations, old clothes, high school yearbooks, souvenirs from nearly forgotten trips, and the other items relegated to purgatory in the dusty corners of the attic.

Jason slowly scanned the floor with the flashlight's beam.

Then it lit up something just beside him that made him yelp in surprise and nearly stumble back down the wobbly steps.

It was the elf, propped up so that it sat against the box, the box into which Jason was sure he'd stuffed the doll before leaving the attic. Its painted smile grinned at him.

"Creepy as hell," Jason muttered. He took a few more steps up into the attic, grabbed the elf, and jammed it into the box where it belonged. He made a point of folding down the tabs at the top of the box and making sure they stayed closed.

Then he returned to bed.

Jason woke to the sound of his daughter screaming, "Mommy! Daddy!"

Sarah was already up and hurrying into the hall without her robe, her pajamas twisted and disheveled around her.

Jason looked at the clock as he got out of bed: 1:47. *One of those nights*, he thought as he headed into the hall.

Jason found them on the bed, illuminated only by the little ballerina nightlight beneath the window. Katelyn was curled up in her mother's lap.

"There was a little man in my room," Katelyn sobbed.

"It's okay, sweetie. There's no one here," Sarah said in her most soothing voice.

Jason smiled. "Where did he go?"

"I don't know." There was still a whiny tone to her voice, but the tears were over. "I just saw his little eyes, and then they were gone."

Jason flicked on the lights. He stood, looking down at his wife and daughter, and brought a finger to his chin. "Hmmm...I'll bet...the closet." He walked over to it and took the knob. He turned back, a finger pressed to his puckered lips, and signaled for Sarah and Katelyn to be quiet.

Then he ripped the door open and kicked at the clothes that hung inside, copying Bruce Lee's kung fu vocalizations as best he could.

Katelyn giggled.

"Hmm..." Jason said, turning back to his little girl. "He

---

seems to have run off…scared of the old man."

Then something caught his eye, something that made the smile abruptly drop off his face.

In the wooden rocking chair at the far corner of the bedroom, mixed in with teddy bears and stuffed animals and decorative pillows, sat the grinning elf in his dusty red and green suit.

"You okay, Daddy?" Katelyn asked.

Jason forced himself to smile. "I just wish I'd been able to catch him and beat him up for scaring my little princess."

"It's okay. As long as you made him go away." Katelyn reached out for the pink sock monkey that she'd slept with since she was only a baby.

Sarah slid the girl from her lap and tucked her back in.

Jason flicked off the light as Sarah kissed Katelyn on the forehead. He went over to the rocking chair and grabbed the elf by the head. He held it behind his back as he went over for his turn to kiss Katelyn goodnight.

He stopped Sarah in the hall. "How did this get in her room?" he asked, holding up the wooden doll.

"Must have snuck around to make sure everyone's behaving," Sarah said with a tired smile.

"What?" Jason asked in a harsh whisper.

"Relax, weirdo, it was a joke," Sarah said. "Katelyn must have seen it and taken it or something." She went back into their bedroom.

Jason looked down at the doll in his hand. He headed down the hall, stopping momentarily beneath the attic stairs, wondering what he would find if he pulled them down and went up to investigate the contents of that cardboard box.

Then he decided against it. He walked into the kitchen, opened the cabinet under the sink, and chucked the old doll into the trash bin.

Jason woke to the sound of Matthew crying in slightly distorted notes through the baby monitor. "Again?" He

---

looked at the clock: 3:13.

"I'll go. You have work tomorrow," Sarah said, already getting out of bed.

Jason laid his head back against the pillows. He closed his eyes and saw the elf's painted smile in the darkness. He got out of bed and hurried out of the room.

He found Sarah holding Matthew, rocking the baby gently as she hummed a lullaby to him.

"What's the matter? I told you I'd get it," she whispered sleepily.

Jason turned the light on.

Matthew started crying again.

"What are you doing?" Sarah's tone was equally annoyed and bewildered.

Jason's eyes were frantic as they scanned the room. "Just making sure." He looked under the crib, in the toy box, and in the hamper full of dirty clothes.

"What are you looking for?" Sarah asked. She'd turned Matthew, pressing him gently against her chest and rocking him in long, wide movements. The boy was quieting back down.

"I'm looking…" Then he saw it. On the changing table, all but the grinning face hidden behind the changing pad. "Ha! I'm looking for that!"

Jason strode over and snatched up the doll.

"What the…" Sarah stopped.

"I threw the damn thing in the trash after I took it out of Katelyn's room," Jason said, shaking the doll out in front of him.

"Yeah, but…" Sarah stopped.

"Exactly," Jason said. He rushed out of the room and Sarah followed quickly after, still holding the dozing baby. Jason stormed down the hall.

"What are you doing?" Sarah asked.

"Getting rid of it."

Jason unlocked the front door and threw it open. He'd

had every intention of tossing the doll in the big trashcan in the driveway, but his eyes were drawn to the noose that hung from the dogwood tree in the yard.

He looked down at the elf. He shook his head and decided that even he'd think he was crazy if he lynched a wooden doll in his front yard.

He stepped out into the cool air; the concrete felt freezing cold against the soles of his bare feet. He cut left just outside the door and walked over to the big, green, plastic trashcans at the end of the driveway. He opened the lid of the closest one, threw the doll face first onto the black garbage bags inside, and slammed the lid down.

Jason went back inside. He closed the door, deliberately locking it and sliding the deadbolt into place. Then he checked both locks.

Satisfied, he headed back to bed.

It was a clicking sound. Something was tapping on the hardwood floor of their bedroom.

"Now what?" Jason looked at the clock: 4:38. He reached out for the light; his shifting weight disturbed Sarah.

"What's the matter?" she asked.

"Better not be that damned elf," Jason said, half kidding. He switched on the light.

Sarah gasped.

"You've got to be kidding me." Jason threw the covers off and got out of bed.

The elf sat against the wall just inside their bedroom, its glossy black eyes watching them, its painted grin smiling at them.

Jason grabbed the doll. "Where the hell did you get this thing?"

Sarah shrugged. "I've had it since I was little."

Jason walked out, carrying the doll in a tight fist. He went down the hall to the kitchen.

Sarah followed and found him rummaging through

88

drawers.

"What are you looking for?" she asked.

He grunted and held up a long, thin stick lighter. He pressed the button on it and, with a click, a flame sprouted at the end of the black tube protruding from the handle. "This."

"I don't understand. It's just a toy," she said.

"Bullshit, just a toy," Jason said. "Come on."

He led her to the front door. "Still locked," he said as he slid open the deadbolt. He unlocked the door and smiled at the noose when it came into view.

Sarah followed him down the concrete steps but stopped at the edge of the lawn.

Jason strode over to the dogwood. He stuck the elf's head into the noose and tightened the knot. Then he stepped back.

"Are we sure there's not another explanation for all this?" Sarah asked.

Jason turned to respond but was stopped by a sound like wood snapping. He turned back to the hanging doll.

The black eyes were now angry slits; the painted grin had turned down into a scowl.

"Holy shit," Jason whispered. He pressed the button on the lighter.

The elf's hand shot up. It pointed at him. "Naughty!" The elf's voice was raspy and loud. It coughed the word out like it was hacking up a piece of phlegm. "Naughty," it repeated.

Jason stabbed at the doll with the lighter.

The old cloth covering the doll's body went up quickly. The carved wood beneath blackened and finally caught fire as well.

The small, carved hand remained extended, accusing Jason. "Naughty," the elf whispered.

Then the hand fell.

Jason stood there and watched it burn. The flames burned down to a gentle smolder, and the elf looked more like

—

a misshapen lump of charcoal than a doll. It remained hanging from the blackened rope, the fibers fused together around the doll's neck.

Jason walked back over to Sarah.

"Are you just going to leave it there?" she asked.

"Yeah...for now," he said. "Tomorrow I'll get some lighter fluid and burn the damn thing to ashes."

Sarah nodded.

"What the hell was that thing?" Jason said.

"It was just supposed to be a toy...a Christmas decoration," Sarah said.

Jason's alarm blared. He smacked the button at the top of the clock and then looked at the time: 6:30. He groaned as he got out of bed.

"Call in sick," Sarah said, her face still pressed into her pillow.

"And tell them what, I was fighting an evil doll all night?"

"I'd go with stomach flu," she said, "but, whatever."

Jason grunted and walked out into the hall. He peeked in at Katelyn and then Matthew. They were both still sleeping. Then he headed for the front door.

He slipped the deadbolt and unlocked the door. He opened it and stood there, looking out at the decorated yard.

He was quiet for a moment, but then he exhaled forcefully and cursed.

The charred rope hung from the dogwood, its fibers blackened and stiff, the length of it swaying in the late autumn breeze. The loop at its end was empty.

Marc Sorondo lives with his wife and children in New York. He loves to read, and his interests range from fiction to comic books, physics to history, oceanography to cryptozoology, and just about everything in between. He's a long time student and occasional teacher. For more information, go to MarcSorondo.com .

DIRTY DYBBUK

By Anna Taborska

630,720,000 seconds without sex. And each of those seconds like a lifetime. For time has no meaning in the abyss. Hundreds of years can go by in a moment or a second can drag out for a thousand years. And that's a long time to go without sex. A very long time.

'Boys don't make passes at girls who wear glasses.' The less than friendly expression had stuck in Mitzi's mind since primary school so that, when her likewise short-sighted friends moved on to contact lenses, Mitzi wore her thick-framed spectacles with added determination. For Mitzi had no intention of having passes made at her by boys. Absolutely no way.

Mitzi was almost twenty-one now and studying English at Oxford University. Sadly there were no women's colleges left; the last one – St. Hilda's – had opted to admit men in 2006 – a financial necessity rather than a matter of equality and fraternity. So Mitzi frequented New College – one of the oldest colleges in the university – where she was a dedicated member of the Jewish Society and the Women's Group. At the end of every term, Mitzi would return home to Golders Green – the leafy and pleasant part of London in which she'd lived all her life.

It wasn't that Mitzi disliked boys or that she was a lesbian – God forbid. Not at all. But Mitzi came from a good family – a respectable, middle class family – and when the time was right for her to marry, her parents would ask a *shadkhan* to pick out a suitable young man for her.

The abyss was long and deep. Inside it were chained the angels that had rebelled against the Lord. Some of them had taken human women as their brides and fathered giants that ransacked the earth. The lust and suffering of the trapped angels drew her to the abyss, but the flames that raged there barred all entry. She floated through the forbidden places, but always made her way back to the human realm. How she envied the women their flesh, with the infinite capacity for pleasure that it brought. How it angered her seeing prudish schoolgirls and pious old maids who kept their legs together and shunned the touch of men. They didn't deserve the soft skin and the heaven between their thighs that had been so brutally snatched from her. Some spark of consciousness within the hungry tormented spirit that was once human drove her relentlessly to her earthly roots. The ties that bind drew her inexorably back to those whose flesh was of her own. And after twenty years of torment that only a disembodied nymphomaniac could understand, she finally found the home that she'd been longing for.

Mitzi had been feeling light-headed the night before and had gone to bed early. She awoke suddenly at dawn as a jolt of energy shot through her body. Startled and confused, she sat up and looked around the room. Then she remembered: it was her birthday! She was going shopping with her best friend, and later her parents were taking her out to dinner at Six 13 – her very favourite restaurant. But something was not quite right. She was feeling tense in an odd, albeit rather pleasant sort of way, and her thoughts turned inexplicably to the blonde blue-eyed *goy* from her staircase in New College. Mark – that was his name. Mitzi tried to push the image of the young man's muscular form from her mind and fought hard against the strange sensations that were taking over her body. But she was battling with a will stronger than her own, and soon she closed her eyes and sank back onto her pillow, her hand straying downwards beneath the sheets.

92

The girl had put up an impressive struggle, but she was young and ripe, and in the end susceptible. The joy of having such a lovely firm body to exploit was indescribable. She was almost able to forget that this fine youthful frame wasn't her own. And there were so many men out there, and so much pleasure to be had.

'Rise and shine with Night Light glow in the dark condoms'. For Hannah Goldblatt, the shopping trip had become a surrealist nightmare. She had gladly agreed to accompany Mitzi – her closest friend since primary school – to check out a few shops on the Finchley Road. The idea was to help Mitzi choose some clothes for her summer term at Oxford, and break up the hard work of shopping with a bite to eat at Daniel's Bagel Bakery. But no – at the last minute Mitzi had insisted that they go to Camden Market, catching Hannah off guard, and using the fact that it was her birthday to bully her friend into going along with her heinous plan. And not only were they now far from home, surrounded by Goths, drug dealers and overexcited tourists, but they were standing in front of the Sex Emporium, an unhealthy glint in Mitzi's eye.

"Let's go," pleaded Hannah. The unfamiliar area made her nervous and more than a little frightened, and she was convinced that everyone who walked past was staring at the two unhip Jewish girls in front of the adult store.

"You go if you want," Mitzi told Hannah, "I'm going in." And she did. Hannah looked around fearfully, spotted three youths in black leather jackets across the road, and hurried in after her friend.

An hour later, a traumatised Hannah emerged from the sex shop with a dazed expression, carrying the bags that Mitzi was too overloaded to manage on her own: bags of kinky nurse and nun outfits, edible undies, a Rampant Rabbit and curry-flavoured condoms.

"I'm thirsty," Mitzi smiled warmly at her pale and silent

friend. "Let's go to the pub."

"You can't go out dressed like that!" Mitzi had come downstairs in her new tight black miniskirt, high-heeled shoes and clinging low-cut red top, and was now facing down her shocked parents in a scene reminiscent of an old Western.

"It's my birthday," she stated firmly. A compromise was finally reached in the form of a cardigan that covered the top half of Mitzi's assets, and the family party left for dinner, but the atmosphere during the meal remained tense.

Over the next few weeks, the relationship between Mitzi and her once doting parents continued to deteriorate, as the young woman took to staying out late and coming home stinking of alcohol, with her lipstick smudged and bits of grass stuck to the back of her jacket. The last straw came in the form of a Thursday evening phone call from the next door neighbour. Mitzi's mother answered the phone.

"Vera," Mrs. Rosenberg said coldly. "I don't know quite how to say this, but I'm afraid you have to do something about your daughter."

"What do you mean?"

"Simcha is only sixteen."

"What are you saying?"

"I'm saying that Mitzi's been flashing over the garden fence."

"Flashing?"

"Her… boobies."

Mitzi had been feeling restless all morning. There'd been no post, so no postman to flirt with, and no prospect of any male company all day. It was very warm for late April, and Mitzi sat in the garden, trying to read a college textbook. Then she heard voices – young male voices – and remembered the kid next door. Without even realizing that she'd stood up, Mitzi found herself peering over the garden fence. She had the distinct feeling that something bad was going to happen, and

—

94

she tried to turn around and go back to her deckchair, but it was too late.

"Hi, Simcha," she heard herself say.

"Hi, Mitzi." Simcha smiled and walked over to the fence.

"Who's your friend?" She grinned past Simcha at the freckly teenager seated at the outdoor table, sipping a fizzy drink.

"Oh, that's Aaron."

"Hi Aaron," said Mitzi, feeling increasingly nervous and trying hard to find a way to end the conversation.

"Hi," the boy waved.

"Would you boys like to see something?" Mitzi asked.

"Sure," Aaron got up and joined Simcha at the fence. And that's when it happened: before she knew it, Mitzi had her top hoisted all the way up over her naked breasts, the fear and excitement overwhelming as the boys stared, then giggled, then turned and fled as Mrs. Rosenberg's shriek of horror split the sultry air behind them.

"I don't know what's got into you!" bemoaned Mitzi's mother.

"Look, darling," the serious expression on her father's face caused Mitzi no end of amusement. "Your mother and I were wondering… are you taking drugs?" Mitzi laughed in an unearthly, lascivious manner. There was something familiar about that laugh, but Mitzi's mother couldn't quite place it.

"The blood tests were negative," Doctor Warner told Mitzi's parents. Of course, your daughter might have taken a drug that metabolised quickly out of her body, but the lab certainly didn't find any sign of any of the more common substances. You know, it's not infrequent for young women of Mitzi's age to have psychological problems. I have a friend who's an excellent psychologist. I can put you in touch with him if you like."

"It's nothing more than a healthy appetite for life," Dr. Friedmann told Mitzi's parents, winking at the girl when they weren't looking. Mitzi winked back, uncrossing and re-crossing her legs in a manner worthy of a sleazy Hollywood movie, and giving her psychologist a tantalising flash that reminded him of all the fun they'd had in their two months of £220 per hour therapy sessions. "But I'll be happy to go on working with Mitzi… and I can give you a big discount."

"That won't be necessary, Doctor," said Mitzi's father. "Thank you all the same."

Mitzi's parents watched in horror as their only child flirted outrageously with all their male friends – and their sons, brothers, cousins and fathers. They stopped inviting men to the house, and succeeded admirably in beating Mitzi to the door or distracting her when the postman rang. But then disaster struck.

With everything that was going on, Mitzi's mother had totally forgotten that she'd booked the gardener for his monthly visit. She and Mitzi's father had gone out to run some errands and got back to find raunchy music blasting from Mitzi's bedroom. They hurried upstairs, with a growing feeling of unease, and found the perplexed, but delighted gardener tied to a chair wearing nothing but his boxer shorts and being given a lap dance by their daughter who was proudly sporting her edible undies. Needless to say, this was not a sight that any parents should be forced to endure, and the poor gardener was promptly untied and given his marching orders. They couldn't lock her in the house, as she was an adult, but Mitzi's parents knew that they had to act fast. They had to save their daughter before she went back to college, where she would be beyond their control and where there was no telling what kind of trouble she'd get herself into.

"I know it sounds crazy," Mitzi's mother told her husband, "but that's not my daughter – that's not Mitzi." But it wasn't until Mitzi dyed her hair a particularly offensive shade of peroxide blonde, and the unmistakable family resemblance glared her defiantly in the face, that Mitzi's mother realised the full implication of what she'd started to suspect on a subconscious level.

"I think a *dybbuk* has entered my daughter," Mitzi's mother told the Rabbi.

"Nonsense!" he replied. But his scepticism vanished as Mitzi – who'd been standing quietly behind her mother – lifted up her top and gave the holy man a quick flash of her bare breasts.

"It's my late sister," Mitzi's mother continued, thankfully unaware of her child's actions behind her back. "She was a prolific whore from the day she turned sixteen to the day she got hit by a truck… I suppose there's one in every family."

So it was that with considerable hesitation the Rabbi consented to perform a banishing ritual. For many days he negotiated with the spirit of Mitzi's aunt to depart the young woman's body before getting her into no end of trouble. The *dybbuk* said that it would leave only if the Rabbi performed lewd acts with the girl, and it took all of the Rabbi's strength of character to push from his mind the images that the misguided spirit planted within it.

The holy man bored her to tears. Sometimes his droning voice and inane arguments wearied her so much that she actually thought about leaving her beautiful fleshy home just to avoid listening to him a moment longer. But there was no way she was going to relinquish her last chance at happiness.

The Rabbi did everything in his power to persuade Mitzi's aunt to leave the innocent girl and move on. But all his attempts came to naught. And then an extraordinary opportunity presented itself.

—

97

"Rabbi, we need your help." The recently wed couple stood before him; the young man sweating and embarrassed, his wife visibly distressed. "All we want is to live a good life in the eyes of God," the young man said.

"And to bear children in his image," added the woman. Her pale cheeks were tinged scarlet with shame, and when she briefly lifted her eyes from the floor, the Rabbi saw that there were tears in them.

"But, you see Rabbi," the man carried on, "my wife just can't bear when I touch her."

"It's not you; it's me," the young woman interjected in her husband's defence.

"I am gentle and I try to give her pleasure..."

"But, I just can't, Rabbi... even the very thought of it makes me sick."

The Rabbi couldn't sleep that night. He tossed and turned, and scanned his memory of *halakhah*, trying to find the right path for all his supplicants. And then it came to him: he would bake two proverbial *challot* in one pan! If he couldn't persuade the dirty *dybbuk* to move on to the next plane of existence, then perhaps he could talk it into moving to a more suitable home.

And so, not only was Mitzi liberated from the burden of unwanted wantonness, but the troubled couple became eternally indebted to the Rabbi – for many fine children, and countless nights, mornings, and even lunchtimes of the most satisfactory wedded bliss.

And Mitzi's aunt had no complaints.

Anna Taborska is a British filmmaker and horror writer. She has written and directed two short films (Ela and The Sin), two documentaries (My Uprising and A Fragment of Being) and a one-hour television drama (The Rain Has Stopped), which won two awards at the British Film Festival Los Angeles in 2009. Anna also worked on seventeen other films, and was involved in the making of two major BBC television series: Auschwitz: the Nazis and the Final Solution *and* World War Two behind Closed Doors – Stalin, the Nazis and the West. *Anna's short stories have appeared in various anthologies, including* Best New Writing 2011, Best New Werewolf Tales Vol.1, Best Horror of the Year Volume Four, The Best British Horror 2014 *and* Year's Best Weird Fiction Volume One. *Anna's short story "Bagpuss" was an Eric Hoffer Award Honoree, and the screenplay adaptation of her story "Little Pig" was a finalist in the* Shriekfest Film Festival Screenplay Competition, 2009. *Anna's debut short story collection,* For Those who Dream Monsters, *was released by Mortbury Press in 2013, with a novelette collection (working title* Bloody Britain) *to follow. You can view Anna's full résumé here: http://www.imdb.com/name/nm1245940/, watch her films and book trailers here: http://www.youtube.com/annataborska and learn more about her short stories and screenplays here: http://annataborska.wix.com/horror .*

WEREGOAT

By Pamela K. Kinney

Alvin Middleton knew he was in trouble when, on the first night of the full moon, he changed into a goat.

Heart pounding, he roamed all night, avoiding being hit by vehicles and chased by barking dogs. When dawn chased the night away, he huddled naked against a lamp post. Not only that; he smelled foul, too.

Hoping that no one saw him, he snitched a sheet off a clothesline in some stranger's backyard and wrapped it around his body. He bolted for home, his bare feet finding every sharp stone along the way.

Once there, he took a hasty shower and threw on some clothes, then anointed the bottom of his sore feet with salve. As he chewed on a week-old donut, he surfed the Internet on his laptop to discover what his problem was. He found lots of articles on lycanthropy concerning werewolves, plus other mythology about werepanthers and every other kind of werething, but nothing about weregoats.

Alvin rubbed his upset stomach. Always a nervous guy, this situation made the gas worse.

Had he been cursed? He wasn't a sorcerer, couldn't do magic if he tried. And to his knowledge no one in his family had this ability, and he damn well hadn't been born a weregoat! He hadn't been near any kind of a goat for years, in fact, any kind of barnyard animal, so he knew he hadn't been bitten by one. Hell, he hated the nasty odors of the barnyard — they always made him queasy. So why had he turned into a goat last night?

He stood and, after a stop at the bathroom to pop a couple of pills, he tramped to the living room. Thumping down on the couch, he rubbed his sweaty palms on his pants.

Would he change for the next couple of nights of the full moon? Could someone shoot him with a silver bullet and kill him? Would he be doing this for the rest of his life?

He shuddered.

What if he got a blind date set up and just as he was about to make his move on the woman he morphed into his smelly, goaty self? Bad enough that he couldn't get a date to save his life, but once his new lifestyle came out of the barn, he'd definitely be dead to the opposite sex. How downright embarrassing it would be if, at the next Shriners meeting, he shifted into a goat.

The Shriners meeting! Oh God, that was tonight.

Last night had been the waxing of the full moon, but tonight it would be the real deal. He'd have to call and make some excuse, even though this was his chapter's meeting where the members voted for their officers and he was on the ticket for president.

To be honest, if he attended tonight and changed into a goat, that would be the end of any chance of being elected president of the Shriners. He'd be drummed out of the group altogether. Not only that, they probably would call Animal Control on him.

Why couldn't he have changed into a wolf? At least chicks dug werewolves these days — look at all those paranormal romances on the bestseller lists. But no, he became the first weregoat ever. A loser no matter what skin he wore.

Deciding to take this new phenomenon like a werewolf would, he went to the library and checked out all the books on the subject he could find. From them, he wrote himself a list of things to buy and use — helpful stuff for the next metamorphosis.

Alvin bought chains and manacles to constrain himself

———

to his bed to get through the night. Once the full moon had passed he would search for someone to help him. A witch, maybe. Otherwise he might repeat this aberration every month for the rest of his life. And if he didn't find the help he needed, well . . . he didn't know what he would do. Memory of how he smelled this morning, like a barnyard gone wild, made him gag.

He'd shoot himself before he went through another night of this.

After dinner that night, he walked into his bedroom and took off all his clothes, folding each piece and placing them into a neat pile in his dirty clothes bin. He shackled himself to the bed, making sure that the other end was secure, and sat down on the floor to wait for the moon to rise.

His gaze caught the brilliance of the full moon as it shone through the glass of the bedroom window. An itch started in the upper part of his back, between his shoulders, and Alvin couldn't reach to scratch as his hands were handcuffed. His back against the bed, he tried to rub it like a bear did against a tree.

It didn't help.

The itch grew worse, spreading to his arms and the lower part of his back. From there it raged like a wildfire, covering every part of his body, including his genitals. Suddenly, and without any warning, the bones and muscles in his body screamed with pain as they began to stretch, trying to remold themselves like modeling clay out of control. Alvin shrieked. The yell grew shriller and shriller until it no longer sounded human, but more like the ba-ba of a goat. To his horror, his feet and hands hardened, his toes and fingers melding together and becoming shiny black hooves. His legs and arms grew hairy with rough, wiry hair. Horns sprouted from the top of his head.

No longer a man, Alvin rolled over onto all four hooves and shook his head. The moonlight splashed his face and reflected in his eyes. Something tugged at his consciousness, impelling him to find a way to get unchained.

An insidious whisper blew into his ear, saying over and over, *"The Shriners meeting."* He tugged at the chain. It didn't work. Bleating, he reared on his fore legs and kicked out with his back legs at the bed. Instead, he tripped and fell on his snout, catching the edge of the blanket covering his bed with his horns and ripping it.

Several more attempts later, the handcuffs on his back legs broke apart. For once, he felt glad about being a cheapskate and buying the lowest priced product he could find. A few more yanks, and the ones on his forelegs snapped, too.

Free! Trouble was, he would be late for the Shriners' meeting and the election tonight. Clip, clop, clip, clop. He stopped and looked down at his hooves. Hey, he had four hooves, much faster than his normal two feet.

He smashed through the glass of the bedroom window and bolted down the street. His next door neighbor's big German shepherd loped from around the back of the house, barking and snarling furiously. The dog's jaws snapped at the back of his heels, only biting air as Alvin sped up. Bleating in fear, he broke into a gallop, until finally he left the mongrel far behind.

Maybe he'd make it to the meeting in time after all.

Cars and trucks jammed the parking lot. It looked like a full house for the special meeting tonight. Alvin peeped from behind a bush. Men wearing red fezzes headed into the temple. He'd forgotten his... How would he even get a fez on his head, much less over the horns?

Once everyone was inside, he snuck around back to enter by the back door.

He found it unlocked and butted it open, finding no one inside.

Humph! When he made president, he would do something about that. If a weregoat could get in, who or what else might be able to?

Just as he passed a room with a door slightly ajar, he heard laughter and then the whiny voice of his opponent, Justin Plimpton. Alvin placed an eye at the crack.

Justin was a fat, balding man who always seemed to wear his clothes tight. He overflowed a chair opposite a tall, thin man with greasy brown hair who slumped on a couch.

Justin snickered. "I don't see Alvin Middleton here tonight, Parker. The spell must have worked. Best damn thing I ever did, paying you to cast it on him. With no one else opposing me, I'm sure to be a shoo-in for the presidency."

The other man said, 'Yeah, but, you still owe me five hundred bucks for the job. You only paid half of the thousand we agree on. Just because I'm a warlock doesn't mean I can magic money out of the air. There are rules, you know."

Justin lit a cigar and took a puff. "I'll give you a check after I win tonight. I told you that before. Want to make sure Middleton doesn't come in at the last moment, in human form." A wreath of cigar smoke circled his head.

Parker glowered. "You better, or else! I cursed Middleton to be a goat, but there are worse things I can turn you into."

Justin forced his girth out of the chair as he tried to keep a hold of the cigar. "Just to show my faith, I'll get that check for you now. But you stay in here. Okay?" He took another puff of the cigar and blew out smoke. "I don't need any of those fools in the auditorium seeing you and asking questions about what you're doing here."

He took out a checkbook, scribbled in it, tore the check out, and handed it over to Parker. The warlock glanced at it, then stuffed it in his pants pocket. Justin waddled out the door.

Alvin ducked behind a trashcan. He didn't want Justin to see him, not yet anyway. It became hard though, as delicious odors from the can wafted to his nose. Remains of a bun with mayonnaise and wilted lettuce lay at his hooves. It must have fallen out of the trash. He bent his head down and nibbled at it. He had never tasted anything so delicious before. Just as he swallowed the last bit, he plopped down on his tail in disbelief.

God, I just ate something from the trash! Just like a smelly old goat.

He really needed to get this curse off him quick. Especially before the stink from the trash grew into an enticing aroma again.

He ducked into the room. The warlock did not see him. Not until Alvin stood in front of him. Before the man could do anything, Alvin butted him in the stomach and knocked him down to the floor. He planted his snout in the man's face, baring his teeth.

"It's you," said Parker. "Damn, the curse worked! I wasn't sure it would."

Alvin just uttered a baa and glared, placing all of his hooves on Parker's chest and groin. He applied special pressure at the groin area.

Gritting his teeth, Parker spat out, "Okay, I can see you are not happy being a goat. But when Plimpton hired me, it was a chance for me to prove I could do magic like my father and grandfather before me. You understand?"

Alvin snorted, blowing hot air in the warlock's face. He placed a hoof on the man's throat and pushed. Parker's eyes bugged out and his face paled. The weregoat took the hoof away.

Parker's voice came out a squeak. "No, I guess not. Look, I don't like Plimpton either. He's a hog all the way. How about I help you out and I still get to keep the money he paid me? I'll uncurse you and put the whammy on him. At least you're proof I can do the magic."

Alvin hopped off Parker and watched as the warlock got to his feet, dusting himself off. The man withdrew a small, dog-eared leather book and opened it, placing a finger on a page.

"Lumbo, nix de juno. Les copeach."

Alvin started shaking and fell to his belly, all four legs splayed out. Agony spread through his body and head. If he thought the pain from the metamorphosis was bad, this felt worse. He ought to get up, pain or no pain, and kick the warlock in the—

He blacked out.

Alvin rolled over onto his back, smiling. He had the most vivid dream of himself and a super model. He woke up when he realized that would never happen to him, not in a million years.

He laid on a hardwood floor and not his bed. Another thing not normal for him, he was nude. When he went to bed, he always wore his checkered pajamas. He sat up, splinters from the floor jabbing his derriere.

He remembered everything.

His hands touched human flesh everywhere and not one goat hair. He was back to normal. Naked as a newborn baby, but back to being human. That's when he saw the warlock.

Parker flashed him an amused look. "It worked. You're 100% human again."

Alvin went to the closet at the other end of the room and lucky for him, he found a pair of pants and a shirt to slip on. Big and baggy, he rolled up the pants so not to trip when he walked.

"Look, Parker, you can put the whammy on Plimpton, but wait until he's up there at the podium, giving his speech. Then stick it to him when I give you the signal."

Parker grinned, his face having the unsettling look of a hungry shark at that moment. "Sure. I can do that."

"Thanks."

No shoes in the closet. Nothing he could do about that. After Parker cursed Plimpton, being a barefooted human would be a better choice for the voters than whatever Plimpton became. A fez lay on a shelf. Alvin snatched it.

"When I tip this fez at you, that's when you use your

magic on Plimpton," said Alvin, then placed the hat on his head and walked out of the room.

He stepped onto the stage just as Plimpton stomped up to the podium. The other man was startled to see a human Alvin. Alvin beamed at him and wiggled his fingers in a wave as he settled into one of two chairs next to the podium.

Sweat beading his forehead, Plimpton cleared his throat and turned back to the audience, his fez perched at a jaunty angle on his head. He began to speak about why they should vote for him. Out of the corner of his eye, Alvin saw Parker peering from behind the curtain. He tipped his fez at the warlock. Parker began to mutter something under his breath.

Now the show would begin. And with a full moon in the night sky tonight, no way Plimpton would get out of this curse.

Plimpton took a sip of water from a water bottle he had, choked, and spit out the water, then hunched over as if in pain. He dropped the bottle and it hit the floor, the liquid spilling across the stage. His meaty hands gripping each side of the lectern; he straightened and began to talk again.

Instead of words, grunts of a pig came out. A loud hiss of shock rose from those sitting in the audience. Alvin giggled.

Plimpton tried again, but the same piggish grunts slipped out. The lectern crashed to the floor. He dropped and lay there, shaking. People rushed to help him, but they gasped and backed away.

Alvin leaped to his feet, craning his neck over them to see what they saw.

Plimpton got to his feet and hands . . . no, to his hooves. His clothes had shredded from the change and hung in tatters. No longer human, he had become a large, pot-bellied hog.

Alvin strolled over, Parker right behind him. Plimpton gave both a wide-eyed look of fright and turned tail and ran offstage, squealing. That was the last time Alvin ever saw him.

By default, Alvin won the election. Though human again and president of the Shriners, his love life was still pathetic.

But anything was better than being a goat and pathetic too.

As for Parker, Alvin heard that the warlock performed a curse on the wrong person, a Mafia boss in New Orleans. His angry men took Parker out by getting a voodoo priestess to turn him into a mouse. They fed him to an alligator, which happened to be the Mafia boss.

It couldn't have happened to a better person.

Pamela K. Kinney is a published author of horror, science fiction, fantasy, poetry, and nonfiction ghost books published by Schiffer Publishing. Her latest fiction includes "Devil in the Details," in Harboring Secrets *anthology and "Let Demon Dogs Lie" released in* Southern Haunt: Devils in the Darkness *anthology March 2014. She has a horror and dark fantasy tales collection in print and download,* Spectre Nightmares and Visitations, *along with other stories and poetry in magazines, anthologies, and ezines. One horror story, "Bottled Spirits," is a 2013 WSFA Small Press Award runner up.*

Under the pseudonym, Sapphire Phelan, she has published erotic and sweet paranormal/fantasy/science fiction romance along with a couple of erotic horror stories in both print and eBooks.

Also an actress in plays and films, she also a casting director for an indie film, wrote a horror screenplay for another indie film, and co-producer for Paranormal World Seekers *by AVA Productions.*

She admits she can always be found at her desk and on her computer, writing. And yes, the house, husband, and even the cats sometimes suffer for it!

Find out more about Pamela K. Kinney at http://www.PamelaKKinney.com

HABITAT FOR INHUMANITY

By Paul A. Dixon

The hundred-year-old Victorian mansion hulked in the October moonlight. Four stories and a turret, plopped smack in the middle of Seattle's well-to-do Madrona neighborhood, squatting on half an acre with a commanding view of Lake Washington.

"Doesn't look like an undead habitat," Deagan muttered, idling his unmarked Ford to a stop behind the dozen black-and-whites that had responded to the 911 call. "More like a bed and breakfast."

It was a quarter past one, forty-five minutes since the call came in. Deagan swiped his phone to life, found the recording and hit play, hoping maybe he'd missed something the first time through.

"911 emergency dispatch," the operator said, her voice tinny over the phone's speaker. "May I have your location, please?"

"My name is Mr. Stevenson." The caller's voice was faint as a ghost, and he spoke in ragged gasps. "I am the caretaker at Madrona Unlife."

There was a brief pause. "That's at 3215 Norman Avenue East, Seattle?"

"Yes," the caller said. "Norman Avenue, yes."

"Thank you, sir. A unit has been dispatched to your location. What is the nature of your emergency?"

"They killed me," the man said.

There was a brief pause. "I'm sorry, sir - can you repeat

that?"

"I said, I've just been murdered." The caller's voice faded, as though the last of his strength were leaving him. "It was… it was…"

A click, and the line went dead.

They killed me, Deagan thought. *They.* It was an odd thing to say. In his not inconsiderable experience, murderers usually acted alone.

Of course, the whole thing was damned odd.

He pocketed the phone and eased the door open, the Ford and his back creaking together in protest. A crowd of uniforms were milling about on the sidewalk; no one seemed to know quite what to do. Deagan sympathized. Far as he knew, undead didn't much welcome outside attention in any form. Whoever responded to a 911 call from a place like this? He couldn't remember having heard of such a thing, not in his thirty years on the force.

He spotted Sergeant Mary Angelo breaking from the pack, a five-foot-nothing bundle of energy striding over to meet him. Good, he thought, giving her a wave. She was just a kid, but he'd seen her work before. She knew her business.

"What've we got, Sergeant?" he called.

"You're going to love this, Lieutenant."

"I doubt it, but tell me anyway."

"One dead caretaker and two suspects." She was close enough now to lower her voice, and for him to catch a whiff of her perfume. "Both tenants here," she said. "Vampire and a werewolf."

"A vampire and a werewolf?" He shook his head, and a little burst of pain flickered in his left temple, just behind the eye. Just his sinuses, or the shadow of an impending migraine? It was getting hard to say these days. "Tell me you're kidding."

"Afraid not. The good news is they're eager to talk," Mary Angelo said. "Each of them says the other did it."

"Wonderful. You pull their files?"

The sergeant shrugged. "Not easy with a place like this. Once they ask asylum and move into a habitat, they get full privacy rights."

"Hmm." Deagan scratched his chin, thinking. "What about our dead caretaker? He is really dead, I assume?"

"Very. He was basically the butler here, near as I can tell. Did odd jobs around the place, looked after the grounds, that sort of thing. It's an old statute on the books. Every habitat has to have someone who is actually alive inside."

"Interesting gig."

"If you say so." The sergeant produced a labeled Ziploc bag from inside her jacket, which jingled when she handed it to him. "Got his possessions right here, if you want to have a look. A smart phone, a key of some kind, and a handful of coins."

Deagan took the bag, and eyed its contents. The phone was unremarkable: last year's Samsung. The key was made of pewter, a long cylinder with a single post at the end and a handle with some sort of engraved knotting that made it look like a prop from a cheap Halloween store.

He grunted, nonplussed, and poured the coins into his hand. What he had taken for loose change turned out to be a half dozen gold Sacagawea dollars. "Now that's interesting," he said. "Our caretaker a coin collector?"

"Who knows?" Mary Angelo said. "Some people like to hang onto two dollar bills for luck. Maybe he did the same thing with those."

"Yeah, maybe." Deagan returned the coins to the bag, and tucked it into his jacket. A cloud drifted across the full moon, and he glanced around, feeling a touch of unease. The night was much darker without the moonlight. Other than a single streetlight, the only illumination came from the red and blues on top of the squad cars, which made the mansion's yellow paint appear sickly, and somehow far older.

He dug in the jacket's other pocket, feeling for the half-opened pack of Camels he always kept with him. "This place has a lot of square footage," he said. "Anyone else in there?"

"Probably." Mary Angelo shrugged again. "We didn't make it past the living room. That's where we found the body, and our two suspects arguing. I figured the rest should wait for you. Hey, you need a light?" she asked, seeing him working at his cigarettes.

"I don't smoke."

"Then why do you have those?"

Deagan almost smiled. "Let me tell you a little story," he said. He gestured for her to follow, and together they started up the sidewalk toward the house. "I knew a detective once, worked narcotics. This was years ago. Had himself a peanut allergy – a real bad one. This guy, he always kept a king-size Snickers bar on his desk. 'Just in case,' he liked to say. Like, things got bad enough, he had an easy way out."

"Funny guy."

"I thought so too, at first." Deagan pushed his way through the front gate, which was flanked on both sides by an eight-foot hedge. A flagstone path stretched before him, leading through a carefully weeded rose garden to the front porch. "But really it was – what do you kids say these days? – kind of a punk move."

"I'm thirty-five, sir. And I don't think anyone has said that in ten years."

"You're thirty-five? Jesus."

A coal-black cat chose that moment to chance across the path. Deagan watched it disappear into the garden, shaking his head. "Talk about clichés," he muttered. "Anyway, the point is, I knew he wouldn't last. It was just a cry for attention – he burned out quick. But this?" He showed her the Camels. The pack was worn smooth, the cigarettes inside crumpled beyond use. "Last pack I ever opened. I'm into yoga now. Helps my back. And wheat grass, for the digestion. See, I figure the key is to outlive the job. Which is exactly what I'm going to do, even if it kills me."

Sergeant Mary Angelo didn't say anything to that. In

Deagan's experience, people usually didn't.

When they got close enough, he was able to make out a cop on the porch, shining a flashlight on a pair of civilians. His brain took the inventory automatically. Male, Caucasian, late thirties, five-ten, dressed like a telecommuting Seattle tech worker: shorts, t-shirt, sandals and wool socks. And the female, also Caucasian, but fashionable: skirt, sweater, stockings and pumps. Early twenties maybe, but hard to tell; she had the palest, smoothest skin he had ever seen.

"Your suspects?" he asked.

"Yup." The sergeant gave him the tiniest smirk. "Even if it kills you, huh?" she said. "I guess you'd better get up there and interview the vampire."

Deagan frowned at her. "That should've been my line," he grunted, stuffing the cigarettes back into his pocket. Wondering how his career had come to this, and what it meant, getting out-quipped by a kid like that.

Then he took a deep breath and climbed the stairs.

Up close, two more facts about the woman came to light. First, she was also holding a crystal goblet, half filled with a suspicious-looking, dark colored liquid. And second, once he caught her gaze, Deagan saw that she was possessed of crimson eyes, which glowed softly in the dark.

Christ, he thought. Okay, then. Start with her. "Hi," he said. "I'm Lieutenant Deagan. Can I have your name, miss?"

"Elena," the woman said, lurching toward him and holding out a hand. "Elena Calineshku." The words came out slurred, as though she were drunk.

Deagan glanced over at the cop with the flashlight, who gave him an expressive shrug. "I'm sorry?" he said, taking her hand.

The woman smiled, making a point of showing him her fangs. "Calinescu," she repeated, this time enunciating with exaggerated care. "Vith two 'c's".

Her hand was cold, clammy, and strong as hell. Deagan

worked his fingers free as quickly as seemed decent, and retrieved his phone from his belt. C-a-l-i-n-e-s-c-u, he typed, which the phone corrected to "Calzones". He sighed. He'd eaten a cheeseburger for lunch, and skipped dinner as a penance.

"Uh huh," he said. "So you're the vampire?"

"Isn't eet obvious?"

"One doesn't want to assume."

"But I didn't do it," the woman said. She spun, nearly losing her balance, grabbed at the wooden railing for support, and waved the goblet at Sergeant Angelo's other suspect, who was scowling at the porch deck. "He did."

"Did he now?" Deagan turned to the man. "And your name, sir?"

"Taggart. Jamishon Taggart." The man's speech was as slurred as the vampire's. "Get that damned light off me, will you?" he added.

Deagan nodded to the cop, who obligingly lowered the beam. "Which makes you the werewolf."

"No," Taggart said. "I am a lycanthrope."

"What is that, exactly?"

"I am an eternal being." The man looked Deagan in the eye for the first time. His skin was almost as pale as the woman's, and now that Deagan saw him clearly, he couldn't help noticing the bloodstain on his shirt. "Gifted and curshed by the bite of another of my kind," the man continued. "Fated to take animal form with each shycle of the full moon, until the dawn comes, or I feed on human flesh, or drink of human blood."

"I see," Deagan said. "And what animal form do you take specifically, if I might ask?"

"That of the noble wolf."

"Mmm hmm." Deagan glanced back down at his phone. W-e-r-e-w-o-l-f, he typed, which the device accepted with surprising grace. "Full moon tonight," he observed, nodding toward the lake, where the moon continued its dance with the

---

116

clouds.

"Yesh," Taggart said. "There is. But I didn't do it." He glared at the young woman, his lip curled back in a snarl. "That blood-drinking bitch did."

"You are calling me a beetch?" Elena snarled back. "Ha! His blood is all over you!"

"His blood is in that glash you're holding," Taggart retorted. "And we both know you were the one that killed him."

"You lie like you smell," the woman sniffed.

"I lie - what?"

"Like a dog." She smiled in obvious satisfaction.

Deagan decided he'd heard enough. "Right," he said, raising his hands. "Let's just take it easy. Officer, mind the porch, and don't let anyone in or out. Sergeant, you're with me. Let's all go inside and have a look together, shall we?"

"Fine by me," the werewolf said.

"And me," added the vampire. "I have nutheeng to hide."

"Good," Deagan said. "I'm glad that's settled. After you, Miss Calinescu, and you, Mr. Taggart."

Deagan watched them go, and took a last look around the porch. Then he shook his head and, wondering what exactly he had gotten himself into, followed them inside.

The living room was dark, the only illumination provided by a pair of lamps mounted on the walls, and a handful of coals glowing softly in the fireplace. Deagan blinked in the dim gloom, his sense of unease growing.

Here he was, stepping across the threshold, entering into the eldritch dwelling of ancient undead - and it was murder that had brought him to this place.

Slowly, his eyes adjusted. The room came into focus. A long slate coffee table dominated the space, around which black leather couches and love-seats had been scattered, bedecked with plush gray pillows. Wooden speaker cabinets were tucked into the corners of the room, and an enormous flat-screen television was mounted on one wall.

So much for the house of the damned, Deagan thought. The place looked like it had been furnished at an Ikea.

Except, of course, for the whitewashed brick fireplace, in front of which the caretaker's body lay outlined in tape, resting in a pool of blood.

Deagan crossed the room and knelt beside the corpse. In spite of the voice on the phone, the victim wasn't an old man at all. He didn't even look forty. He wore black jeans, and a black t-shirt from a band Deagan didn't recognize. His face was relaxed, so peaceful in death that he almost seemed to be smiling.

"You see?" Taggart growled. "Look at his neck! I told you she did it."

Deagan bent closer. Sure enough, there was a bite mark - a pair of pinpricks, two inches apart, positioned directly over the carotid. There was also, Deagan saw, a much larger wound on the inside of the man's left thigh. His pants were torn, and there was a ragged tear in the flesh, as though he had been bitten by a wild animal.

He gave Jamison Taggart a mild look.

"Wasn't me," the werewolf said.

"You sure about that? He called just after midnight. Wouldn't you have been a wolf then?"

"Yesh," Taggart admitted. "But I was at work."

"Uh huh. What is it you do, exactly?"

"Well," Taggart said. It seemed to take him some effort to gather his thoughts. "I work in forenshics," he said finally. "Kind of like you, Lieutenant." He gave a short, barking laugh. "Except I am a forenshic accountant."

"A what?" The pain flickered in Deagan's temple again, and he winced. Definitely a migraine, he thought. He had a few hours at the most, and then would need a good, long rest.

"A forensic accountant," Taggart repeated. "I hunt for companies with accounting irregularities, and short-sell before they get caught and their shtock price crashes."

"Sounds a bit predatory," Deagan said.

"Wolf."

"Right." Deagan sighed. "You do this kind of work at a computer, I'm assuming?"

"I do my besht thinking in my true form," Taggart said. He straightened proudly. "So I had a special laptop made."

"Eet has paws buttons!" Elena laughed, pantomiming mashing an imaginary keyboard.

Deagan opened his mouth to respond, thought better of it. "That pay pretty well?" he asked Taggart.

"Who do you think buys all the stuff for our house?" Taggart said.

"And has zuch sheety taste?" Elena added.

"Let me see if I understand," Deagan said, before Taggart could take the bait. "Two hours ago, you were a werewolf, sitting at your computer, doing – whatever it is you do."

"Yesh," Taggart agreed.

"And now you have the blood of a dead man on your shirt. But you say you had nothing to do with your caretaker's murder?"

"Look, I am what I am, okay? I smelled the blood on the floor; I had a drink."

"You see!" Elena said.

"But he was dead when I found him! I certainly didn't do – that," Taggart said, pointing at the ragged gash on the caretaker's thigh.

"Mmm hmm. And you," Deagan said, turning to address the vampire. "Are holding – in fact, drinking from even now, a glass of the dead man's blood."

"So?" the woman said. "Vat did you have for lunch? A cheeseburger, I bet. I can smell it on your breath."

Deagan nodded in spite of himself, cringing at the memory.

"Does zat mean you murdered the cow?" she asked.

"Mr. Stevenson had bled out by the time I smelled him from my room. So I also had a drink, so vat? I am a vampire. I do zis all ze time."

Deagan looked at the pair, for a long moment not trusting himself to speak. "Sergeant?" he said at last.

"Yes, Lieutenant?" Mary Angelo's voice was pure innocence.

"Would you be so good as to take Miss Calinescu's dinner, a swab of Mr. Taggart's chin, and a sample of the dead man's blood, and have them sent off to the lab?"

"Of course, Lieutenant," Mary Angelo said. "Looking for anything in particular?"

"First, let's establish a match between all three, just for the record. Then test it for everything they can think of. Alcohol, narcotics, the works. Now…"

But before he could continue, a tremendous clanking sound erupted from behind the closet door. "What the hell?" he cried, spinning to look.

"That's Davey," Taggart said. "You'll want to be careful of him."

"Our house skeleton," Elena added.

"He lives in the closet?"

"Oh yes," Elena said. "Ve never let him out. He does like to rattle his chain, though."

The noise came again, a crunch of metal smashing into wood. Deagan edged across the room, eyeing the door warily. His .38 was a cold lump in its holster, offering little in the way of comfort.

He reached out, testing the door, and was rewarded with another enormous crash.

"Don't bother – it's locked," Elena said.

"I assume the caretaker had the key?" Deagan asked.

"Yes – his key opens everything in ze house. It iz, how do you say, a skeleton key? But I wouldn't open that door, if I were you," she said, giving him a toothy smile. "He bites."

"She's right," Taggart added. "Davey is very dangerous -

much more so than the rest of us. No one goes in there, except Mr. Stevenson."

Deagan looked the door up and down. He was contemplating opening it anyway when a dark stain on the handle caught his eye. "Sergeant," he said. "Give me some light over here, will you?"

He hadn't been sure what he was seeing, but in the flashlight's beam it was unmistakable. The handle was smeared with blood, and more had dripped onto the floor.

"Well will you look at this?" he said quietly. Carefully, he retraced his steps, stepping back to Stevenson's body. The trail of blood was faint but unmistakable, now that he knew where to look.

Mary Angelo came to stand beside him. "You think someone drug him across the room?" she asked.

"Or maybe he used the last of his strength to walk that far," Deagan said. "You said your men didn't make it out of the living room?"

"That's right."

"And we have no idea who else lives here."

"True," she agreed. "Though the killer has to be one of those two, don't you think? Judging from the wounds?"

"Maybe," Deagan said. "Then again, maybe not. Get those samples off to the lab, will you? And you two," Deagan said, forced to raise his voice over the ruckus still coming from the closet. "We're up to a vampire, a werewolf, and a skeleton. You mind telling me who else lives in this place?"

There was an awkward pause. "Ve really can't," Elena finally said.

"It ish private," Taggart agreed. "Shouldn't have told you about Mr. Jones, actually. Just didn't want you opening that door."

"I thought the skeleton's name was Davey?"

"Yesh," Taggart said. "Davey Jones."

"The Davey Jones? With the locker?"

"Sort of," Taggart said. "The drowned men always call

themselves that. It's about the only thing they ever say. Dead men tell no tales, you know."

"You have got to be kidding me."

"Death is no laughing matter, Lieutenant," the werewolf said.

"Don't I know it. Now you two listen to me." He turned to Elena. "You, Miss Calinescu, have got a dead caretaker, with a bite wound in his neck. And you, Mr. Taggart," he said, "an admitted werewolf…"

"Lycanthrope."

"…werewolf, have a caretaker who has apparently been attacked by a wild animal of what could easily be the canine variety. Whereas I have an entire host of uniformed officers outside and some questions I'd like answered. So let me ask you again, unless you'd like to head down to the station right now: who else lives here?"

The vampire and the werewolf looked at each other. "Vell," Elena said. "There is the ghost in the attic."

"And the four zombies in the basement," Taggart added reluctantly.

"Ve are down to three. You remember the incident with the chainsaw?"

"Ah, right. And of course our witch, Esmerelda."

"Let me guess," Deagan said. "The black cat I saw out front?"

"Oh no," Taggart said. "Her name is Zoe."

"And what is she?"

The werewolf looked confused. "She's a cat."

"Ah." Deagan sighed. "Pet of yours?"

"Why would I have a pet cat? That's absurd." Taggart looked at Elena. "Who am I forgetting?"

"The ghouls," Elena said. "Half dozen of them, I zink, around back."

"Right. I doubt you'll get much out of them, Lieutenant. I assure you this is all a waste of your time. The murderer is obviously here in this room."

"You're probably right," Deagan agreed. "But I may as well get started. Sergeant, give me your flashlight, will you? I'm guessing I won't be able to see a damned thing in this place."

"It is true, our kind hate and fear the sun," Elena said, somberly.

"Then it's a good thing you live in Seattle." Deagan nodded to Mary Angelo, who handed over her flashlight. He smacked it in his palm. Its weight felt more reassuring than the pistol holstered at his side. "Now," he said. "Why don't you show me the way to the attic, and this ghost of yours?"

Three and a half hours later, Deagan was ready to number himself among the walking dead. His feet ached appallingly, and his migraine was flitting bat-like around the edges of his vision, threatening serious violence.

The dawn was still far away and a light rain had begun to fall, spattering the windows and making his time outside inspecting the grounds even more miserable.

Elena and Taggart had long since left him, preferring to keep away from the rest of the tenants. Deagan could hardly blame them. He wasn't sure why he'd bothered with the interviews – he should just take the two suspects he already had in for questioning, and call it a night.

At least now, save for Davey Jones in his closet, the work was almost done. All that remained to inspect was the caretaker's room, here at the end of the second story hall.

Deagan gave the door a gentle push, which swung inward on well-oiled hinges. Inside, the décor was more of the same. Desk and dresser were a perfectly matched, cherry-finished set. A double bed sat in one corner, covered with a black comforter emblazoned with a skull and crossbones, while posters from various goth bands adorned the walls.

Deagan began working his way through the desk drawers, his brain once again taking inventory. Black eyeliner. A handful of silver jewelry – necklace and crucifix, a couple of rings. A bag of cat food, and a pair of bowls.

And also, at least fifty more Sacagawea dollars, in a brown paper bag.

No skeletons awaited Deagan in Stevenson's closet – just a double curtain rod hung neatly with rows of jeans, t-shirts, sweaters and sweatshirts.

When he finished his search Deagan sat wearily on the bed, trying to think. So the man had a cat, listened to depressing music, and liked to wear black. It made sense, living in a place like this.

But what the heck were the coins for?

Eventually he hauled himself to his feet, made his way downstairs, and flopped down on the couch, staring at the caretaker's body, trying to piece it all together.

Two suspects; two wounds, one perfectly matched to each.

What had happened in this place? His cop instincts told him something was off, but he couldn't put his finger on it.

Just then the front door banged open. He started, thinking it was the skeleton he was hearing. But no – it was just Mary Angelo, back from her trip downtown.

"How'd you make out?" she asked, shrugging off her soaking wet jacket.

"You don't want to know."

"That bad?"

"Where would you like me to start?"

Mary Angelo glanced around the room. "How about the zombies?"

"All right." He found the recording of the interview on his phone and hit play. A low moaning sound trickled out of the speaker. "Sorry," he said. "That's the ghost. Hang on." He fiddled with the phone, tried again with a different track.

"Braaiiins," said the phone.

"Hmmm," the sergeant said. "I'm guessing the ghouls were no better."

"You guess correctly."

"What about the witch, Esmerelda? You get anything from her?"

"A couple of recipes." Deagan sighed. "Not to my taste."

"Well cheer up, Lieutenant, because I have good news." Mary Angelo sat down onto the couch next to him. "All three samples match."

"So both Elena and Taggart fed on him."

"Looks like."

"Doesn't mean they killed him, though."

"Maybe not," Mary Angelo agreed. "But we've also got an explanation for their slurred speech. You were right to have the labs screen for pharmaceuticals. Turns out Mr. Stevenson's body was pumped full of Percocet."

"A painkiller?" Deagan frowned, rubbing his temples. Actually, a little Percocet didn't sound half bad. "That's odd," he said. "He was a young guy. He shouldn't have needed anything like that."

"Maybe he was addicted to it." Mary Angelo shrugged. "It happens."

"Don't I know it. Still, though – I wonder."

"What?"

"Well, Stevenson was basically a glorified butler, you said."

"Yeah. So?"

"So it was his job to take care of this place – and not just the house, but the tenants living in it. I went through his room, and the kitchen, and I can tell you he had everything he needed to do just that. There is some pretty grim shit in that fridge, Mary Angelo, including what I really hope is venison, you know what I mean?

"But we have to assume he knew the job. He even had a saucer of milk for the cat – and she's just a cat. And Elena and Taggart said he was the only one who went in the closet..." He trailed off, thinking.

"Well, if a vampire wants blood, and a werewolf wants flesh, what does a skeleton want?" Mary Angelo asked.

"Not just a skeleton," Deagan said. "Taggart called him a drowned man. A Davey Jones."

"Okay. So what would a drowned man want?"

Then it hit him. "Gold," Deagan said, jumping to his feet, all weariness forgotten. "He'd want gold coins, which is exactly what Stevenson had in his pocket, and in his room." He took a long, hard look at the closet door. "I think he went in there before he died."

"And what? Lost control of the skeleton, got bit, called 911 and died before we got here?"

Deagan shook his head. "Doesn't make sense," he said. "The leg wound I could imagine, but the wound on his neck? That's a bite mark."

"Maybe Elena bit him afterwards. Maybe he was laying on the floor, and she finished him off."

"Maybe," Deagan said. "And then Taggart comes along and licks some more blood off the floor. But why the Percocet?"

"He could've taken it after the attack."

"I suppose," Deagan said. "But it looks like he didn't make it past the fireplace. And it's not like he had a bottle on him."

"You're right. None of it makes any sense," Mary Angelo said. "Maybe we should just take them all in and call it a night."

Deagan thought about it. "Not yet," he said. "I'm going to go in there myself. Nothing in this house likes the light very much – I bet between the flashlight to keep him at bay, and the gold coins to keep him happy, I'll be okay, even if it's only for a second."

"That's a hell of a bet."

"I'm not about to ask you to make it with me. Go on outside, Sergeant."

"You know I can't do that!"

"You don't have a choice. It's an order. And besides," he said, softening his voice. "If I'm wrong about this, pistols aren't going to do either of us any good anyway."

"I thought you wanted to outlive the job."

Deagan smiled. "Don't we all," he said. "Don't we all. Now get out of here, will you?"

Mary Angelo protested to the bitter end, but eventually Deagan got his way. He clicked the door shut softly behind her and turned to regard the closet. The skeleton had been quiet for the last several hours, but he had no illusions the thing was asleep.

Or ever slept, for that matter.

"Right," he said to himself. "Nothing for it."

He slipped the caretaker's key into the lock, and carefully turned the latch.

Click.

The door eased open an inch, then two, and Deagan shone his light inside – directly into the face of the waiting skeleton.

Bleached white bones glinted in the flashlight's beam, a horror show of protruding jaw and over-large teeth, frozen in a rictus smile. Empty orbital sockets gaped at him, and a black pit yawned open in the center of its face where a nose should have been.

"*Dead... men...*" the skeleton intoned. It was so close! Deagan had to move, but he couldn't take his eyes of that face.

"*Tell...!*"

The skeleton lashed out, wrapping its chain around Deagan's ankle, jerking him off balance and dropping him to the floor.

"*No...!*"

Deagan banged his hand on the doorframe as the skeleton jerked him into the closet, losing his grip on the flashlight. It skittered away, the beam flashing wildly, coming to rest against a leather bag near the back of the closet.

"*Tales!!!'*" the skeleton shrieked in triumph. The thing reached a bony arm over Deagan's head and yanked the door shut, and then scrabbled at his throat. Its fingers were cold as ice, and wickedly strong. Deagan fought for air, desperate, trying to think.

Of course - the coins! He dug in his pocket and grabbed a handful, even as the skeleton dug its bony claws deeper into his windpipe. Vision fading, he flung the coins as hard as he could, sending them clattering in all directions.

"Gold!" the skeleton cried. It wheeled around, releasing him. Deagan worked at the chain, trying to free his ankle even as the skeleton smashed about the tiny closet, scrabbling after the Sacajawea dollars.

At last the chain came loose. Deagan grabbed the bag and dove for the bag for the door. The skeleton lashed out with its chain, catching Deagan in the back. Jacket and flesh tore and Deagan cried out in pain. The skeleton swung again, but before the blow could land he had hold of the handle. The door swung open, and he spilled into the living room.

He slammed the door shut just as the skeleton smashed into it from the inside. The door buckled savagely; there was no way it would hold for long. Acting on sheer impulse, Deagan grabbed for the key, which he had left in the lock, and twisted as hard as he could, nearly snapping the thing in two.

The lock clicked, and the skeleton immediately fell still. Deagan thought he heard it say "Gold..." one last time, and that was all.

"Christ," he said. He rubbed at his back, wincing as his fingers found the gash the chain had left. It was going to need looking at, and his head felt like it was about to explode.

At least he had what he came for. Hands shaking, he upended the bag, dumping its contents onto the floor: a leather punch, a pair of scissors, a scalpel, and, Deagan noted with satisfaction, a half-empty prescription bottle of Percocet.

Technically the drugs were evidence, but even so. One or two wasn't going to make any difference, and the migraine would be put off no longer. He shook a couple of the pills from the bottle, and swallowed them dry.

"I'll be damned," he said to no one in particular, as the pain began to fade. "The butler really did do it."

Elena and Taggart found him in the living room. "Ve have a proposal, Lieutenant," the vampire said without preamble, looking nervously out the window at the approaching dawn.

Deagan stared at them dreamily. "Up past your bedtime, aren't you?"

"Yes," she admitted. "But I am also, how shall ve say, feeling better. Thinking more clearly, than before."

Percocet must've worn off, Deagan thought. Too bad for her. The stuff was wonderful.

"I'm listening."

"Ve have agreed that one of us must have committed the murder," she continued. "And attempted to frame ze other. Eet ees no secret that werewolves and vampires do not get along, as I'm sure you have learned from interviewing the other members of our little household."

"Go on."

"Neither of us has any wish to leave the grounds. Ve are both convinced the other is lying. Perhaps ve are wrong. Perhaps it was Esmerelda, playing one of her tricks. Or Davey, or our ghost. It doesn't matter."

"Only our caretaker knows who his murderer was," Taggart joined in. "Therefore, Elena will raise him, and we will simply ask who did it."

It was all Deagan could do not to smile. "That will add a member to your little family, will it not?"

"It vill," Elena said. "Eet is regrettable, but cannot be helped. He has been after me to turn him for years. So, he ees going to get his vish."

"Well," he said, trying not to laugh. "There is the question of the legality of all this."

"We are in an undead refuge, Lieutenant," Taggart said. "The rules are a bit different here."

"True, true." Deagan pretended to think about it. "So what do you want me to do?"

"All you need do is watch, and monitor ze proceedings," Elena said. "He will rise, and ve will all have our questions answered."

"Fair enough," Deagan said. "Do what you gotta do." He waved an arm airly at the corpse on the floor. "I'll just rest here on this sofa. It's ugly as hell, but actually kind of comfortable," he said, smiling as he closed his eyes.

"Lieutenant. Lieutenant!" Deagan awoke to find Taggart standing over him. "We're ready for you," the werewolf accountant growled.

"Right." Deagan found his feet and made his way to the fireplace, where Elena was drinking from a bottle, the origin of whose contents he didn't care to guess. There was a gash on her wrist, and her sleeve was soaked in blood.

As was the caretaker's mouth. Who, Deagan realized, was coming to life before his very eyes. First Stevenson flexed his left hand, and then his right. Then he sat up, resting his softly glowing eyes on each of them in turn.

His gaze settled at last on Elena, who was regarding him with distaste.

"You turned me, then?" he said.

"I did," she acknowledged. "I never vould have, as vell you know, but it was necessary."

Stevenson's mouth broke into a wide smile. "Excellent," he said. "I imagine we have a great deal to talk about."

"Yes, yes," Elena said impatiently. "You are my child now, I am your immortal patron, we have eternity to contemplate the meaningless of it all. But first..."

"First," Taggart chimed in, "the detective here has some questions for you."

"Actually, I don't," Deagan said.

"Vat?"

"What?"

"I imagine," Deagan said, "that your man's testimony will exonerate both of you. Your caretaker did the deed himself, isn't that right, Mr. Stevenson?"

"I did," Stevenson said. "And now that I am alive again – or rather, undead – I claim asylum in this habitat."

Deagan nodded. "Figured you might," he said, even as the vampire and werewolf stared open-mouthed at the newest member of their household. "Now if you will excuse me, I am going to go outside and have a smoke."

Mary Angelo was waiting for him. "So that's it?" she asked, when he had related all that occurred.

"That's it."

"How are we going to write it up?"

Deagan gazed out over the lake, pondering. Dawn had come at last, and the cold October rain had ceased for the moment.

"Well," he said. "It's not like Stevenson faked his own death – he really did die. So I guess we just call it a suicide."

"Fair enough," Mary Angelo agreed. "Though I'm still not sure I understand that whole business with the skeleton."

"Stevenson needed a place to hide the evidence," Deagan said. "He figured the closet was the one place no one could ever search. So he drugged himself, used the leather punch, God help him, to make the bite marks on his neck, and the scissors and scalpel to make the wound on his leg. Stuffed everything in the bag, opened the closet door, gave Davey Jones a handful of coins to keep him busy while he stashed the evidence. Then all he had to do was call 911 and bleed out."

"Knowing Elena and Taggart would find him."

"Right. Stevenson would've known Taggart would be in wolf form – that's why he waited until midnight of a full moon. He had to figure each would assume the other had done the deed, and they'd do anything to see the other take the fall."

"Pretty clever. Hey, you want to grab breakfast?" she

asked. "I'm starving."

Deagan laughed. "Sure, why not? Then I need to get home and update my resume."

"What for?"

"Well…" Deagan hesitated, embarrassed. Then again, he may as well tell Mary Angelo where he was going as anyone. "I figure they're going to need a new caretaker in this joint, right? Sure, the skeleton is a bastard and the zombies aren't much better, but what the hell - I work with dead guys all the time anyway.

"And you have to admit, he may not have been into wheat grass and yoga, but at least Stevenson found a way to outlive the job."

What you should know about Paul Dixon: He began his professional career as an oceanographer before suffering a crisis of faith and winding up a digital marketing technologist – all while nurturing an underlying passion for the craft of writing. Now his goal is to bring those three things together: to use technology to raise awareness and find solutions for the environmental issues that threaten our livelihood as a species, starting with the health of the global ocean, and to write to educate, inform, and of course to entertain. Paraphrasing Winston Churchill – if not the arts, then what are we fighting for?

Where you can find him: He lives with his wife and daughter in his Seattle hometown. But unless you're willing to search through every coffee shop in the city (and they've got a lot of them), it's probably easier to find him on his blog at www.paul-dixon.com, where he maintains links to his writing alongside scattered thoughts about everything from running marathons to the experience of re-watching Star Blazers as an adult.

He can also be tracked down on Facebook at www.facebook.com/sunstealer, or on Twitter at @paul_a_dixon – but only if you're into that sort of thing.

THE HEARTLESS BOY

By Edward Ahern

Tom Willman was born experiencing no strong feelings, in fact no feelings at all. No love or affection. No hate or dislike. Certainly no fear. The closest he came to emotions were pleasing or displeasing sensations.

Tom's parents, desperate for a smile, had him tested for a litany of diseases, but he proved to be uncaringly above average. They quit trying to show Tom affection by the time he was six, and by the time he was ten were providing only what was legally required of them.

He ate because the tastes were good and food kept him alive. He avoided the harmful and the idiotic, so no drugs or gluttony, but also no designer water or wandering chickens. He exercised and bathed because his body felt better, and exhibited an attractive trimness about which he was oblivious.

Girls in high school viewed Tom's indifference as cool and his trimness as attractive, feelings heightened once they discovered that his lack of emotion gave him extraordinary staying powers. Tom viewed his frequent sex acts as pleasant consensual exercise.

The person who tried hardest to know Tom best was Arthur Lausten, the high school psychologist. Lausten, with no significant life of his own, compulsively coached people on how to live better. His recurring daydream was perching in a confessional and prescribing atonements.

Tom was required to attend frequent sessions with

Lausten, who toiled through hundreds of hours trying to etch Tom's stainless steel persona with the bristles of a verbal toothbrush.

"Tom, you appear to be neither sociopathic nor psychotic, but except for satisfying basic biological requirements, you're completely indifferent to your humanity."

"What's your point, Mr. Lausten?"

Lausten was desperate. He pulled out a large folding knife, flipped open the blade and waved it in front of Tom. "What would you do if I threatened to stab you?"

"Run."

"And if you couldn't get out of the room?"

"Ask somebody to reason with you."

"And if that didn't work?"

"Hit you with this book end."

"How do you feel about me right now?"

"That question is inane."

Early in his freshman year a bully had cornered Tom on the football field. Tom let the boy hit him twice before retaliating, knowing that in order to avoid discipline he had to have the boy's aggression witnessed. Then he broke enough of the boy's bones that he would be unable to be aggressive again for several months. The onlookers noticed that Tom's expression had remained calm.

At the graduation ceremony, Tom was approached by several girls and avoided by most boys. Tom perceived both the attention and avoidance as irrelevant. An unknown young woman was among those who approached.

"Mr. Willman, I'm Raissa Pandorapolis. I have a job offer for you." The young woman curved aesthetically and looked no older than he was, although her eyes had the worry lines of middle age.

"Ah."

"Am I correct that you'll be leaving home and are looking for work?"

"Yes."

"Am I also correct that you've had difficulties with pre-employment screening?"

"The human resource departments tell me that I'm inhuman."

"Not me. Please join me for lunch while I explain my offer."

Once seated in the restaurant, Tom began his questioning. "What sort of job is it?"

"I own and operate a- call it an entry portal- and need help running it. You'd be a gatekeeper/doorman to handle the rush hour traffic.

"It's night shift work, with the traffic occurring between 11 p.m. and 3 a.m. Outside of those hours you're free to pursue your own interests, or do nothing at all. The clientele is a nasty lot, but can't harm you if you're careful. Given your indifference, I'm hoping that you can ignore their vicious comments."

Tom's parents had ordered him to vacate their house immediately after graduation, so he needed work and a place to stay. "What's it pay?"

"$30 an hour, six nights a week. You stay at the house rent free. Payment is in cash, off the books, so you won't need to pay taxes. You merely let the, ah, personalities in and out. They're universally ugly and surly, but you should be able to ignore their abrasive traits."

Suspicion was a way of thinking which Tom's condition encouraged. "That's three times minimum wage for a menial job. What's the catch?"

"There are a couple niggling conditions of employment. You'll swear an oath of secrecy under penalty of immediate death, and failing to get the commuters in and out promptly is equally fatal. In other words you treat them like cattle and keep your mouth shut. You're really quite well suited to the job."

"How long would I have to sign up for?"

Raissa smiled. His question meant he was leaning toward acceptance. "The secrecy agreement is forever, but the initial term of employment is one year. Oh, and you can't have any visitors in the house, and can't bring in any kind of communication device- no phone, camera or tablet."

Having no emotional distractions, Tom's logical and intellectual capabilities were formidable. He reasoned that his expenses would be minimal and at the end of a year he should have at least $50,000 dollars in cash.

"For that kind of money it must be crooked. I've got no interest in going to jail and becoming somebody's bum boy."

"It's abnormal or paranormal, but not illegal. At worst, you'd be driven crazy or torn to shreds."

"Am I the first person you've hired?"

"No there've been two others, a vicious sadist and a nearly catatonic recluse. They both died screaming in anguish, so I changed my hiring criteria. Tell you what, I'll stay with you for the first week. If you can't handle it you'll get paid for the week and just have to keep your mouth shut."

Tom was terminally neutral, but sensed Raissa's sharp-edged emotions. He assumed she'd lied and would kill him if he tried to leave after the first week. It was the only way she could be sure he wouldn't talk. But Tom lived entirely outside of human emotions, and doubted anything he encountered could break through to him. Raissa needed him. Badly, or she wouldn't be making accommodations.

"All right," he said, "we'll try it for a week. When and where should I show up?"

"I'll pick you up this evening," she said. And did. They drove for almost an hour before stopping. Raissa walked Tom into a house and locked the door behind them.

Tom looked around at a great room with shuttered windows that took up most of the ground floor. A large jagged hole in the floor made most of the room unusable. Tom looked over the edge, but the hole dropped into blackness with no visible bottom. On one edge of the hole a large circle and symbols had been painted on the wood floor. The circle contained a lectern, easy chair and battery operated lights.

"Where's the hatch or lid for this thing?"

"It's, ah, symbolic. Step into the circle and stand at the lectern."

Tom did so, and saw there were two bronze tablets on the reading stand.

"At 11 p.m. you read the left hand tablet, at 3 a.m. you read the right hand tablet. What could be easier? Just make very sure you don't step outside the circle before 3 a.m."

He stared at the tablets. The top half of each had unrecognizable characters. The bottom halves had English gibberish syllables. He glanced at Raissa.

"The top parts are in Mycenaean Greek, pre-Phoenician characters. That's for my use. The bottom half is the pronunciation guide in English. You don't need to know the meaning, but you do need to pronounce everything perfectly. Otherwise you'll be killed. Not by me, by the commuters. It's as if you'd left them off at the wrong stop. Imagine how annoyed you'd be. Sorry, you don't get annoyed, do you?"

"No. Okay, I'll be killed if I step outside the circle while I'm working, and killed if I make a mistake in either reading. Recite one of them to me."

Raissa stepped so close to Tom that he could feel her breath on his ear as she spoke.

Tom turned his head to look at her. "And you've been able to recite these for a long time without being hurt?"

Her expression deconstructed into sadness, as if she looked into the eyes of dead relatives. "For a long time. I was just a happy, inquisitive girl, but look at me now, trapped timelessly with evil for company, never to know love or have children. Is it any wonder that I'm testy?"

Tom, emotionally clueless, said nothing. Raissa's face wrinkled into what he knew to be anger. "All right, simpleton, recite the incantations for me until I think you've got them down. Let's see if you can last the night."

Raissa commandeered the easy chair, leaving Tom to stand at the lectern. By the third repetition he pronounced the syllables correctly. Tom asked more questions.

"How many of these beings are there?"

"Do you know your Christian bible? Of course not. The phrase "My name is legion" has no meaning for you. Thousands, Tom. Single entities transmute into several, and none. A swirling porridge of personified evils. Oh, except for one prissy little bitch."

"Who's that?"

"The exception that makes everything worse. The hope that you can endure these defilements. Sorry, of course not you, Tom."

"How will I know when it's exactly 11 p.m?"

"There'll be a gong. You'll have three seconds to start or be burned to ash where you stand."

Tom, of course, viewed death merely as a timing issue. "Okay."

"I almost forgot. Once they see that it's you at the lectern and not me some of them will probably double back and try to shock you into stepping out of the circle. You do, you die."

"Got it. Do I need to do anything between 11 p.m. and 3 a.m?"

"Stay alive. Oh, and the jug next to the lectern is in case you have to urinate. Do not, under any circumstances, piss into the pit."

The gong rang, and Tom's mouth strained to utter the harsh sounds. The pit's blackness seemed to glisten, then break into shards. A suppurating odor washed into the room, but neither Raissa nor Tom vomited. Shapes boiled out of the pit, changing without pause from deformities to demons to grotesqueries for which Tom had no descriptive words. They spoke.

"Fresh meat."

"A pretty boy this time."

"Raissa lusts for him."

"Play with us, pretty boy."

Tom turned around and looked back into the room, now filled with apparitions. The shapes had exaggerated breasts and vulvas and penises. The smells of rutting overrode the aromas of rot. The shapes were now all pleasing and Tom felt his skin tingle as tactile sensations seeped through the protective circle.

He stood without words or expression. The shapes screamed and distorted themselves into broken, exposed bones and oozing lesions. The smell of pus ruled.

Tom was curious, another of his few human traits, and began to categorize the shapes and scents. The hoarse howling intensified at this indifference, punctuated by ear shredding screams. Raissa sat quietly, watching the apparitions swirl. Tom got the impression that she was acquainted with all of them. After several minutes they dispersed outwards through the walls of the house.

Tom turned to Raissa and noticed that she was staring at his ass. "Where are they going?"

"Into your world to inflict pain and terror. There's never enough of them to go around. Ah, here comes Miss Prissy, late as always."

A slender white shape emerged from the pit. The woman was gracefully formed, but Tom thought her to be androgynous. "Who's that?"

"Hope. The bitch follows around after the evils and applies a little zinc oxide to the humans who've just been seared. Keeps them from committing suicide, which they'd be better off doing."

A lurking apparition charged the protective circle, spewing yellow gobbets, but for Tom the bile was merely sour snot and he asked it, "What's your name, slime ball?"

Raissa sucked in air. "Careful. Exorcists ask for a demon's name, Tom. Doormen just keep their mouths shut."

The slobbering, evil figure was contorted with rage. Tom ignored it and stepped over to Raissa. They looked like teenagers on a first date. "I think you've been going about this all wrong ."

"Excuse me!"

"For one thing, Pandorapolis sucks as an alias. Look Pandy, we don't learn much in high school, but we do get some rudiments of mythology. All you've done for two millennia is run these ethereal bed bugs through chutes, when you could've been whipping them into something more interesting. It's past time for you to screw with their deformed little minds. You clearly hate the way you're doing things now."

"You can't talk to me like that! I'm a demi-god."

"Don't think so. You're just a human trapped into being timeless. I doubt you've had sex for several hundred years. We could fix that though, the chair is big enough."

Raissa sputtered. "I'm going to kill you right now."

"Don't think so. Let's let the week run out and see where it gets us."

Raissa paused. "What do you mean 'screw with their minds'?"

"If you're bored and frustrated with a couple thousand years of herding evil cattle, think what they must feel like. What happens if you give them a day off? Or let them sleep in an extra half an hour? Or let them know they can work at half speed and you won't report them? Or, maybe best of all, let them concoct their own deviltry rather than using an obsolete play book they're bored with?"

"My curse is immutable."

"Seriously? You're already cursed, what more can happen to you? If something does happen at least it would be a change."

Tom reached over and touched Raissa's shoulder. She didn't pull away. "Tomorrow night I'll talk to one or two of them and see where we get to."

"You'll kill us both!"

"You can't die and I'm indifferent."

140

The next night Tom picked out a blobular evil with open sores mounded like barnacles on an oyster shell. He turned to Raissa. "Okay, I can't control it without knowing its name. What is it?"

She huddled back in the easy chair. "Alaputrius."

"Hey, Alaputrius! What're you tasked with tonight?"

The beast glowered but answered. "Drunkenness that causes self-maiming accidents."

"And you do that every night?"

"Yes ape, since beyond memory."

"Okay, tonight you're doing initial drug addictions among middle aged, overweight men."

"That's Foulbreathea's job. She'll disembowel me."

"Might be an improvement. But tell her/it that it's okay for you to change jobs for one night and if she has any problem with it to talk to me."

Like all classic evils, Alaputrius had no sense of joy or contentment, but he had plenty of greed and thwarted envy. "Wow. Okay, then. I'm on my way."

An hour later Foulbreathea stormed in and Tom mollified her by letting her cause bed wetting among adolescent girls at sleepovers. The assignment changes spiraled and by three a.m. over fifty imps had been short circuited.

By the end of the week over 1,000 evils had been transposed, and even Tom's considerable analytical powers were strained keeping track. Hope kept wandering in and out of the pit in confusion. Raissa had begun laughing at the changes, and on day five they began sharing the easy chair in post 3 am trysts.

On the last day of the week Raissa looked down at a naked Tom. "I'm not going to kill you."

"I presumed as much. How many of these suckers are there?"

"More than you can count, tight buns, call it half a million."

Tom noticed that the pit had started a rolling boil, throwing off steaming mounds of black pitch. "Raissa, is it supposed to do that?"

"Zeus Rex, no! Watch out!"

An ebon figure rose from the pit and without hesitation floated into the mystical circle. Its voice was rolling thunder. "I've received an employment discrimination complaint from Hope."

"That bitch," Raissa interjected.

The thunder resumed. "Hope's pretty dense, but I gather that you two have been shuffling my deck without permission."

As the figure spoke the pitch slid off it, leaving what looked like a nude, fat-saggy Arthur Lausten. "Not much to look at, I know," it said, "but it's the most distasteful image I could find in your mind.

"What am I going to do with you two rutting little animals? Killing you creates dysfunction, and if I administer excruciating pain you'll lose focus during the procedures."

Tom's expression had remained calm. "You're the Deus Ex Machina."

"One of them."

"You're missing out on a great opportunity."

Lightning flashed and the almost Arthur Lausten glared. "Explain yourself very quickly."

"For two thousand years the same evils have been inflicted on the same people, night after night. The humans get used to it. What we're doing is making the evils of the world truly random- the drug addict becomes a miser, the murderer becomes self-abusive, but just for a night. They'll never know what's coming next."

The figure could be seen to think. "It is the same amount of evil, after all," Tom added.

"Hmmm. All right, take a few hundred years to try it out. Let Hope in on the action so she'll get off my back."

The figure vanished and the pit resumed its

---

impenetrable blackness. Tom turned to Raissa.

"For a being that powerful it's really stupid, isn't it?"

"Shhh. Just enjoy things. It's like a party where we get to mess with all the guests."

Tom paused. "You understand that I'll never feel affection or love for you, that we'll always just be sexually active acquaintances?"

"I've been in worse relationships."

Ed Ahern's life has been enjoyably haphazard. He's been able to do most of the immature things he wanted to do when he was fourteen. After graduating from university he was, in approximate order: a naval officer specializing in diving and bomb disarming; a newspaper reporter; an intelligence agent working in Germany and Japan; an international sales executive for a Canadian paper conglomerate and a major U.S. trading company, and now a fiction writer.

He's lived in six countries, visited another seventy five, and speaks four languages (Japanese badly). His free time is misspent fly fishing and shooting.

UP ON THE HOUSETOP, GARGOYLE PAWS

By Jonathan Shipley

"So what did you do with the cursed mahogany candlestand?" Marianna asked over coffee and cake. "I mean, the options are fairly limited."

"They are," her brother Justin agreed. Lean with salt-and-pepper hair, he always managed to look suave, even under pressure. "I couldn't leave it in the shop, so I . . . took it back to the apartment."

Marianna gaped. "You what? You're living with cursed mahogany --"

"It's not as bad as it sounds," Justin said quickly. "I placed a properly blessed silver bowl on it, filled with Holy Water, where I'm growing rowan shoots. That ought to counteract a curse in multiple cultures. And it seems to work. At least I'm not kept awake at night by dark emanations."

"It's creative but reckless," she said firmly. "And if I had a better solution, I would tell you to get that thing out of your apartment immediately. But I don't," she added with a sigh.

"At some point, if the cursed antiques start accumulating, I promise to locate a quicksand bog to dump them into. But so far, it's been manageable. Thank goodness most curses are breakable."

Marianna just shook her head and took another bite of plum cake. Dealing with curses was a crazy job, but someone had to do it. Technically, of course, cursed objects weren't in either of their job descriptions. She was a rare books dealer, and Justin was an antiques dealer. But the fact that both of them dealt with old, unusual things and both had a bit of witchiness in the bloodline sort of pushed them that direction. They could deal with these dark, sometimes dangerous things better than the average shop owner.

"More cake?" Ella asked, stopping by their booth in the diner. Sam & Ella's was a thoroughly pleasant 50's diner, heavy on nostalgia but still healthy in its offerings. The plum cake, a specialty of the house, was both low calorie and gluten free. The diner shared space in the Asheville shopping strip with Marianna's bookstore and Justin's antique shop, which made it a convenient meeting place for the siblings.

"Please," Justin nodded, holding out his empty plate. He was partial to the plum cake.

"I'll see if I can manage an extra-large slice," Ella began, then turned as the door opened to admit a frantic man, thirtyish, with tousled hair. "I suspect he's looking for you," she said, beckoning him over.

"It's awful," he moaned, pushing into the booth beside Marianna and massaging his temples.

"Hello to you, too, Craig," Marianna sighed. Craig Wilbury was the Biltmore House Assistant Curator for Oblique Decorative Arts whose job was to poke through the attics and basements and catalog the forgotten odds and ends that had been tucked away there since George Vanderbilt built the huge chateau. They'd gotten to know Craig very well over the last year. Dark things turned up regularly in those attics and basements, and he had a hard time coping at times.

"And what is it this time?" Justin asked pleasantly. "Dueling pistols that discharge on their own? Poisonous teacups? Murderous claw-footed chairs?" It sounded like sarcasm, but those were actual cases they'd worked on together.

"Gargoyle," Craig groaned. "A winged wolf-like creature on the rooftop of the west façade -- or at least it used to be on the rooftop."

"I think you mean a grotesque, not a gargoyle," Justin

commented. "If it's a carved creature that's not a downspout, it's a grotesque."

"And thank you for that pedantic clarification," Marianna shot back, then turned to Craig. "So what happened to the gargoyle?"

"The grotesque," Justin murmured under his breath.

"It's gone," Craig sighed. "And no one knew it until the Rooftop Tour this morning. Empty spot on the parapet with only a steel bolt to show where it used to sit. And yes, we checked the terrace below to see if it had fallen, but nothing. The other logical possibility -- that someone snuck up to the roof and stole it -- strains the imagination. That's several hundred pounds of limestone you would have to sneak down five flights of backstairs. So I came to you for some less logical possibilities."

"You suspect it spread wing and flew away?" Justin asked.

"I don't suspect, just wonder," Craig shrugged. "I mean, isn't that what gargoyles do in folklore?"

"Supposedly they protect their building by warding off evil spirits, but coming alive and flying is--"

"Commonly depicted on Saturday morning cartoons," Marianna offered. "That may make it more urban myth than folklore. But flying off and not returning its perch by dawn is not part of the package. That's just odd. The whole thing about gargoyles--"

"Grotesques."

"-- is that they work behind the scenes unnoticed by humans. For all we know, the rooftops of Biltmore may be a hotbed of activity after sunset."

Craig groaned again. "Can you please find the missing wolf-thing, whatever you want to call it? If it's found soon, everyone will gladly stop asking how and why and just accept that it's back."

"We're on it," Marianna assured him.

The two-seater electric maintenance cart was more substantial than a golf cart, but still a light enough vehicle to traverse the grounds where no road led. "So you obviously have a plan," Justin said as they zipped through the gardens towards the woodsier sections of the estate. "Why the spyglass?" He held up the brass specimen from his shop questioningly.

With anyone else, it would have binoculars, but with Justin, a nineteenth-century spyglass was conveniently on hand. "We need a straight line of sight back to the west roof," Marianna explained. "As long as we have that, we're on track."

"Because?" he prompted.

"Because there are gargoyles--"

"Grotesques."

"-- at intervals all around the house. Assuming the stone guardians theory, that ought to mean that each . . . carving is responsible for the segment of the estate it is facing--"

"-- and if it's not on its perch, should be somewhere in its assigned segment of ground. That actually makes sense."

"Oh, thank you," Marianna muttered.

"So that's a limit on radius, and there should be a limit on distance as well," he continued. "Presumably this was a reaction to a nearby threat, not something on the Tennessee border."

They kept going past the formal gardens and into the acres of pine forest with its fresh, woodsy scent. Estate foresters kept the area cleared of brush, so the cart had enough space to dodge around the boles of trees. "Strange about Biltmore having stone guardians, don't you think?" Marianna asked as she turned and checked their relative location to the House with the spyglass.

"Indeed I do. It means that someone had to plan it into the fabric of the estate. It could be George Vanderbilt himself, or it could be the architect Richard Morris Hunt. But I haven't heard of either of them being associated with the supernatural in that way."

"What if it was someone down the chain of command?" she suggested. "The stone carvers, for instance? Most of them were brought in from Europe and probably came up in the old apprentice, journeyman, master system. Combining a charm of protection in the stonework may have been the Old World way of doing things. Even over here, you find coins hidden in the studs of old frame houses as good luck charms. Or the protective hex symbols on the barns of the Pennsylvania Dutch. It all seems to be the same mentality of protecting what one has built."

"And if one carved creature is active, then probably the whole host of carvings on the roof as well. I don't think I'll ever look at the Biltmore's silhouette at dusk in quite the same way." He fell silent a moment, then added, "If we accept all this as somebody's plan of defense for the house, then we also have to assume that it's been activated time and time again during the House's hundred-and-twenty-year history. But no one's noticed."

"Before the estate started giving Rooftop Tours, it wouldn't have been very noticeable if a statue or two went missing every so often," she suggested. "Or maybe the gargoyles all came back home in time."

Justin gave a tight nod. "I'm thinking the latter. And that raises the uncomfortable question of why this one didn't return. But I suppose we can ask it. That looks like a misplaced bit of statuary up ahead, don't you think?"

Marianna nodded. A piece of stonework with outstretched wings looked decidedly out of place in a forest clearing. And the gray-yellow limestone was a match for the House itself. As they drove nearer, she tensed. Did that fallen tree limb next to the statue just move?

It did.

"Justin, stop," she whispered savagely. "I think that's a boa constrictor ahead."

"Florida may have feral pythons, but there are no boa constrictors in Appalachia..." he began, then suddenly fell

———

149

silent. He'd seen it, too. He brought the car to a halt, and whipped out the spyglass. "Merciful heavens," he muttered. "It's a huge snake with several hundred pounds of stone statue sitting on it. What we're seeing is the tail lashing about." He slipped out of the cart. "I'm going in for a closer look."

"Don't!" This was more than Justin being reckless this time; this was her psychic nerves prickling. She was sensing things about this snake, and none of them good. "Whatever it is, it has to be both supernatural and dangerous if the gargoyle went after it."

"There is that," Justin admitted. "Perhaps instead of closer, I'll circle around at a distance to see what the other half looks like."

For Justin, that was a huge concession, but Marianna was so tense she could barely sit still. She pulled out her phone to do what she did best -- research. Huge snake . . . Blue Ridge Mountains . . . local folklore. She would have gladly settled for an escaped boa constrictor from a zoo, but she doubted it would be that simple. In her world, nothing ever was.

By the time she sifted through the first batch of search results, Justin was back. He looked shaken. "Some sort of horned serpent -- more like antlers than horns, actually."

"But you kept your distance, right?" she demanded. This was confirming the worst of her search.

"Most definitely. Considering how deadly the Saharan horned vipers are, I was not about to get near to their oversized cousin." He glanced at her taut expression. "What did you find?"

"Uktena," she murmured. "Roughly the Cherokee equivalent of a basilisk. So let's go. We can't do anything here without better preparation."

The drive back was quiet with only snatches of conversation as an idea occurred to one or the other of the siblings, then was quickly discarded. A basilisk was no poisoned teacup and quite possibly out of their league

150

entirely. At the service court of the House, they traded the maintenance cart for Justin's SUV and headed out to town. They ended up back at Sam & Ella's for strategy and more plum cake.

"It's deucedly inconvenient, you know," Marianna grumped as she kept scrolling through articles on her phone. "European monsters all come with easy recipes for their destruction, but with Native American monsters, it's always something difficult. The uktena has to be shot with an arrow of sacred wood directly through the diamond on its forehead, the diamond being the center of its life-force. How can you shoot it through the forehead without looking at its eyes?"

"I don't think we could manage a bow-and-arrow solution anyway. But if a uktena is like a basilisk, then what about trying to kill it the same way?" Justin suggested. "What's the worst that could happen?" He winced. "Forget I asked that."

"Well, if it was me," Ella said, appearing to pick up their plates, "I'd just spray the whole thing down with hydrochloric acid until it dissolved away like the slug it is."

"Thank you, Ella," Justin said, deadpan. "The cake was wonderful, as usual." But the moment he was gone, he leaned over to his sister and whispered, "We're getting careless in public."

Marianna wasn't listening. "What if," she said slowly, "someone" -- it wasn't going to be her -- "sprayed down the uktena with the same concoction you used to counteract the cursed candlestand -- blessed silver, Holy Water, and rowan wood? That has to be a lethal combination to anything from the dark side."

"Holy Water mixed with silver nitrate and essence of rowan bark, rowan being a sacred wood in many cultures," Justin murmured. "That just might work. We'll need a delivery system that allows us to spray from a distance, but --"

"Don't include me in that 'we'," she said firmly. "I'm officially drawing the line at giant snakes."

"Craig, then," Justin nodded. "He probably has an old hand-pump anti-fire device somewhere in that endless inventory of his. Give us an hour before calling in the National Guard." He was already moving toward the door.

That might or might not be a joke, depending on how you looked at it. If the experts couldn't deal with the giant supernatural serpent, then it might take the National Guard. It was going to be a grim hour. Marianna stayed where she was in the booth. She'd rather worry here with matronly Ella cooing encouragement than alone in her bookstore.

When Justin and Craig showed up fifty-eight minutes later, they both looked subdued. Well, Justin looked subdued; Craig looked shell-shocked. He knew about the supernatural because he kept running into it in the strange crates in Biltmore's attics. But he'd never had to deal with the nitty-gritty before.

"Yes, success," Justin announced, sliding into the booth. "The pump let us keep a safe distance, and once we sprayed the diamond on its forehead, the rest turned into amorphous, green slime."

"Too much detail," Marianna shot back. "If I wanted guts and glory, I could have gone along."

"Understood. Craig and I are assuming the winged wolf will be back on its perch come morning, now that its mission is completed. And it was the darnedest thing, wasn't it Craig?"

Craig just grunted and shook his head.

"There was a moment at the end when I swear the statue turned its head and looked directly at us. Do you know what that feels like to be stared at by a gargoyle?"

"Grotesque?" Marianna suggested.

Fort Worth writer Jonathan Shipley creates short stories and novels in the genres of fantasy, science fiction, and horror. In the writing profession, there are two huge challenges. One is the writing itself, and the second is getting the works published. In terms of output, he has written over a hundred short stories in a vast story arc that ranges from Nazi occultism to vampires to futuristic space opera. On the publication front, he has had several dozen short stories published in magazines and anthologies, including the Bram Stoker Award-winning After Death *horror anthology A full listing can be found at* **http://www.shipleyscifi.com/publishedworks** *and most of these publications can be purchased at* **http://www.amazon.com/author/shipley** .

When not writing, Shipley works on the restoration of his 1916 historic home and collects antiques to go in it.

—

SEVEN MINUTES

By Jason Norton

Billy Hayman was reasonably sure there was no patron saint of Spin the Bottle, but throwing caution to the wind, he offered up a silent invocation.

"Please don't let it land on Sandy Bradshaw again. She smells like meatloaf and litter box," he prayed to whatever deity might be overseeing the outcome of adolescent party games.

It was his most crucial spin of the evening. He'd already landed on all four girls in attendance once. Their ensuing mandatory kisses had all been indistinguishable; nervous and quick, bubblegum lip gloss-coated-peck-on-the-lips exercises in awkwardness.

This spin was crucial. Second time around and you're closet bound. Seven minutes in Heaven, alone in the dark, anything goes. Regretfully, or perhaps thankfully, 14-year-old Billy Hayman didn't really know how far "anything" went.

His cousin Jeff had given him a few ideas. The magazines Jeff had shared (no, not the National Geographics, doofus; the ones from under the mattress) bore testament to the potential end result of "if you show me yours," though Billy found little resemblance in these eighth-grade girls and their glossy, staple-bound counterparts.

He could live with Carlie Libman, should it land on her. She had nice eyes and long hair, which he considered a plus. Short hair on a girl was a definite no (one more strike against

Sandy Bradshaw). It would be a definite score if it landed on April Dawes. By his estimation, she had big boobs and according to Jeff, that constituted her "a keeper." Last was the new girl, Samantha Cooper (he was pretty sure that was her last name, at least that's what he thought he heard Mrs. Vincent introduce her as in home room). Her face was okay and the vague outline of her figure, hidden beneath a baggy Led Zeppelin t-shirt and bellbottoms, looked tight and trim. But her biggest asset was mystery.

Rumors had spread like wildfire since her arrival at Newton Middle ten days ago. Most alleged that she was a military brat, relocated here because of her father's transfer to Kingsville Naval Base. Of course most of those same stories implicated Mr. Cooper as a SEAL who would soon be deployed as a squad commander for secret anti-terrorist missions in Belgium (or was it Switzerland?). Billy couldn't reconcile how an elite super-commando would end up at a base where no SEAL teams were headquartered, or why anyone would feel the need to terrorize the waffle (chocolate?) capital of the world.

Sam's older sister had reportedly run off with the circus as a teen, driving her mother to a liter per day habit. In an ironic twist of fate, Mrs. Cooper had reportedly been featured in a national print ad campaign for Mothers Against Drunk Driving years before. The students swore they'd heard she rarely ventured out in public nowadays unless there was a wine festival nearby.

According to the guys in fourth period gym, Samantha had gotten kicked out of her last school after getting caught in a stairwell with a freshman who had his hand up her shirt. Billy was branded a "dork" when he called BS on the rumor, pointing out that hardly any schools combined junior and senior high students anymore for that very reason. Of course, if it were true, and she was generally inclined to such behavior...well, that would certainly make Seven in Heaven interesting.

The bottle decelerated, wobbly but slow enough now that Billy could easily discern the stamped white Dr. Pepper lettering from its orangey-red background. Greg had notified them at least three times since the game began that no one was to throw the bottle away once they were done—his mom would ground him for a week if she wasn't able to send a full six pack of empties back to the market for deposit.

Greg was always worried about getting in trouble. To hear him tell it, he was constantly one C minus/broken family photo/Sunday school prank away from solitary. Billy was flabbergasted when Greg had called him about the party. It would've never gone down if Greg's parents hadn't been out of town for the weekend for one of his dad's dental conventions. Adam, Greg's older brother, had been left in charge. He was gone by the time Billy and the other kids arrived.

"He said he didn't give a rat's patoot what I did, as long as I didn't burn down the house or have the cops show up," Greg had said, trying to impress Billy with more than a hefty hint of bravado in his voice. But Billy noticed the Wild Man's reluctance to fully commit to reckless abandon: their "crazy" beverage choices for the evening consisted of Tang or Fresca (coasters mandatory). He was also fairly certain that the Great North American Badass—whether captive or free-running— was not inclined to include the word 'patoot' in its common parlance.

Thus far, the party had lived up to all of Billy's expectations, if not Greg's.

Though it had indeed been the torrid mixture of Cheeze Curls, black lights and the Bay City Rollers Greg had eagerly anticipated, the closest he'd gotten to any "action" was when Sandy Bradshaw came out of her pants (no thanks to any of his advances). She'd guffawed a gusher of Fresca through her nose at the "Does this taste funny to you?" punch line of

April's joke about cannibals eating a clown. Sandy was sure she'd be grounded if her mother found her brand new jeans soiled when she came to pick her up, so, being the consummate gentleman (and constant horndog), Greg offered to let her wear a pair of his gym shorts until he could wash and dry her pants. He immediately regretted not giving her last year's pair; they had shrunk nearly two sizes thanks to his mother's insistence that they be washed daily.

Billy had contemplated cutting and running within the first half hour. His best friend, Adam Grady, was supposed to be there but an unforeseen thirty-minute vacation to the principal's office yesterday had spurred Adam's parents to ground him for a week.

Billy had walked to the party, as had most of the kids. It was that kind of neighborhood. Everyone knew everyone because everybody lived on top of everybody. None of the parents had blinked an eye at the announcement of the party — of course none of the kids had told them Greg's folks were going to be gone. But most of the adults had watched Greg grow up on the little league fields and cafetorium elementary school graduation stage and knew he was cravenly harmless. They would've likely sent their kids even if they'd known Dr. and Mrs. Libman were absent. Party at Greg Tolliver's? What's the worst that could happen? You get a teen-free night on the town and your kid comes home with a Pixie Stix buzz.

Billy hated Pixie Stix. He also hated Greg's hypersensitive opposition to just about anything that constituted party fun. Thus far, no one else at the party had gotten to even consider Billy's suggestions to bum shots off of Dr. Libman's conveniently unmarked decanters or test the integrity of the basement windows by blasting Boston through the Kenwood at 30. At least he'd agreed to Desperately Seeking Sandy's suggestion of Spin the Bottle.

It was down to its last few turns; three—maybe four?—rotations left. The girls giggled as it swung their way, a soda-twinged divining rod potentially pointing Billy Hayman to the pubescent hormonal oasis that he would likely never have discovered otherwise.

One turn. Two.

Carlie, April, Sandy (shit), Sam, Carlie, April, Sandy (double shit), Sam, Carliiieeee, Aaaapprilll, Sannnnn(shit)nnnnn(duck shit)dddd(shit and shit and piggly wiggly diddly shit)yyyyy, Sssssaaaammmmmm.

Sam.

That would work.

Carlie and April let out giggling "ooohs." Sandy soured, looking as if Ed McMahon had shown up on her front door with a giant cardboard check then realized he had the wrong address. Greg played it as cool as he could, which meant he gave Billy a wink that only Carlie and Sam noticed.

Billy wasn't gushing, but the congenial smile he gave Sam at least conveyed his appreciation for his fortune. She, on the other hand, looked as enthused about spending Seven minutes in Heaven with Billy Hayman as she would have about hanging the last few missing sheets of pine paneling in the Tollivers' basement.

Greg stood, finally posturing to the genuine role of host. "Well, all right; here we go!" he said, slapping and rubbing his hands together like a carnival barker coaxing his next Guess-Your-Weight rube onto the scale. "All righty, you two; right this way!" Greg said, guiding the two of them to the corner closet as excitedly as if he were the one about to lose his Spin the Bottle virginity.

Billy stood first, wondering if he should offer his hand to Sam and escort her to the closet thusly. Wasting no time, Sam hopped up and headed toward the corner. Dumfounded, Greg trotted in her wake.

Greg flung the squeaky door open with the Vegasworthy flair of a stage magician. "Voila!" he exclaimed; his grandiose hand gesture failing to elicit the awe he'd hoped for in his guests. When he caught Billy's "there's a bear behind you" thumb wag, he understood why. The closet was crammed to the gills with winter coats, all manner of small appliances, a tool box, two coolers and what Billy was pretty sure was a saddle that was too small for horses, but just right for, say, a donkey. He wasn't going to ask questions.

"Aw, geeze. Sorry guys," Greg apologized. "My dad throws everything in here. Last summer we found a raccoon trap in here. It still had little bits of fur and tail in it. Dad forgot he left it in here until we noticed the smell. It was kind of like if The Abominable Snowman far—"

"Hey, Greg," Sam cut him off. "What if we use your closet instead?"

Greg looked slightly confused. Billy recognized that face. It was the one Greg wore throughout the near totality of Mrs. Langley's pre-algebra class.

"You mean the one in my room?" Greg clarified.

"That's the one," Sam answered, gently veiling sarcasm behind what sounded like genuine enthusiasm. Billy was impressed. He wagered Sam had used the same tone to sweet-talk her way out of more than a few disciplinary beatdowns from Sgt. SEALAssassinSuperspy.

"Well...yeah. Sure, we can use that one. I've just gotta'...clean up a little," Greg said, inwardly distraught as to whether he'd left Mr. Pookles, his teddy bear, peeking out from the covers.

"Dude, nobody cares, as long as there aren't any dead animal parts in cages," Billy said, eliciting a giggle from the girls—except stone-faced Sam.

"Well, okay," Greg conceded sheepishly. "Follow me."

The lucky couple fell in line. They'd barely taken two steps when the girls snapped to attention, giving chattering chase. Billy flashed a glare over his shoulder. "What?" April asked. "There's no way we're missing this."

160

For Greg, the basement-to-second-floor-trek had never seemed so long. With every step, sweat percolated in his armpits. He hadn't begun using deodorant like the other guys in gym class just yet; his mom argued it wasn't necessary for a boy his age, despite his pleas and the sweet-onion reek that seemed to be baked into each of his shirts by day's end. Soap and water, detergent and 'softener; they were plenty enough for a young Tolliver man, she insisted.

He rattled on as they ascended the stairs, hoping to keep the trailing kids from focusing on the dampness welling at the crack-seam of his corduroys. If the others discovered his secret; if they learned the truth—that each night he violated the ultimate code of adolescence, having his mother tuck him in with the stuffed animal that his Gammy had brought back from Romania ten years ago—he could kiss all hope for social acceptance—much less dominance—down the sweet patoot throne.

Billy meanwhile, was wrestling with his own nerves. Apparently this was not Sam's first rodeo, based upon her indifference to the whole scenario. He, on the other hand, had never even come close to kissing a girl the way he'd seen grown-ups do it in movies. The millisecond smooches he'd handed out downstairs were about as daring as the ones he gave his mom each morning before heading to the bus stop. Greg's tepid Fresca had more zing.

But to really lay one on a girl? He knew more about French than he did French kissing and that wasn't saying much; he'd yet to pass a test in that class.

Jeff had provided a little insight. Billy knew, for example, there was some level of tongue involved, but to what degree, he was not exactly sure. He imagined it must entail about the same effort as trying to squish away the top third of an ice-cream cone—but probably more like the soft-serve variety than its hand-dipped cousin. Jeff also mentioned something about a swirl that he'd dubbed, "The Spiralicious."

It was based upon the ancient teachings of Tibetan monks and was only intended for the most adept practitioners, apparently. He'd warned Billy to stay away from it until he was more experienced, lest he assuredly entwine himself in a girl's braces or choke her to death.

God help him if she expected him to round first base and head for second. God help them both. For Billy, bras were like platypuses; he knew they existed, but he'd never seen one up close and in its natural habitat. If he were left to be the one to remove hers, chances were good that at least one of them would end up in the triage ward at Idlewood General.

The other girls' muffled snickers passively taunted him from behind. He thought he heard Sandy whisper something about "barely a handful" and he could've sworn he caught the phrase "fresh squeezed" at some point, though he couldn't attribute it to any particular source.

Throughout the ascent, Sam remained as stoic as ever, only glancing back at him once in a gesture which Billy surmised a gut check. He took it as somewhat of a challenge, and as they summited the final step, he swallowed the butterflies corkscrewing up his throat; determined to give Samantha the best seven minutes in Heaven this side of Glory.

"Well, here we are," Greg said, pressing his dampened back to the closed door of his room so snugly that the knob rattled. "You're sure you guys don't want me to tidy up a bit?" he asked, hopeful.

"We're good," Sam said, reaching around his death grip to push the door open.

Greg belched a whale-song sized gulp of dread that he hoped only echoed in his mind. Apparently the other kids didn't hear it, as they barreled into the room wildly enough to nearly bowl him over. Frantically he gave a quick scan of the bed, noticing the football-sized lump concealed beneath his NFL bed sheets (thankfully, his Star Wars ones were in the wash). Once Sandy finally lumbered her way across the threshold, Greg dove for the bed while the others perused his room. As soon as their backs were turned, he quickly slid Mr. Pookles out from under the covers and stuffed him under the bed, breathing a silent sigh of relief as he stood to preside over the ensuing festivities.

"All righty then, let's get on to the getting it on," he bellowed, obviously amusing himself with the quip more than anyone else. He led Billy and Sam to the closet, flinging the door open with the same pomp and circumstance as in his original basement performance. Greg's closet was likewise cluttered, but not nearly to the same degree, and the telescope and assorted woodwinds cases would be much easier to navigate than the heap of electronics from downstairs.

"Okay, so just to make sure we're all clear," Greg began, looking to unnecessarily explain the rules.

"We know," Sam broke in. "Billy and I go in the closet and shut the door. We stay in there in the dark for seven minutes and anything goes."

"Right, Billy?" she added, eyeing him with a challenging smirk.

"That's right," he returned, with as much valor as he could muster. "Anything goes."

"We'll be right out here to time the whole thing," Greg said.

"Yeah, and we'll hear everything," April said, eliciting a chorus of tittering catcalls from everyone else.

As Billy turned to give them a "very funny" scowl, Sam took his perspiring hand. The mere gesture sent tingling needles up his arm, returning him to the impending, exhilarating trauma.

"Okay, loverboy," Sam said.

"Let's do this."

When Billy was seven years old, he and his family vacationed in the Great Smoky Mountains. After the obligatory stop at Georgia's Rock City, they toured the clammy bowels of Forbidden Caverns in Sevierville, Tennessee. Once their group had gotten all the way into the middle of the cave, the tour guide shut off the dim overhead lighting, shrouding them all in complete, absolute darkness. The guide explained how it was a common, nightmarish occurrence for Indians to begin exploring the caves with a well-lit torch, only to be left stranded in the black if the rippling winds inside gusted too fiercely. Braves would walk with their backs to the wall so they could feel their way out should their torches ever extinguish thusly.

Standing there in the pitchy blackness of the closet, Billy wondered if he would likewise have to let his fingers do the walking if he wanted to get out alive. He could barely see three inches in front of him; the razor-thin echo of light from Greg's room barely permeating the interior of the closet. One thing was for sure, it must have been one heck of a well-insulated house if the contractor had hung all the doors so tightly.

He felt Sam's breath, hot and moist in front of his face, and caught the distinctly noxious aroma of a recently-finished orange Tootsie Pop. When her tongue entered his mouth, he suddenly thought he'd finally discovered the one human who could finish one without biting.

Screw you, Mr. Owl.

He stood his ground, manning up as best as his instantly-weakening knees would allow and fired a return volley that he was sure would send her head spinning. Damning discretion, he threw the entire arsenal he'd always imagined himself having her way. He was pretty sure that he utilized at least three different forbidden forms of the Spiralicious within the first eight seconds of their kiss. The jarring clink and her reflexive "Ow!" froze him, as he realized he'd bumped her teeth with his.

"Sorry," he apologized.

"It's okay. Just relax," she told him.

The giggles rang from outside. "What are you doing in

164

there? It's not supposed to hurt!" he heard someone (it sounded like Sandy) bellow.

Billy reached for Sam's face to try to steady her for his less rambunctious second attempt. Things went much smoother. He wasn't exactly sure of what he was doing, but he seemed to be hitting his stride, despite the nauseating union of cocoa and citrus that would throw a lesser man off his game.

He felt Sam's hands upon his back, working up between his shoulder blades (the scapulae, if he remembered Mr. Swanson's biology unit correctly) and over his shoulders (deltoids, thank you very much).

Then they were back down again, at his lower back, just above his jeans. Instantly, they found their way to the back of his neck. Then her hands were on top of his, coaxing them down from her face to her neck to her…

He could barely believe it; he could barely stand. Samantha Cooper, mysterious and dangerous, was giving him the green light to second. The rumors about her must've been true.

He was about to find out just what constituted "anything."

"I can't hear anything," April said, squatting with her ear firmly against the closet door.

"What's going on in there?" Carlie yelled through the door, to no response.

"We'll never know if Sandy keeps chomping on those chips so frickin' loud," April said.

Unbeknownst to the rest of the group, Sandy had apparently smuggled a tube of Pringles from the basement, figuring that if she couldn't participate, she could at least enjoy some portion of the auditory floor show.

"What?" she managed to eke out, through a crumbled mouthful of potato, wheat starch and flour while reclining on Greg's bed.

"Stop eating for two seconds, Sandy. Geeze, I thought you'd be more interested. After all, this may be the closest you get to Seven in Heaven," April followed.

Sandy swung a half-playful/half-irritated swing at April with the nearly-empty Pringles can. April beat her to the punch, swatting the cardboard tube from Sandy's hand. It hurtled from her grasp, tumbled to the floor and rolled under the bed.

"Hey, there was still a couple of halfsies in there," Sandy said, leaning over the edge to retrieve her piecemealed snack.

Greg rushed back into his room; his momentary absence spent answering nature's Tang-induced call.

"What did I miss?"

Suddenly he stopped short, catching sight of Sandy's apparently headless form leaned across his bed. He immediately realized the horrific implication.

"What the heck is this?" Sandy said, producing not only the displaced can, but Mr. Pookles, as well.

Greg's face went ashen.

"Holy crap, Greg! You still have a teddy bear?" Carlie exclaimed, bursting with mocking laughter. The other girls echoed her taunting jeers.

"Geeze, Greg; even I don't sleep with a teddy bear and I have—you know—girly parts," Sandy cackled. April and Carlie kept chortling, Sandy along with them; the three of them now indifferent to the activity behind the closet door.

Greg screwed up his limited supply of courage and bolstered his only defense.

Honesty.

"My grandmother gave him to me when I was little. I was scared to sleep by myself because I was sure there were monsters under my bed and in my closet. Mr. Pookles helped protect me," he tried to explain.

"Yeah, but you're like fourteen now. Don't you think it's time to give it up?" Sandy jibed. "I mean what kind of a baby are you?"

"I bet his mommy still tucks him in every night, too," April chimed in.

"Probably wipes him every time he poops," Carlie added, "I mean, if he's out of diapers by now."

They all erupted into their most raucous round of laughter when Sandy curled up on the bed, nestling Mr. Pookles against her chin as she popped her thumb into her mouth and shivered in pantomimed terror.

Enraged, Greg burst into tears. He grabbed Mr. Pookles from Sandy and stormed out of the room, slamming the door behind him. "I hate you!" he screamed at them, as he planted his hip into the sidewall of the bookcase on the far side of the landing. "I hate you all!" he yelled again, muscling the heavy wooden unit across the doorway with an enraged strength that belied his meager frame.

The girls continued to concoct new insults, despite the fact that Greg was long since gone. They were so busy laughing, they'd failed to hear the scrape of the bookcase along the wooden floor; they also missed the thumps of his descending footsteps on the stairs.

In fact, the only time they really gave any attention to his absence was when the lights went out.

Billy had practically summited Everest; he'd bested two clasps on Samantha Cooper's bra. His shaky-handed blindness had made it an awkward adventure, but he had overcome. He just hoped he could get through number three before his seven minutes were up. He pressed onward, determined to triumph in conquest.

Just as he tugged at the third clasp, he heard the screams.

Startled, he pulled away from Sam. "What the heck was that?" he asked her.

"The girls. Something's wrong; open the door!" she said, fumbling to reconnect her bra strap.

Billy fumbled for the doorknob in the darkness. Ironically, it had been a lot easier to locate the more taboo portions of Sam's anatomy.

"Here," she said, finding it before he could. She turned the knob.

The door refused to open.

"It's stuck, Billy!"

"Here, let me try," he said, feeling for her arm, tracing its length to her fingertips. He twisted as hard as he could, feeling the knob rotate, but the door wouldn't budge.

The growl came from somewhere behind him. It rasped thick and heavy, gurgling below the surface. An underlying bottom note trilled acid and edges.

Billy whipped around in the tiny space, bumping his head into what he assumed was a shelf. Trickling warmth snaked into his eyes. As if it wasn't tough enough to see already, now he had bloo...

Sam screamed a millisecond before he did when the glowing green eyes appeared all around them. Billy suddenly realized why it seemed like Sam's hands were all over him earlier.

They hadn't been her hands at all.

Billy was probably the biggest loss of the bunch. Greg had liked him, but in retrospect, he'd never really proven much of a real friend. Billy had always teased him too; not as badly as the girls, but a real friend wouldn't have picked on him at all.

The girls all deserved it; maybe not Sam, but the rest of them definitely had it coming. At least Sam was the new girl; not too many of the other kids would really miss her.

It had been a long time since he'd appeased them this way. The homeless man--the creepy one that always watched him in the park--had been the last one, and that was nearly a year ago now. He'd followed Greg home without argument, probably confident of what he'd get out of the deal. Joke was on him. His sacrifice had quieted them down for a good three months. But they always came back. Thank God he had Mr.

Pookles.

He'd tell all the parents that their children had left right on time and he hadn't seen them since. If Sandy's mom gave him too much trouble when she arrived, he'd lead her to the bedroom, kill the lights and scram. He wasn't scared of her or any of the parents for that matter. He knew what they all thought of him, that he was weak; that he was a coward.

He hugged Mr. Pookles tightly as he turned off his bedroom light, hunkering down under the covers. He rubbed the inverted star-shaped charm around the bear's neck, silencing the claws scraping on the underside of his footboard—their friendly reminder that even with tonight's offering, he couldn't get rid of them so easily.

"You're my best friend, Mr. Pookles," Greg whispered to the fuzzy little bear.

"As long as I've got you, I'm not afraid of anything."

Jason Norton is a lifelong fan of science fiction, comic books and monster-under-your-bed stories. He is a certified personal trainer and massage therapist. When he's not playing volleyball, he studies wilderness survival skills. Honest. Not even he could make that up. Jason and his wife live in Powhatan, Virginia. He has a son, two cats and two dogs. He prefers the son.

His work has appeared at/in Bewildering Stories, Fiction Vortex, Gothic City Press, Daylight Dims, e- Horror, The Horror Zine, Inner Sins and Dark Moon Digest. He currently has stories awaiting publication at Nightmare Illustrated, KnightWatch Press, Pro Se Press and Angelic Knight Press.

See some of his work at:
http://daylightdims.com/portfoliotaxonomy/volume-one/ and
http://www.darkmoonbooks.com/dark_moon_digest_issues.htm

CLUTTERBUGS

By Adrian Ludens

Eddie Allen settled the camera on his shoulder and focused on television's self-appointed prophet of cleanliness, Lester Baxter. With the top button of his pressed shirt open and the sleeves rolled up, Baxter conveyed the appearance of a man about to tackle a tough project. Steady Eddie knew the truth: the only object his boss would lift during the course of the day was a microphone.

"Hello everyone, and welcome to *Clutterbugs*," Baxter said. "The television show that helps pack rats eliminate their clutter and reclaim their space. I'm your host, Lester Baxter. I'm a professional closet organizer and amateur psychologist. Remember, if you have too much, you need Les! Let's meet today's featured guest." He indicated the white-haired man who had answered the door. Steady Eddie thought he looked like a tree stump; short, weathered, sturdy. "He's a handyman and jack-of-all-trades who neighbors say is away on business quite often, Mr. Carl Ado. Hello, Carl. How are you today?"

"Surprised."

"I bet you never expected the *Clutterbugs* team to pay you a visit! Don't be intimidated by the camera, Carl."

"I'm surprised because I forgot there was a door here." Lord Caruvial Adolamin, known for centuries as Caruvial the White, aka Lord Whitesmith, and (most recently) Carl Ado, was one of the most powerful sorcerers to ever have dwelt upon this plane. Though his powers were awe-inspiring, his memory was not without its failings.

———

"Judging from all the junk we can see piled inside your home, that doesn't surprise me! An anonymous neighbor lodged the first complaint about the state of your home, Carl."

His collections of sacred talismans, magical artifacts, fey relics, and Department 56 collectibles were without equal. Carl felt irritation at the television host's ignorance but brushed it aside.

"City Building Inspector Horace Glimmer's office became involved and they contacted us."

"I thought I sensed Horril Glimmergaunt's fetid presence." Carl scowled and mumbled a series of unintelligible phrases.

"Mr. Ado, I couldn't make out what you just said. Are you gargling marbles, by chance?"

"No. I'm casting spells of concealment."

A look of exasperation tainted Baxter's features. "Please listen, Mr. Ado, because I'm not going to repeat myself."

The old man cupped a hand to one ear. "Come again?"

"I said I'm not going to repeat myself."

"Still didn't hear you."

"I'm not going to repeat myself!"

Carl winked into the camera. Baxter, cheeks as red as a masochist's backside, growled at Eddie: "Edit all that! And I want final approval before this episode airs!"

Baxter took a deep breath and mentally regrouped. "Carl, this is serious business. Mr. Glimmer, in his official capacity as City Building Inspector, contacted us. Since you have been unresponsive, and by extension, uncooperative, today we are here for an ambush clean-up. See those dump trucks? By sundown, they'll be full of junk that we're going to gather from inside your house."

Carl frowned. Baxter grinned. Steady Eddie thought about Tragedy and Comedy clashing on reality television.

"Rodney, come over here." The host called, and a balding man with a barely-concealed paunch approached. "In lieu of friends or family members—because we were unable to locate any—we've asked a local resident, Rodney Gimble, to help spearhead the cleanup efforts. Welcome."

"Thanks. I'd like to say 'hello' to my old lady, Lucille. I call her Lucy. That's 'el-you-see-why' for any wise guys from work who might be watchin'. And to my boy, Derrick, whose name was inspired by the three months I spent workin' in the oil fields of North Dakota. Hey, buddy! Lookit, your daddy's on the TV!"

"Edit that down to 'thanks'." Baxter told Eddie, not even bothering to whisper. "Rodney, this is Carl Ado."

"I gotta stop you there, Mixter Baster. This is Wyomin', not Colorado."

"Rodney, did your mother have any children that lived?"

"You mean outside of Wyomin'?"

"Forget it. Rodney, listen: it's not 'Mixter Baster,' it's 'Mister Baxter'."

"Nice to meet ya, Mr. Baxter." Rodney said, as he turned and shook Carl's hand.

Baxter, his wits astride a mustang galloping down the trail between Furious and Apoplectic, croaked out two words. "Edit that!"

Carl knew he'd been lucky so far. He'd been able to stall the show's host long enough to cast a series of concealment spells, blocking the impending invaders from most of his sanctuary. But he left a few of the seventy-seven chambers open. To these he gave the outward appearance of rooms in a mobile home. Carl mentally weaved a befuddlement spell on the local fellow in order to buy himself a few extra seconds. The wizard used these precious seconds to cast as many individual spells of transformation as he could manage before the host lost patience and turned his team loose.

Carl heard Baxter snarl, "Edit that!" as if it were a powerful spell of his own, and sensed that the gathered throng would invade his refuge in mere moments. He also sensed Horril Glimmergaunt's presence, though his enemy must have cloaked himself in some type of disguise.

"It's *Clutterbugs* cleanup time!" Baxter announced. "I need a volunteer to go in first."

"I will," said a young man with a crew cut and tattoos on his forearms.

Carl immediately scanned the inked symbols to make sure they weren't magical in nature. The one on the young man's right forearm turned out to be an expertly-rendered likeness of a 1950s pin-up model who'd also been a witch (unbeknownst to her generations of fans); alluring, but harmless. Tattooed on his left forearm were a series of Chinese symbols which, Carl realized, translated to the English words: 'foolish', and 'tourist'.

"It means 'Strength and Honor'," the crew-cut man explained proudly when he noticed Carl looking.

"Okay, Mike, you're first. Eddie follows with the camera," Baxter instructed. "Carl and I will be right behind you."

Carl let himself be dragged along by the well-meaning host, who narrated for the camera. "Carl, a stereotypical pack rat, clearly gave up trying to keep his home organized years ago. The floors—where we can see the floors, I should mention—seem to be covered in brown grime. I see three- and four-foot high piles of decomposing trash, and it's going to be a challenge getting anywhere in here."

Ahead of them, Mike emitted a howl of pain and started hopping on one foot. Carl held his fingers in a way that allowed him to pass intangibly through the piles of disguised items to get to Mike's side. He eased the young man into a sitting position and glanced at the injured foot.

"Looks like Mike stepped on a nail," Baxter said. "He'll need a tetanus shot, for sure."

Carl knew the damage was much worse; Mike had impaled his foot on a long, thin spike that had been taken from Golgotha, the hill just outside of Jerusalem, two thousand years prior. It was one of Carl's newer acquisitions, and he hadn't found the time to catalog and file it away yet.

Carl's eyes scanned the room until he found something he could use. He cast a spell of concealment around the object to suit his purposes and then turned to the TV host. "I have a tube of salve that will help stop the bleeding," he said. "Mr. Baxter, if you wouldn't mind grabbing it? It's right there on the desk, the small plastic tube."

Baxter hesitated. Then he gingerly moved forward, scanning the floor as he went. At the desk he paused again, his fingers hovering over an ancient grimoire that Carl had disguised as a bag of Cheetos. "Oh, man, I love these," Baxter murmured, distracted from his mission.

Sighing, Carl cast another illusion, and hundreds of cockroaches burst from the bag of snacks. The TV host tottered back and thumped the camera lens with his head. Carl took advantage of the brief distraction to mentally pull the tiny vial of phoenix tears across the room and into his palm. Within five seconds, he'd removed the spike from Mike's foot and tipped the vial so that a single phoenix tear fell onto the man's gaping wound. The tear proved to be more than adequate; the injured tissue began to mend instantly. Carl helped Mike to his feet and steered him back out to the yard.

"Attaboy, Mike," Eddie said as he filmed. "Way to take one for the team. We'll dedicate this clean-up to you!"

"Oh, please," Carl chided. "It takes more than a single nail to make a man a martyr."

Just then, two other volunteers — a slight man and compactly-built woman — entered. Both wore work gloves and carried plastic garbage bags. "We're running behind schedule," Baxter said. "Let's get this show on the road."

"I wish this show would hit the road," Carl murmured. He turned, intending to cast a disorientation spell on the pair, when another worker jostled past him. The momentary distraction was enough; the woman plucked up an item and ruffled Carl's feathers.

"How 'bout we toss this ratty, old pillow?" she asked. "It feels flat and uncomfortable to me. I can't imagine why you'd want to keep it."

Carl swallowed hard and shook his head. She had found an item he had not ensorcelled. If she looked inside the silk pillowcase, he'd have further explaining to do. "I can't part with it. It's a gift my grandmother gave me just before she died battling her greatest foe, Therstina Carsaadi."

Baxter and the members of the cleanup crew in the room stared at him blankly. "Thirsty who?" the woman holding the lumpy pillowcase asked.

Carl's mind raced. "I beg your pardon; I slipped back into my native tongue for a moment. I meant to say that my grandmother battled thyroid cancer."

"What language was that?" Baxter wanted to know. "Italian? French? Fat-free Ranch?" One of the other volunteers guffawed.

Affecting sudden deafness, Carl hurried to the woman, who still held the silk pillowcase. His grandmother had indeed given to him. It wasn't meant to be used as a pillow, however. Ensconced inside it were several dozen feathers harvested ten centuries ago from a griffin that had died in the Altai Mountains of Scythia. Carl had no intention of parting with them for the sake of a third-rate reality show. He gave the woman a polite smile and pried the pillowcase away from her clutching fingers.

"How can we clean up if he won't give up anything?" one of the other volunteers complained.

"For a hoarder like Carl, his possessions are a source of pleasant memories," Baxter recited. He tilted his face toward the ceiling and his hands clasped behind his back. "They are always around for him to look at to cheer himself up. It's an easy relationship—to use the term loosely—to maintain. Many hoarders, or clutterbugs, as we like to call them, carry within them a deep-seated sorrow or angry resentment of the outside world that may indicate any variety of mental disorders."

Carl took advantage of Baxter's on-camera soliloquy to conjure up a stack of boxes in one corner of the room. "All of this can go," Carl announced.

Several volunteers immediately formed a line. The person nearest the boxes lifted the first one from the stack, turned, and handed it off to the second person in line. As each box gradually made its way to the bed of one of the waiting trucks, the first person then lifted the next box. Carl suppressed a smile. He'd interwoven a regeneration spell with a conjure spell so that as long as he concentrated, there would always be another stack of boxes behind the first.

Any pleasure Carl felt was as short-lived as an intelligent sitcom, however. A second group of clean-up volunteers had entered an adjacent room and the wizard hurried after them. He entered the room in time to see a volunteer climb onto a magic carpet disguised as a treadmill. The carpet lifted and transported the surprised man face-first through the window and into some lilac bushes. Then, riderless, it dropped back to the ground. Before Carl could warn or stop her, a third volunteer picked up what appeared to be an outdated phone book. The most-definitely-not-a-phone-book fell open and a tremendous wind began to blow. The wind raged angry, blind, and stupid. The volunteer cleaners were flung in every direction.

Teeth gritted in frustration, Carl cast an elongation spell. Always a hit with the ladies for reasons better left to the imagination—the spell allowed Carl to reach across the room and slap the Tornado Tome shut. The room's objects and occupants floated, fell, and tumbled to the floor.

The wizard's exhalation of relief caught in his throat when he heard Baxter speak.

"Now that we've finished that project we can move on to new business."

Carl hurried back to the first room to see the host wiping his brow, though he hadn't helped lift any of the conjured boxes. Carl mentally chided himself. He'd placed so much of his focus on the dangerous events unfolding in the next room that he'd let the spells creating the never-ending stacks of boxes dissolve. Now the sweating volunteers had turned their attention to other, less-stringently protected rooms.

Invaluable amulets, ineffable talismans, supernatural artifacts, and fey antiquities were carried away by unknowing hands. Carl darted his gaze first left, then right, unsure of what to save first.

"Give me that!" Carl shouted. He darted forward and pulled a long, heavy object from the grasp of a muscle-bound volunteer. The fellow thought he'd been vacuuming the carpet. Only Carl saw that he'd been carving long gouges in the floor with the tip of Caledfwlch, better known as Excalibur. "That's not even mine. It's just on loan from my friend, uh, Merle N. and he'll kill me if the tip had been dulled." Carl hurried from the room and down the hall. On the way he recast the transformation spell on Excalibur, causing it to look like a toilet plunger to anyone who saw it. He created a spotless, new bathroom in an unused recess in the wall. Carl dropped the Excalibur-toilet plunger into the waters of the toilet bowl. Carl knew its positioning had looked much the same on the day Arthur had plucked it from the hand of the Lady of the Lake.

Frantic screams ruined his brief moment of satisfaction. Carl held his fingers together again and slipped through the wall, back into the first room. Some numskull had dropped a hive of flaming hornets, and the ill-tempered creatures clouded the room, preparing to descend on everyone and everything with their fiery stings.

To protect the volunteer cleaners, Carl unleashed a frost spell so cold he extinguished the entire nest. "You fools!" he shouted, finally at the end of his rope. "Do you have any idea what I just did, thanks to you?" Carl spun his gaze from one surprised volunteer to another. The men and women all stared back with varying degrees of confusion. A few shook their heads.

"I just destroyed the only nest of flaming hornets in the entire city!"

"Oh, come now, Mr. Ado," a new voice chided. "They're far too stupid to understand the importance of the 'burbs and the bees."

Carl narrowed his eyes in recognition at the mushroom cloud of a man who approached. "Horril Glimmergaunt; you've finally decided to reveal yourself."

"City Building Inspector Horace Glimmer has arrived," Baxter narrated for potential viewers. "Let's hope he can put a stop to Carl Ado's outrageous distractions and protestations."

"I have assumed this mendacious terrestrial job so as to strip you of as many of your trinkets as possible," Glimmer said. He swept his unruly hair away from his eyes and sneered down at his nemesis. "I have all the proper documentation."

"It's meaningless, and you and I both know it."

"Certainly, but they don't."

"We end this now." Carl said. "But know this: as we battle, I will continue to weave spells of concealment and transformation against the eyes of your unwitting helpers."

Carl and Horace, seeing each other as Caruvial and Horril, lapsed into a more natural conversation—for them, at least. Their magical nature kept them slightly out of sync with the rest of the mortal plane, including of course, the volunteer cleaners and the crew of *Clutterbugs*.

"Then you waste your spells, fool. Your annihilation will be at my hand."

"I think Carl just challenged Mr. Glimmer to a spelling bee a few moments ago," Baxter explained. He glanced distractedly into the camera. "And now the City Building Inspector has responded by accusing Carl of urinating on his hand. Doesn't make sense, but that's what it sounded like to me. Mr. Glimmer has produced a lit cigar from inside his sleeve. Carl has wrapped himself in an entire roll of paper towels. Wow, that was quick. Mr. Glimmer has pushed the lit cigar against Carl's chest and—no! I'm wrong; Carl's not inside the paper towels at all. Sure fooled me. There's Carl! He's throwing handfuls of what appears to be kitty litter at Mr. Glimmer. The building inspector is flailing around like he's on fire! Are you getting all this, Eddie? Give me the thumbs-up if—wait a second! Mr. Glimmer has brushed the litter away. He has Carl on the run. Carl's just grabbed a can of spinach from the windowsill. He's squeezed it open just by flexing his hand. This is so surreal, ladies and gentlemen." Baxter's words poured from his mouth and he sounded like the track announcer at a horse race. "For some reason I assumed he would eat the spinach, but Carl is smearing it on his skin instead. He's making symbols. I see a cross on his forehead, now he's making an ankh on his right bicep. Mr. Glimmer meanwhile, has taken something out of his pocket, a piece of gum, I think. He's chewing it while Carl continues smearing spinach symbols on his skin. I see what looks like a ship's anchor on his left forearm. I think Carl's going to try to punch Mr. Glimmer! Glimmer doesn't appear concerned; he's busy blowing a bubble. Unbelievable! Carl's punch was absorbed by the bubble Glimmer blew! This is just too bizarre for words! Eddie, are you getting—oh, real mature. Don't flip me the bird! I'm just doing my job by making sure you do yours."

Baxter paused and mopped sweat from his brow. Around him, the *Clutterbugs* volunteers had gathered to watch. Most tilted their heads in bewilderment, like dogs trying to understand commands spoken in a foreign language. Carl stopped moving. A grinning Mr. Glimmer stepped toward him with what appeared to be a rubber spatula clasped in one hand. He thrust the object toward Carl's chest, but paused in apparent surprise when nothing happened to his adversary.

180

Eddie, Baxter, Rodney, Mike, and all the others gaped in astonishment as well, but for a different reason. Carl Ado, they saw, now wore a robe of green velvet and conical, symbol-covered hat. Mr. Glimmer wore a black and red tuxedo, complete with top hat, tails, and spats. Cast about the room were a variety of items that most of the volunteers could not readily identify. The lone item in the room that everyone could agree upon was the rubber spatula in Glimmer's outthrust hand.

"You released all the spells of concealment," Glimmer said.

Carl grinned and nodded.

"But this never changed," Glimmer stared at the spatula.

"It did change. It was a spatula originally. I put a transformation spell on it to make it resemble the kris dagger, Setan Kober, which killed Arya Penangsang, the mighty viceroy of Jipang, then concealed it from the others."

"You mean the big, curvy knife I grabbed…" Glimmer said.

"A spatula is a spatula is a spatula," Carl said.

"Are you paraphrasing Shakespeare?" Glimmer's nostrils flared as he asked the question. Carl shook his head.

"Gertrude Stein, then?"

"No."

"Ronnie Milsap?"

Carl rolled his eyes.

"Who, then?"

Carl paused and cast a pointed look around the room. "They can't know."

Glimmer leaned forward. Carl cupped a hand around his mouth and brushed the dark sorcerer's ear with his outstretched pinky.

"*Abra cadaver.*"

Horril Glimmergaunt collapsed to the floor. His centuries-old frame rotted away to dust in seconds.

"Someone should sweep that up and get it out of here,"

Carl said. "No use keeping it."

The battle and resulting clean-up had taxed Lord Caruvial Adolamin the Whitesmith more than he'd care to admit. In fact, he now had a wizard-strength migraine, one that no magic could diminish. Lord Caruvial finished erasing the memories of all the volunteers, tended to their various injuries, and retrieved all of his mystical relics. Then he decided to put himself in a state of suspended animation for a few hours in order to rest.

That's why he never noticed the events transpiring on the other side of another of his many magical doors. This particular entrance to his sanctuary, situated thousands of miles from the one he'd just defended, was also the focus of a different group of people.

"Welcome to *Storage Auction Battle*! Today's lot is unit number thirteen. The winning bidder will get access to everything inside. Do with it what you will. Let's start the bidding!"

Adrian Ludens is the author of Bedtime Stories for Carrion Beetles, *a collection of short stories available from Amazon and Smashwords in various formats. His fiction has been published in* Alfred Hitchcock Mystery Magazine, Woman's World, Blood Lite 3: Aftertaste, *and* Blood Rites, *among others. He lives in Rapid City, SD with his family. Visit him at adrianludens.com .*

THE GHOST OF OUR LADY OF PEACE

By Columbkill Noonan

Anfernee Antonius Abercroft III went to a dance at the Our Lady of Peace Catholic Girls' School, and it killed him. The dance itself didn't kill him, of course; that would be ridiculous. No, more precisely, it was the punch that he drank at the dance that did him in. Or, even more precisely, it was the wine that his dimwitted friend Julius had snuck into the punch. Because, you see, Anfernee is, or, more precisely, was, terribly allergic to wine.

So, when Anfernee unknowingly drank the punch that had been spiked with the wine, he quickly went into anaphylactic shock. His hands and feet got all tingly; his tongue and his throat did the same, and he began to wheeze. Frightened and embarrassed, he crept behind the bleachers in the gymnasium where the dance was continuing on, completely unconcerned about the fate that was befalling poor Anfernee. As he crouched beneath the wooden seats of the bleachers, his airways swelled and closed as he struggled to breathe. Finally, the lack of oxygen overcame him. Anfernee passed out, and, when he woke up, he was dead.

For a while, he was quite confused. It was very dark and cramped where he was, but somehow he could see quite well despite the lack of light. He knew that something was terribly wrong, because it seemed that he was not altogether *together* anymore. He himself seemed to be in one place, but he could quite clearly see his own body, right there next to him.

He looked down at his thin, gangly body, just lying

there, arms and legs weirdly akimbo, and wondered what in hell had happened to him. Several times, he tried to get back into his body. He carefully sat down on himself, and tried to arrange his ghostly limbs in the twisted fashion of his real limbs. When that didn't work, he sat up, made some adjustments, and tried again. But of course, none of this worked. Once you're dead, you're dead, and, no matter what anyone says, you can't get undead no matter how many times you sit in your own dead body.

So, soon enough, Anfernee gave up trying to get back into himself. He just sat there staring at himself for a very long time, feeling completely despondent. He reached out a hand to stroke his pale, pimply face to which, though it might not look like much to other people, he was quite attached. Still, depressed and confused as he was about not being able to be in his body anymore, there's only so long one can stare at one's own corpse. So, after a couple of hours, Anfernee gave up sitting next to himself, and crawled out from under the bleachers to see what he could see.

What he saw was that the dance was long over, and everyone was gone. The bleachers had been pushed back into the wall of the gymnasium, so that Anfernee's body was completely hidden, tucked neatly away behind so many rows of collapsible seating. "Hunh", said Anfernee, seeing this and wondering how long it was going to take for someone to find his body.

As he stood there quite stupidly for some time, looking at the bleachers and feeling confused and despondent all over again, he felt a tap on his shoulder. Surprised, he turned around and saw another ghost standing behind him.

"Hi there, brother," said the other ghost. "I'm Spencer."

Anfernee just stood there, staring, aghast.

"Let's try this again," said Spencer, putting on a mockingly stern face and pointing his finger at Anfernee. "And remember, it's customary to say hello and offer one's name when someone else introduces himself to you."

"Oh, geesh, sure, I'm sorry," stuttered Anfernee. "It's just, that, well, you're kind of a ghost, and I was trying to work out if I still ought to be scared of ghosts, you know, now that I seem to be one and all."

Spencer laughed. "You're a silly fellow, aren't you, brother? Well, let's have your name then," he said, rolling his hand in the air to urge Anfernee along.

"Oh, oops, sorry, of course! I'm Anfernee," said Anfernee, extending his hand to shake Spencer's.

"Well, Anfernee, you really should…wait, it's 'Anfernee'?" asked Spencer

"Yes, Anfernee Abercroft III," replied Anfernee.

"Oh, so your da's name was Anfernee, too?"

"No, my da's name was Alan," said Anfernee.

"Alan? Really? You're not pulling my leg?"

"No, no, my da is Alan, and I'm Anfernee," said Anfernee, getting a bit frustrated with his new friend's obtuseness.

"Well, then, how can you Anfernee Abercroft III if your da…" began Spencer, then stopped when he saw the blank look on Anfernee's face. "A bit mental, that," he muttered to himself, raising his eyebrows and shaking his head.

"My Mum wanted to be creative, she says," Anfernee offered, not understanding why his name warranted such a long discussion.

"Of course, of course. Sorry then, brother. Anyway, as I was saying, you really need to go through the door and get yourself signed in and such. I think you might be quite late already, really."

"The door? What door?" asked Anfernee, looking around.

"Well, THAT door," said Spencer, pointing to the exit door to the gymnasium. Or, rather, what used to be the exit door to the gymnasium. Now, the neon sign above it that should have read "EXIT" said "Newly Dead Sign-In", in letters that were quite small.

"Well, that's not very noticeable, is it?" Anfernee said, annoyed that government ineptitude seemed to extend into the realm of the dead. "How's anyone ever supposed to see that?"

"Enough griping already," said Spencer, rolling his eyes, pushing Anfernee towards the door. "You need to hurry up and get your ghost power."

"My ghost power? What's that?"

"Well, every ghost gets a specific power that they can do while they're a ghost. Choose carefully, because it will be the only thing you can do. And since you're late, you'll be lucky if there's any left at all."

"What do I even need a ghost power for?"

"Well, for one thing, it gets really boring being a ghost. Yeah, there's a few of us here to keep each other company, but it's still nice to get attention from somebody alive once in a while. But really, the most important thing for you right now seems to be that you need to get people to find your body, and if you don't have a power, how are you going to let them know where you are?"

"Why do they need to find my body?"

Spencer sighed in a dramatic, beleaguered fashion. "Because, silly, if they can't find your body, they can't give you a proper burial. And if they can't give you a proper burial, then you're, well, stuck. Like the rest of us here." He glanced pointedly over at the bleachers. "And it seems to me that nobody is going to find you under there until they pull those bleachers out for the basketball games next fall. So unless you want to hang out here in this gym until basketball season…"

Still, Anfernee hesitated, uncertain. Going through that door seemed quite final, an admission of being, well, dead.

"You'd really best hurry up", said Spencer," or seriously, all the good ones will be taken. Trust me, I should know. I waited too long, too, and my ghost power is terrible. Quite an embarrassment, really."

"Why, what did you get?"

"I got the ability to turn on battery operated electronics. I can't do just any electronics, oh no, that would be too useful. Nope, just the ones that run on batteries. Doesn't suck as bad now that smart phones and such have come along though. And I did have some fun in the 90's with those virtual pet things all the kids had. But it would be nice if I could do more than just turn them on. Gets old quick, I gotta tell ya."

"Oh," said Anfernee, "I'm sorry. That sounds dreadful!"

"So, go on then," said Spencer, shooing him on. "I'll be here when you get back, give you a hand getting your bearings and such."

Anfernee reluctantly let Spencer push him through the door. As soon as he passed over the threshold, he found himself standing in a brightly lit lobby. Across the room from him was a large desk, at which sat a stern-looking lady, wearing black-rimmed glasses with rhinestones at the corners and a tight bun in her hair. She gestured impatiently to him, saying, "Well, come on then, it's almost time for me to close. Took you long enough to get here, didn't it?"

"I didn't know, I just…"

"Yeah yeah yeah, you didn't know," the woman interrupted. "Can't you read signs? Well you're here now, so let's get on with it." She gestured briskly at a table set up to the side, on which stood cards, like the place cards one gets at a wedding that lets one know where to sit. There were only two left. "Those are the ghost powers that we have left. Go ahead and choose yours, and bring it back to me so I can get you signed in."

Anfernee made his way over to the table, and picked up the first card. On it was written, "The ability to change the time on clocks. Not the digital ones, mind you, only the old fashioned ones with the hands and such." Discouraged, Anfernee put that one down and picked up the other one. This one said, "The ability to croak the word 'Groch' at whatever volume you wish." He put that one down, as well.

Turning to the lady at the desk, he asked politely, "Excuse me, but do you have any others? These cards here don't seem to be much use to me, after all."

The lady looked at him over the rim of her glasses. "Guess next time you die you won't dilly-dally so long, will you? That's all that's left, so pick one, or I'll pick it for you."

Chastised, Anfernee picked up both of the cards and considered them again. The clock one seemed ridiculous. He couldn't think of one useful thing he could do with such a power. The croaking one seemed quite absurd as well, but at least it was a way to communicate, of sorts. So, croaking it would be.

He picked up the card, handed it to the lady, who brusquely wrote his name and the contents of his ghost power card at the end of a long list. She dismissed him, waving him back towards the door he had come through, and he walked back through it into the gymnasium. When he turned around to look at the door again, the sign at the top had changed back to "EXIT." So, there would be no appealing his ghost power, it seemed. No, he was stuck with "Groch."

Spencer was sitting on the bleachers in the gym, waiting for him. "Well?" he asked, enthusiastically. "Did you get a good one?"

"I can say 'groch'", replied Anfernee.

"'Groch', you say?" asked Spencer dubiously. "And just what are you going to do with that?"

"Well, it's all they had left!" Anfernee snapped, disheartened and irritated by the whole process of being dead. "It was that or changing the time on clocks, which is even more stupid."

"Ok, ok," soothed Spencer. "No need to get your ectoplasm in a bunch." He sat thinking for a moment, scrunching up his face and stroking his chin in a caricature of contemplativeness. Then he brightened. "Well, I can't think of anything just now, but at least people will be able to hear you. We'll come up with something, brother."

"We'd best," said Anfernee. "I don't want to wait until basketball season. Won't I be quite disgusting by then? And besides, I hate basketball."

"No worries, we'll have you sorted out before then, I'm sure. Now let's show you around the place, shall we? School's about to start for the day, and it's best to get the tour done before the halls are swarming with students."

Anfernee nodded, and followed Spencer as he led the way out of the gym and into the hallway. As they walked up the long corridor, lined on either side with ranks of boring grey lockers perforated every few feet by doorways to classrooms, Anfernee realized that, consumed with consternation at his own problem, he had neglected to ask Spencer anything about himself. Embarrassed by his rudeness, he asked, "So, how long have you been here?"

"Oh, I've been here since the 80's," Spencer replied. "Quite a long time, really."

That explains the parachute pants and combat boots, thought Anfernee. "How did you, well, what I mean to say is…" Anfernee broke off, unsure if it broke ghostly etiquette to ask someone how he had passed away.

Spencer laughed airily. "How did I die, you mean? No need to be shy, I've been dead so long I'm quite used to it." He looked off into space as though recalling a fond memory. "I was trying to sneak into the dorms to see a girl. Mary Catherine was her name. Oh, but she was a cutie. Blonde ponytail that swung back and forth when she walked, prim little pearls around her neck, smelled like flowers." He shook his head, rousing himself from his reverie. "Never mind her, she's long gone now. Probably old and grey and wrinkly, smelling like mothballs. Anyway, I never made it to the dorms. I didn't know that they were getting ready to build an extension of the school building, and I tripped over some construction tools and fell into a big ditch. Hit my head on a block of concrete, and, well, here I am."

"Where, exactly, are you? I mean, uhm, where is your

body? How come they haven't found you yet?" asked Anfernee, thinking that thirty years was a terribly long time to wait.

"They went and built the new Art Wing right over me. I'm underneath the concrete basement floor. Tried for years to just stand over my own self, turning on the electronics of anyone who came down to the basement, thinking somebody might be smart enough to figure it out and dig up the floor. But no, they just thought it was electrical interference from the breaker box down there. Brought in an electrician to fix it. Useless, really. I'll be here until they demolish the school. Unless, maybe, you could try saying 'groch,' over my body?" Spencer asked hopefully.

"Of course, I'd be happy to," agreed Anfernee, not wanting to disappoint his new friend, although he failed to see how saying 'groch' would make anyone think to break open a concrete floor.

"Anyway," continued Spencer, "we have plenty of time for that. Gesturing towards the hallway in front of them, he said, "We're just coming out of the English Wing now, and we'll pass the office and continue on to the Science Wing over here on the left."

"The office?" Anfernee asked, feeling an idea begin to form in his head. "Where is that?"

"It's that door there, straight ahead," said Spencer, pointing.

Anfernee's mind raced. The office was where the adults were, the ones that knew what they were doing. In any school, it was where a student went if he had a problem. And Anfernee most certainly had a problem.

Without any further thought, Anfernee raced down the hall and ran headlong right through the office door, ignoring Spencer's warning calls behind him, telling him to wait. Sure enough, the nun who was in charge of the office had arrived just moments before, and was settling down at her desk to begin getting ready for the day.

Anfernee ran right up to her, and yelled excitedly, "Groch!"

The nun looked up, and glanced around the office. Seeing nothing, she shook her head and went back to shuffling papers around on her desk. "Groch!!!!" he said louder, and the nun looked up again, nervously. The headmaster emerged from his office.

"Did you say something, Sister Agnes?" he asked.

"No, Father Marion," she said. "But I thought I heard something too."

Encouraged that people were noticing him, Anfernee put even more effort into it. He stuck his face right up against Sister Agnes' ear, and yelled, "Grooooooooch-ahhhhhch-ahhhch!" as loud as he could, just as several other nuns entered the office through the front door.

Sister Agnes jumped, then fainted dead away onto the ground. The other nuns screamed, and clung together like frightened hens. Father Marion, eyes wide, pulled himself together and went to stand over Sister Agnes. He waved his hand in front of her face, and shook her by her shoulders.

"Urk", said Sister Agnes. Opening her eyes and sitting up, she shook her head groggily, then gripped Father Marion's hassock. "A demon, Father Marion! You heard it too, didn't you?"

"I heard it!" chimed in one of the nuns by the door.

"Me too!" echoed the rest.

"Indeed, I heard it too!" said Father Marion. "A voice most evil and foul!" He whipped out his crucifix, and wielded it aggressively in front of himself. "I exorcise thee!" he shouted. Anfernee, stunned at this unexpected turn of events, and quite insulted at being called evil and foul, stood there uncertainly. "In nomine Patris, et Filii, et Spiriti Sancti, I compel thee. Begone!"

As the priest spoke, a wind began to dance about Anfernee. A mere tickle at first, it built in strength until at last, when the priest cried, "Begone!" the wind became so strong that, with a mighty blast, it blew Anfernee right through the door. He landed in a heap in the corridor, and looked up to see Spencer standing over him, shaking his head in amusement.

"Groch!" Anfernee cried, and rushed towards the office door, thinking to try talking to them again, to make the nuns and the priest see who he really was. But the door repelled him like the wrong sides of two magnets, and he bounced backwards to fall ignominiously again and again. He screamed in frustration, and beat his fists in futility upon the floor.

"Ah, brother," said Spencer sympathetically. "Your first exorcism! And it was a fine one, too. Quite dramatic!" Spencer began to giggle. "And I must say, you looked quite funny, flying through the door like that, your face all surprised and such."

"But why can't I go back in?" wailed Anfernee. "I need to talk to them!"

Spencer clucked, shaking his head. "Yeah, you gotta be careful with that. Once you get exorcised from a place you can't ever go back. You get exorcised from enough places in here, you'll end up like poor old Harry."

"Why, who's Harry?" asked Anfernee.

"Well, he got exorcised one too many times and now he can't go anywhere. He's stuck in a locker on the third floor. Got exorcised from the hallway up there, and had nowhere to go but into that damned locker. Now he's just trapped in there. Can't do a thing about it. It's even more terrible because his ghost power is to open drapes. There aren't any drapes in that locker, let me tell you," said Spencer, shaking his head ruefully.

"So what do I do now?" asked Anfernee dejectedly. "If my power gets me exorcised, then how am I supposed to get them to find my body?"

A group of girls walked past as Anfernee was talking. "Hello," said an electronic voice, interrupting Anfernee's complaints. "What can I help you with?" Yet another electronic voice chimed in, and then another. The girls all stopped, checking their cell phones and looking startled.

Anfernee saw that Spencer was not paying attention to him and was instead watching the girls with amusement, and immediately figured out what was happening. "Spencer! Stop turning on phones while I'm trying to talk to you!" he cried in frustration.

"Sorry brother," Spencer apologized, looking sheepish. "A bloke needs to have his fun when he can. Anyway, no use crying over being exorcised. It happens to us all. Just be more careful in the future. Let's go back to the gym and rest a bit. We can finish the tour later."

Anfernee agreed and the two ghosts returned back to the gym. Spencer went off into a corner and amused himself by turning on the electronic timers used for gym classes, and Anfernee sat next to the bleachers, contemplating his future. As he sat there, feeling hopeless, a little grey cat walked into the gym. Vaguely, Anfernee recollected that the school kept a cat as a mascot, and called him Saint Francis of Assisi, after the patron saint of animals.

The cat sidled up to him, meowing, and reached out a paw towards him. Of course, Anfernee thought excitedly. Animals can see ghosts! He felt another idea beginning to take shape. Perhaps if he could get the cat to follow him to his body, the cat might then lead someone else there.

So thinking, he began to edge his way under the bleachers towards himself, beckoning to the cat while he moved. Obligingly, the cat followed, until at last Anfernee and the cat stood in front of his body. Feeling hopeful, Anfernee watched as Saint Francis of Assisi crept cautiously up to his corpse. The cat tapped his dead flesh with a tentative paw, and, getting no response, stuck his head forward to sniff his hand. Saint Francis of Assisi licked Anfernee's thumb and, before Anfernee could react, bared his sharp little teeth and bit the thumb off at the knuckle.

"No!" yelped Anfernee, horrified.

The cat, startled by Anfernee's howl, jumped and ran off, thumb still firmly clasped in his jaws. Anfernee gave chase.

The two emerged from beneath the bleachers, one naughty cat intent on keeping his pilfered meal and one outraged, nearly hysterical ghost.

"Get back here, Saint Francis of Assisi! You drop that thumb right now!" yelled Anfernee.

But, of course, Saint Francis of Assisi did not listen, and being much faster than Anfernee, quickly made good his escape.

Anfernee gave up the chase and stood there, more miserable than before. But he was quickly distracted by the sound of laughter coming from the other end of the gym. Spencer stood there, nearly doubled over with mirth, wiping tears from his eyes.

"Oh my goodness," Spencer gasped, trying to catch his breath. "Oh my goodness. I've never seen anything so funny in my, um, life."

"It's not funny!" chastised Anfernee. "Saint Francis took my finger!"

This prompted another gale of laughter from Spencer. "Oh heaven help me," he cried between guffaws.

Finally, seeing that Anfernee was in no mood for light spirits, Spencer calmed down. "It's all right, brother," he said, coming over to clasp Anfernee's shoulder. "You don't need that finger anymore. See," he said, holding up Anfernee's ghostly hand, "you still have all of your ghost fingers, right? That body isn't you anymore, and you need to come to terms with that."

Anfernee nodding, seeing the truth of what Spencer said. But he still wasn't quite ready to relinquish his attachment to his earthly body, and he definitely did not think it was funny to watch a cat make off with his parts.

"Come now," said Spencer. "I know what will cheer you up. How about if we visit the girls' dorm tonight?"

194

Like most teenage boys would be, Anfernee was quite delighted by this prospect, and the thought of spying on the girls, completely unseen, quickly caused him to forget the indignity that had been inflicted upon him by Saint Francis of Assisi.

After school had let out for the day, dinner had been served, and all of the girls returned to their dorm rooms, Spencer and Anfernee set out on their escapade. They entered the dorm, and Anfernee looked around excitedly as Spencer showed him around. "This hallway goes down to the bedrooms, and right here is the common room, where all the girls hang out," Spencer said, gesturing to a large, dimly lit room furnished with heavy, old-fashioned furniture and decorated in somber colors. "The bedrooms are far more interesting," he continued, with a lecherous wink towards Anfernee.

The two ghosts were about to set off down the hall towards the bedrooms, when they were passed by two girls scuttling excitedly down the corridor towards the common room. "Hurry!" one admonished the other, pulling her along. "We're late for the séance!"

Anfernee and Spencer looked at each other with excitement, and hurried to follow the two girls into the common room. In one corner was a cluster of girls, seated on the floor on a heavily embroidered woolen rug. They were arranged in a circle around an ornate old sconce, with lit candles in each of its three holders. A bowl of sage burned next to the sconce, creating an herbal fog that permeated the entire room. The latecomers hurried up to the circle, and everyone shifted to make room.

Anfernee and Spencer crept closer to see what was going on. All of the girls clasped hands, lowered their heads, and closed their eyes. One girl began to speak.

"Oh spirits of Our Lady of Peace, hear us now!" she said, striving to make her girlish voice sound low and sonorous. "We bid you to come speak with us."

Anfernee looked at Spencer and rushed towards the circle, beckoning Spencer to join him. So excited was he that he barely felt Spencer's hand as he tried to pull him back, and he scarcely heard Spencer's harshly whispered imprecation to wait.

Instead, in his exuberance he ran straight to the middle of the circle, and accidentally knocked the candles over. The girls screamed, and indeed it seemed that the candles would surely catch the rug on fire until several of the more quick thinking ones scurried over to extinguish them. In order to be heard over the tumult that he had created, Anfernee cried out with all his might, "Groch!"

The girls all froze in silence as his voice echoed through the room. Finally, the girl who had been leading the séance stirred. "Stop it, Mary Pete," she said. "We know that's you. You always do that!"

"It's not me!" protested Mary Pete from the other side of the circle. "It didn't even sound like me!"

Frustrated at the turn things were taking, Anfernee summoned all his might and yelled with all his being. "Anfer-neeee!" he shrieked.

Suddenly everyone spoke at once.

"Oh my goodness," said Spencer. "I think you said something other than 'groch'."

"Did you hear that?" said one of the girls.

"What was that?" said another.

"Seriously, Mary Pete," said the leader.

"Anfernee!" cried Anfernee again.

That time, the girls heard him more clearly. "Anne Ferney?" a few of them ventured. "It said 'Anne Ferney'! Go get the yearbooks!"

And so the circle broke, as all of the girls scurried about, trying to find yearbooks, and looking for "Anne Ferney" within them.

"Groch," said Anfernee, standing forlornly where the circle had once been.

"Well," said Spencer, "this is going to be interesting."

Finally, one of the girls squealed with excitement. "I found her!" she called. "She's in the yearbook from 1957. She lived over in the other dorm. Let's go!"

And so all of the girls ran off together to search for the ghost of Anne Ferney, while Anfernee stood disappointed again.

"Tried to stop you, brother," said Spencer. "You've got to plan these things better. Although, I must say, I haven't had such fun since before poor old Harry got banished to the locker." He laughed. "Anne Ferney! Can you believe it? Ha!"

"Humph," said Anfernee. Again, being the butt of the joke, he naturally didn't find it nearly as funny as Spencer did.

"Well," said Spencer, "there's no use looking around the dorm now. You've sent all the girls running around on a wild goose chase. There's nothing for it but to go back to the gym. We can always come back another day."

Anfernee agreed, and together the ghosts made their way back to the gym. Once there, Anfernee sat sadly in front of the bleachers, contemplating his fate. Clearly it was useless to keep trying to get someone to find his body. Every effort he made ended preposterously. And, after all, it was only ten months until basketball season, when they would open up the bleachers, find his body, and give him a proper burial.

He looked over to wear Spencer sat, watching a group of girls walk past with a goofy grin on his face. "Hello," chirped a robotic voice from the purse of one of the girls. "Welcome," said another girl's purse, while tinny electronic music played a scale from another. The girls squealed and fumbled in their purses. "I do not understand 'Eek!'", said the voice from one purse. "Would you like me to perform a web search for 'Eek'?" Spencer laughed raucously at the cacophony of startled girls and confused smart phones, slapping his hand on his thigh. Anfernee sighed and settled down to wait. It was going to be a long ten months until basketball season.

Columbkill Noonan has an M.S. in Biology, and teaches Anatomy and Physiology at a university in Maryland. An avid history buff, much of her writing, which could be best described as "supernatural historical horror", combines historical events with elements of paranormal fantasy. Her first novel, Night Woods, is available as an e-book on Amazon.com. She is currently working on her second novel, which was inspired by a trip to Scotland, particularly by the grim castles and spooky underground alleys of Edinburgh.

In her spare time, Columbkill enjoys hiking, scuba diving, and riding her horse, Mittens. To learn more about Columbkill, and to hear breaking news about her latest works, please feel free to visit her at www.facebook.com/ColumbkillNoonan .

TWO MARTINI LUNCH

By B. David Spicer

"Hello, my name is Gary, and I'm an alcoholic."

The reply from the other fifteen people in the room couldn't have been more monotone. "Hi, Gary." They sounded more dead than I did, which is really kind of funny, seeing as how I am dead. I wasn't there to get sober though, no, quite the opposite. I wanted to tie one on in the worst way, but I needed help.

"Let's see, I've been drinking since, well, since I could pick up a bottle. I never drank to be social though; I drank because I liked how it felt, the burning in my throat, like swallowing a hot coal. I liked how it made the world go away, how all my problems just vanished. Let me tell right now, I've got problems, problems like you can't imagine." I scanned the crowd through the wafting scum of cigarette smoke, looking for the antsy one, the one licking his or her lips, the one that'd bolt for the nearest bar as soon as they got their attendance sheet signed. I've gotten good at picking them out, and I always find one.

"My wife left me to join a free-love hippie commune outside Denver. My son works as an S&M fashion model in Madrid, and my twin daughters work as longshoremen in Portland, Maine. Even my dog left me for a semi-platonic relationship with a stray pot-bellied pig. I've got problems! But after a couple of martinis, they don't seem so bad, sometimes I even smile." That whole story is nonsense, of course, a story I'd made up just so I'd have something to say at the meetings. Over the years the stories change a bit, sometimes my wife left me for another woman, sometimes for a mime. My daughters are sometimes doctors, and my son is sometimes a priest. Truth is, I've never been married, and I've never fathered any children. Even if I had, they'd be long gone by now.

I found my target, a sweaty, mid-forties, white guy in a wrinkled gray suit. He'd just started smoking his fifth cigarette in twenty minutes, and his hands shook. I knew that feeling! Hell, my own hands shook just looking at him. "I'd drunk one too many at a Christmas party, and passed out. I woke up dead." A couple of people chuckled, one or two gave me a blank look, but most of them weren't paying attention.

Lewis, the guy who ran the meetings cleared his throat. "Uh, Gary, what do you mean by that?"

"I mean my heart stopped beating. I was dead!" Okay, that part's true, but I left out the part about how I was still dead. That part's kind of icky.

"You had a heart attack?"

"There was an attack, oh yes." I put my hand over my heart. "I've never been the same since, and I've never taken another drink." Not for lack of trying though! I must have knocked back a couple hundred bottles of bourbon before I gave up. It'd hit my stomach and come right back up. Whiskey and the undead don't mix well. I got tired of throwing up.

Cornelius, my sire, used to laugh at me. "Vampires can't get drunk, you idiot!"

"Then I don't want to be a vampire! I never asked to be one!"

"Neither did I, but you don't see me whining about it! I liked eating cherry pie, but when the plague came through, there weren't many pies being baked. My sire saved me, and I saved you. So quit bellyaching and show a little gratitude!"

I bowed theatrically and hoped the sarcasm of the

gesture showed through. "Oh, thank you, benevolent one! Your munificence is truly without bounds!" Then I flipped him the bird.

He always laughed when I carried on like that. "Come on, kid. Let's find a hot meal." He stood up from his crouch, and his smallness caught me off guard, as it always did. Such a tiny man and one who moved with an unexpected grace. I'd argue with him every chance I got, but over the decades I came to love the little bastard too. I still miss him.

"Fine, you old coot. How do you stay so thin when you eat like a pig?"

He patted his belly. "I only hunt the skinny ones!"

Now, he'd said things like that hundreds of times during our century together, but I never thought anything of it until after I'd lost him. We'd gone into a new nightclub in the 80s, one of those places with the elaborate light shows and thumping dance music. I hung out at the bar, watching (with considerable jealousy) the underage kids getting sloppy drunk, but Cornelius waded right into the writhing mass on the dance floor. The guy looked like a scrawny grampa, but for some reason the women were all over him! If he'd still been able to perform, he could have scored a dozen times that night! That mental image made me a little queasy, and I watched a young woman chug down a Cosmo with envy.

A new song started up and the lights shifted from a lurid red, to the purplish gloom of black lights. The back of my neck seared with pain and I spun around. Cornelius had frozen on the dance floor; he held his smoldering hands palm-up and stared at them, also clearly in pain. The light! Something about the light hurt my skin! I rushed toward the door, turned, and saw Cornelius shoving his way toward me. He made it about halfway before, POOF! he was gone in a puff of ashes.

You need to understand that vampire society is ruled by regional councils, and each council is headed by a figure known as the Magistrate. Anytime one of our kind is killed, whether by sunlight, by a human being, or by any other means, we have to go before the Magistrate and explain how it happened.

Such gatherings are invariably sad, solemn events, akin to funerals, where the dead are mourned by those who knew them, sometimes for centuries. Not that one though, oh no, I wasn't that lucky. I stood there, in front of the Magistrate, in front of the Council of Vampires for the city of Chicago, and explained how my sire had been vaporized by the light show in a dance club, while dancing with girls not yet ripe enough to eat. The Magistrate, a humorless wretch even by undead standards, made a sound deep in his belly that burst forth into a dusty laugh that hadn't been heard since the Fall of Rome. He laughed until he snorted. Ever hear a vampire snort? It's not pleasant.

The whole council collapsed into peals of mirth, holding their bellies as if they might split open. They had to cancel the rest of the inquest because every time they'd look at me, off they'd go on another gut-buster. I didn't think it was funny, and lord have mercy, did I want a drink! I'd never wanted one so badly, not even when I could still swallow it.

After that, I knocked around Europe for a few years, alone mostly, but eventually I met a fellow vampire in Dusseldorf who changed my unlife forever. He said his name was Kummerspeck, but I just called him Speck. Without a doubt, Speck exceeded, by orders of magnitude, the girth of any man, living or undead, that I have ever seen. He lived like a dandy, and had to have his clothes specially tailored, so he tended to stay close to where his tailors lived. He looked like the rotund illustrations of Humpty-Dumpty in children's books. A well-dressed egg of a vampire, as round as he was tall.

I'd known him for a few months before we decided to hunt together. He took me to his favorite spot, an enormous confectioner's shop in the old part of Dusseldorf. "Here is good place, jah."

"Why here? It's full of old people and children. I don't

---

eat kids."

He laughed. "No, but the nectar is sveeter after the chocolate."

"Huh?" I tried to process that, but it didn't work very well. "What are you talking about? Blood always just tastes like blood."

He shook his head from side to side emphatically. "No, no, no! Is sveeter after the chocolate! You vill see! Jah, you vill see!"

We settled on a pair of twenty-somethings who had just shared an enormous chocolate bar. They don't come that size in America, but those two went to town on it, just gobbled the whole thing down. It kind of made me queasy to watch. We followed them through the park until we were each able to catch them alone and take a bite of their nectar, not much of course, we'd leave them alive so we could hunt them again later. Catch-and-release, the vampire way. For the first time in over a century, I tasted something sweet. The vast amount of chocolate, taken so soon before we began our own meal, had increased their blood sugar, and I could taste it! It tasted amazing too.

I looked up at Speck, and he smiled redly. "See? Is sveet, no?"

"Yeah. It really is!" I went back for seconds. The best part? I didn't throw up! I decided Cornielius hadn't known about this technique or he'd have force-fed cherry pie into half the population of Chicago. Too bad, that might have put some meat on his bones, like it clearly had done for Speck.

Not long after that I returned to Chicago. I started hunting near Dairy Queens and Dunkin' Donuts. Halloween became my favorite holiday. Trick-or-Treat! I didn't always want a sweet meal, but it felt good to know I had the option.

Back in my breathing days, when I went to school, biology classes were unheard of. Speck had taught me that the amount of sugar carried in the blood could change the taste, but it honestly never occurred to me that the blood could carry anything else. I can't overstate my ignorance of the metabolic workings of the living, so I felt stupid when I saw the billboard. Of course!

The sign said, "Four drinks can increase your blood-alcohol level beyond the legal limit of 0.8!" I read the sign twice more before the implications of what I'd just read sank in. Blood-alcohol level. "The bloodstream can carry alcohol?"

I found a liquor store and bought a bottle of whiskey. I found a homeless guy in an alley who was more than willing to have a drink. He finished the bottle, and I finished him. I wish I'd washed his neck first. I learn something every day.

He tasted like whiskey. And tacos, but mostly whiskey. As the bum's blood coursed through my veins, the liquor did its work. I stumbled down the sidewalk, singing a tune a hundred years out of date. A couple of patrol cops pulled over their prowl car to interrogate me.

"Sir, what have you had to drink tonight?"

"Uh, just an old man."

The cops looked at each other. "He must mean Old Gran-Dad." He spoke loudly to me, as if I were going deaf. "Sir, do you mean Old Gran-Dad whiskey?"

I blinked a few times. "I don't know if he was a gran-dad, but he needed a bath."

"What?" They both chuckled. "Okay, sir, you'll have to come with us. Will you do that?"

"Sure, you fellas seem mighty nice. I love you guys!"

They smiled and opened the rear door of their prowler. "That's nice, sir. We love you too."

"No, I mean it! I love you guys!" I really did mean it, at least right then.

Well, those two fine, upstanding police officers escorted me to a nice clean jail cell. Fortunately, I sobered up before the sun rose. I had my first hangover in a century, and I realized that I really hadn't missed that part of drinking. In fact, I began to wonder if I could load up some poor bastard with a titanic dose of Tylenol.

I had to shift into my mist-form to get out of there before sunrise, not an easy thing to do even when my skull doesn't feel like it's full of broken glass and molten lead. I made it to my lair just in time, and I slept better than I had since my heart stopped beating on Christmas Eve all those decades ago.

"Gary?"

"Huh?" I looked at Lewis and tried to remember where I was.

"You were telling us about your heart attack."

"Oh! Yeah, guess my mind wandered off." I finished my fictitious story about how my heart had stopped and an old man named Cornelius, who was dressed up like Santa Claus, had saved my life with a timely CPR session. During it all, I kept watching my target smoke cigarettes and look at his wristwatch. After I'd finished speaking, nobody else had much to say, so Lewis wrapped it up with his usual spiel about how we didn't need to drink to solve our problems and be a productive member of society, blah-blah-blah. I'm sure he's right, but I'd heard the speech so many times before that I can recite by heart. Besides, I'm already dead. What's the worst that could happen? Okay, okay! As long as I don't drink in dance clubs, what's the worst that could happen?

I followed my target out the door, down the street and into the bar. I sat down next to him, and he shot me a dirty look. I held up my hands to indicate my harmless intentions.

"Don't worry, we're here for the same thing."

"Are we?"

"More or less. What are you having?"

"A martini. Probably two."

A smile stretched across my face. "Excellent. There's nothing I like better than a two martini lunch."

B. David Spicer lives in Ohio, where he earned a BA in English from Ohio University. He has always been an avid reader and one day woke up and started writing fiction of his own. He writes crime fiction, science fiction and horror fiction and occasionally writes scripts for independent comic book publishers. His short fiction has appeared in several anthologies and journals throughout the country and overseas. In his meager spare time he enjoys reading, hiking and playing boardgames. He shares a house with an imperious cat and more books than any one person should own.

CATTING AROUND

By Logan Zachary

I came home late one night from the bar and saw the big tomcat standing by my back step. There was a patch of blood along his right side, a dark crimson/black slash across his yellow tiger-striped body. There was a bare spot on top of his head and a nick was taken out of his left ear, clotted with blood. The night was close, and the day's heat still radiated off the concrete. My T-shirt and cut offs clung to my skin from my sweat and humidity.

"You poor guy," I said as I saw him. "Are you okay?" I bent down to scratch his neck.

The cat arched his muscular back and rubbed up against my hairy leg, sending shivers up my leg, all the way up my spine.

What was this strange reaction? I know I didn't drink much at the bar. I looked up at the moon, almost full but not quite. Two days to go. I could feel my nerves raw under my skin in the moonlight, itching, prickling wherever it touched me.

I knew how this poor fellow felt. "Did you need something to eat? Drink?" I dug into my pocket and pulled out my keys. I unlocked the back door, and the cat darted into my house. I grew up with dogs my whole twenty-five years on this earth, and after my camping accident, I haven't owned a pet.

I flipped on the light to check on where my guest ran to.

The golden tom sat in the middle of the kitchen looking

at the refrigerator.

I opened the door and pulled out the bottle of milk and a cold beer. A bowl dried in the rack by the sink, and I poured some milk into it and set it on the floor.

The cat raced to the bowl and lapped up the milk. His pink tongue dipped into the cool liquid, and he drank quickly.

I opened the cupboard and found a can of tuna and opened it. I tipped it over onto a plate and set the plate next to the bowl.

The cat stopped drinking and eyed the pink cylinder of fish. He slowly approached and took a small bite. He looked up at me and gobbled the rest down.

I filled a glass with cold water and drank it as I watched the cat eat. I kicked off my shoes and set them by the back door.

The tom cat looked over at me as I bent over. He watched me intently.

I looked back at him as I lined up my shoes. I could feel my tight shorts cling to my backside and I looked back at the cat.

His green eyes glowed in the kitchen light. His pupils dilated.

Was he checking me out? I looked underneath him and noticed he was a big old tom. He must know which way I swung. I opened my beer bottle and took a big sip.

The cat ran into my leg and a mouthful of beer spilled out of my mouth and rolled down my chin to be absorbed into my shirt. I wiped my face and felt the cold wave of beer soak down into my shirt. I pulled the cotton away from my skin and smelled my sweat. "This needs to be washed." I peeled my shirt off and threw it down the backstairs to the washing machine.

The cat looked me up one side and down the other.

I combed through the hair on my chest and looked down at my shorts. I unbuttoned them and slipped them off. My tighty whities clung to my body like a second skin.

"Me-ow," the cat said.

"I'm off to shower and then to bed."

The tom followed me up the stairs.

As I started the shower, the tom looked at the running water, no fear or avoidance in his stare. He looked at me in my underwear, seeming to wait for me to strip and enter the shower. Steam billowed around the tiled bathroom and fogged the mirror.

The tom jumped onto the closed stool and waited.

I turned my back to him and pushed my briefs down. I let the damp cotton fall to the floor as I stepped out of them. I cupped myself as I pulled the curtain around me. The plastic crinkled as I closed it and stepped into the hot, cleaning spray.

"Ahh," I moaned, as the hot water washed my stressful day down the drain. I brought my head back and shook my hair and let the water rinse the sweat away.

The shower curtain rustled.

I opened an eye and peeked over to see the cat pawing at the curtain. I tapped the plastic, and he stopped for a second. I closed my eyes as I reached for the shampoo. I soaped up and the citrus smell of lemons filled the room as my masculine sweat disappeared. The thick foam flowed down my body and as I rinsed off I noticed a dark shadow next to my head.

Images of Psycho filled my mind as the shrilling music played in my mind. I stumbled against the tiled wall and blinked the water from my eyes. Then I recognized the tom cat's body clung to the center of the curtain.

As I made a move toward the plastic curtain, the tom cat slowly slid down the curtain to the floor. Its small nails poking holes as it went.

There goes a dollar ninety-eight.

I turned the water off and grabbed my towel. Running it over my head, and then quickly across my chest and under my arms, I wrapped it around my waist. Padding bare foot across the tile to the wooden floor that led to my bedroom, I pulled the covers back.

The tom cat jumped onto the bed. Its green golden eyes watched my every move.

"Make yourself at home." I pressed the towel against my hairy legs to absorb the last of the water and tossed the towel over a chair next to my bed. Slipping naked between the sheets, I settled down into the down pillow.

The tom curled up next to me, looking into my face as it fell asleep.

I woke the next morning with the tom cat curled up next to my bare butt. I moved my leg and the cat stretched at the same time. I could feel his claws poke into my flesh, but it was an innocent wake up call, not a territorial stance.

Ignoring my naked state, I jumped out of bed and walked to the bathroom.

The tom cat rose at the foot of the bed and watched my every move. His eyes glowed in the sunrise as his tail curled around his legs and the tip rose ever so slowly up and down.

I watched its rhythmic flip as I emptied my bladder, but its gaze held me. I shook and hurried to get dressed. Goosebumps rose over my body as my briefs covered my butt.

"What should I do with you today? I can't keep you locked in the house all day."

The tom walked to my pillow, curled up into a ball and went to sleep, deciding the issue.

Work flew by and on the ride home, I picked up a litter box, two bowls and a box of cat food, along with three pouches of soft food.

The tom met me at the back door.

The house looked fine, and no worse for the cat.

The cat box was set up; the bowls were filled with food and water.

I set about cooking supper as the cat walked around and around my legs. The beer went down smooth and easy as the broccoli steamed, the potato baked with the chicken breast.

———

The kitchen just started to smell of great food as there was a knock on the back door. I turned off the oven and stove top.

The back door opened, and the tom cat stopped and waited. My ex entered, and the tom disappeared.

"Hey," Dave said.

"Hi."

"Not happy to see me?" He slurred his words and alcohol hung in the air. His jeans were skin tight and dirty, days unwashed and unshowered.

"What do you want?"

"Getting ready for supper?" He walked over to the refrigerator and pulled out a beer. His foot kicked one of the cat dishes.

I stood in front of the oven.

"So I have been replaced, already?" He drained half the bottle.

"You were the one catting around." I folded my arms over my chest.

He kicked the empty food bowl out of his way.

I looked around the room, and the cat was nowhere in sight. "I think you need to leave. You're not welcome here anymore."

Dave approached me as he drained his bottle. He towered over me and held the empty over my head. Stale beer breathed out of him. "Not enough food for two?"

"Nope." I stood my ground.

He pressed against me and backed me against the hot stove.

I saw a golden flash across the kitchen floor and across the counter top. It streaked over the cabinets and landed on top of the refrigerator.

Dave stepped on the empty bowl and shattered it. "Still no food for me? You got some for some damn stray, but nothing for me? Are you sure?"

My hand hit the hot burner, and I flinched.

Dave pulled his shirt off, and his body odor rose from

him. He twisted his shirt in his hands and brought it up in front of my face. He wrapped it around his hands and placed it against my neck.

The tom stood on his hind legs, looked down on me as Dave towered over me.

I closed my eyes and felt the wet T-shirt go around my throat. I pushed forward and heard a blood curdling scream.

Dave dropped his shirt and arched his back. He twisted one way and then the other. As he ran around the room, I saw the tom cat dig in deeper into his back, blood ran down his skin as he tried to reach behind him and pull the cat off his back. He ran out the back door and as he hit the knob, the tom cat dropped off and landed on the floor.

I stepped forward to make sure the door was locked and the cat was okay. The scent of fleshly drawn blood hung in the air and sent my nerves on edge, the night before the full moon.

The tom cat looked up at me and meowed. He came into the kitchen and walked around the pieces of his shattered food bowl.

I looked out the window and Dave was long gone, hopefully forever.

"I'm sorry. I'll get you a new one tomorrow." I turned on the oven and opened the cabinet to take out a spare bowl for the cat. "I need to come up with a name for you."

The cat sat at my feet and looked up at me.

"Thank you," I said as I bent down and scratched his ear.

He purred and purred.

I picked up Dave's sweaty shirt and threw it away. Supper would be ready in a few minutes.

I added the last few bites of chicken for the cat and set them in his new bowl. I was tired and ready for bed. The back door was locked and the dishes would wait until tomorrow.

I pulled back the sheets on my bed, and the cat jumped into the opening. He sat and looked deep into my eyes. "You are so sweet." The cat curled into a ball and closed his eyes. I leaned forward and kissed him before heading to the bathroom to brush my teeth. I quickly finished my grooming and flipped off the light.

I stripped and crawled into bed. As I settled into my pillow, I took a deep breath and my body relaxed.

"Kitty, Kitty. Where are you?"

A hairy bare leg brushed against mine, and I jumped out of the bed. My hand reached for the bedside light and turned it on.

A blond tanned man lay in my bed.

I pulled the sheet from my bed and covered my naked body. "Who? Who are you?"

"Me-ouch," the blond said and stretched as he came up onto his elbow. His naked body was amazing, except for a scratch along one side of his body and a cut on his ear.

My arousal started, and the sheet was pressed harder over my lap.

"Hi, my name is Tommy, but my friends call me Tiger." His sleek body arched gracefully on the bed. "Thanks for breaking my curse, and your ex is a real asshole."

I sat up higher and saw even more of his beauty. "How?"

"As near as I can figure, your kiss broke the curse."

"True love?" I asked.

He smiled, "Maybe." He patted the bed. "Come up here and find out."

And I did, all night long, and until the full moon showed Tiger my hairier side. Needless to say, we are still a hairy, happy couple.

Logan Zachary (www.loganzacharydicklit.com) lives in Minneapolis, MN and has over a hundred erotic stories in print. Calendar Boys is a collection of his short stories. Big Bad Wolf is an erotic werewolf mystery set in Northern Minnesota and its sequel GingerDead Man will be out later this year. His stories can be found in: Going Down, Best Bondage Stories of 2013, Tricks of the Trade, Big Men on Campus, Beach Bums, Sexy Sailors, College Boys, Teammates, Skater Boys, Boys Getting Ahead, Homo Thugs, Black Fire, Sweat!, Brief Encounters, Biker Boys, Threesomes, Rough Trade *and* The Spy Who Laid Me.

COSTUMED HERO

By DJ Tyrer

"I can't say I'm impressed with the quality of the costumes." Sally sniffed as she observed the outfits her guests had chosen: most of them wore tacky commercial costumes that predominated between plastic bibs and capes and fangs for Draculas and variations on animals, nuns and witches with loose morals. The few homemade outfits were lamentably poor in terms of quality and imagination. And, these were adults! A lame costume on a kid could be endearing, but not on a grown man.

"We've had some right ones," John agreed. "There was this one guy who came in his underpants. He was –"

"Yes, I think I can guess, and it's not amusing."

John chuckled at her annoyance. "It's just a bit of fun, nothing more."

"Well, people could put in some effort. I spent hours designing and making my costume." She saw the look on his face. "I'm Queen Elizabeth Tudor."

"Oh, yes, I see it now."

"I mean, even your costume is streets ahead of this crowd. It might be rented, but you actually picked out a good-quality one, not some cheap tat. Let me guess... Hmm, the hand protruding from the pocket makes me think either Professor Frankenstein or Herbert West. Am I right?"

"Uh, yeah, Herbert West?" John had no idea who that was. Did he kidnap and kill those girls with his crazy wife? Maybe. The costume had just said 'Mad Scientist' on it.

She smiled, and he felt good. He had fancied his neighbour since he moved in next door, despite being too scared to admit it to her, and was also happy when he pleased her. Which was the only reason he was here – as guest and aide – for he hated fancy dress parties.

"It's a shame."

"What is?" he asked.

"The way people treat Hallowe'en, so frivolous."

"It is?"

"Yes. Once the festival was the Celtic New Year and remembrance of the dead, a solemn day of celebration."

"Can you celebrate with solemnity?"

"Of course you can," she told him firmly. "You have a good time without making a fool of yourself, without getting rowdy and upsetting everyone."

"Like Eddie Smith?"

Sally winced. "Please, John, do not remind me of that man! I still cannot face a bowl of salad without feeling nauseous. But, yes, that is exactly the sort of awful behaviour to which I'm referring."

Just then, an unfamiliar figure stepped through the open front door. Most of the partygoers hadn't bothered with makeup or masks and most of the makeup that had been applied was a crude slathering of pallid grey-white or witchy green, while those who wore cheap plastic masks with their costumes were largely recognisable enough thanks to the lack of effort they had made with their costumes. But, this man, and Sally was fairly certain it was a man, was the part.

"Now, he is good," said John with a whistle, "I'll give you that."

The man approached, looming over then.

"Hello. I'm Sally; welcome to my party. I can't say I can tell who you are..."

A heavy eyebrow rose quizzically. "Bigfoot." The voice was deep, like an avalanche rumbling down a mountainside.

"Oh, yes. Ha-ha. I meant, I couldn't tell who it is inside

216

the costume. I could tell you were the Yeti or something."

"Bigfoot."

"Well, I suppose I'll guess, eventually... Um, well, let me introduce you to John, he's my upstairs neighbour."

"Pleased to meet you," said John.

"And you," said Bigfoot, extending a huge, hairy hand in greeting.

John shook hands and winced in pain as his hand felt as if it were in a vice.

"Ow!" He shook his hand as soon as it was released. "That's quite a grip you've got there! You got some sort of gyros in that suit?"

"Well, I have been working out. I found an abandoned camp in the woods – well, I say abandoned; the hunter ran away as soon as he saw me – and amongst the usual tins of beans and junk, I found this doodad with springs that you can use to exercise your hands. You know the sort of thing, you give it a good squeeze, then relax. Makes a change from bench-pressing redwoods, you know?"

"I can imagine," said Sally with a flirty grin that annoyed John. For a huge, hairy beast, Bigfoot was far too suave for his tastes.

"I mean," the rumbling voice continued, "life can become quite tedious when you live out in the woods. Although, I must admit, things have improved since I got satellite TV and the Internet. I had to get an especially adapted keyboard, of course."

"Of course."

"But, once I had that, it all kind of fell into place. I'm active online; Facebook, Twitter, that sort of thing. Not as myself, of course."

"Of course."

"But, one can be, well, anyone online and that allows me to just be myself." He laughed a loud, booming laugh. "It sounds silly, doesn't it, utilising a disguise to be myself? But, I'm sure you understand..."

"Oh, I do."

"It means I can order online – finally, I can buy the books I want without relying on what I can find in RVs and dumpsters. Also means I can book plane tickets, which is what brings me here – although I had a devil of a time actually getting on the flight!" He laughed again. "I'm staying with Jenny; we met online."

"Oh, you're a friend of Jenny?"

"Yes. She invited me along as her plus-one."

"How nice!" Her tone said she hoped they were more than just friends. So did John, for entirely personal reasons. "Well, I'm glad you came. I really do like your outfit. I must say you really are living the character. Amazing!"

"I'm just being myself," he told her, spreading his arms as if to display his costume. "Anyway, I ought to mingle and allow you to talk to your other guests."

Bigfoot lumbered off and they admired the costume as he went.

"It really is as if there are muscles rippling beneath the fur," marveled Sally.

"It must've cost a fortune!" John nodded, suddenly feeling incredibly underdressed. "I mean who wears such a thing to a fancy-dress party? Outside Hollywood, at least."

That was certainly the reaction of their fellow guests, who flocked around Bigfoot as if he were a celebrity in their midst. In a way, he was.

"He must be a successful man," commented Sally, "well-off and clearly a nice guy. Oh, I do hope he and Jenny make a go of it. They would be perfect together."

"Better than the last bloke she dated." That had been the infamous Eddie Smith.

"Please!" She winced again.

"Sorry. Hey, he's quite a mover, isn't he?"

John meant Bigfoot, who was dancing like a pro to some Daft Punk. He'd imagined the suit must be cumbersome, but Bigfoot was moving with grace and precision.

"Quite amazing," agreed Sally.

"He must have some sort of exoskeleton thingy under there, you know the sort of thing the military were developing. That costume must've cost millions!"

"Quite amazing," she repeated.

One of the partygoers, one of the men who thought a black plastic cape, some cheap plastic fangs and a tacky plastic bib printed with a shirt, waistcoat and cravat constituted a costume, came over to them and said, "Great party, Sally."

"Thanks." The man worked in the mailroom where she worked, but she could never remember his name, had only invited him because not doing so would have seemed rude.

"That Bigfoot is marvelous! A great costume and a fun guy. He told the most amazing joke – did he tell you? About the gargoyle and the lemming?"

"Gargoyle and lemming?" John repeated, bemused.

"Well, it is Hallowe'en... so, you haven't heard it?"

John attempted to redirect the question, but the man just rambled on regardless. Sally took the opportunity to quickly slip away.

"Well, there was this gargoyle on a church, right? And, every Hallowe'en it would come alive for one night. Now..."

John groaned.

Sally was glad to get out of earshot. The man was an absolute bore: even a truly brilliant joke would become tedious drivel when told by him. Besides, she told herself to still her guilt, she did need to circulate, didn't she?

"Hi, Sally – great party!"

"Love your costume, Sal!"

"Having fun? I know I am!"

"Have you seen that Yeti guy? Amazing!"

"– and the gargoyle sees a lemming –"

"Thanks for inviting us, Sally!"

"– and it jumps off the altar –"

The voices were all merging into a babble, and she was finding a smile and nod sufficient to play the part of the gracious hostess, when she spotted an anomaly. Normally, there was a casket on her mantle, made of gold and ebony, worth a fair bit in itself, which contained a vial that was said to contain, in turn, some of Rasputin's blood, taken at the autopsy which had failed to ascertain quite which of several fatal injuries had actually killed him. Her great-grandfather had been a diplomat to the Tsarist court with some peculiar interests. Tonight, however, there was a conspicuous space where the casket should have been and she knew that wasn't because she had removed it to somewhere safe. She should have, she knew, but then, hindsight always allowed perfect vision.

Looking around, she saw a woman poorly dressed as a witch carrying the casket out into the passage and towards the front door.

"Stop! Thief!" she cried, pushing her way through the revelers. Unfortunately, most of them didn't really catch what she was saying over the music and those who did looked around futilely, thinking she was pointing out a particularly fine costume.

"May I be of assistance?" boomed a voice from behind and above her.

Looking round at Bigfoot, she quickly gabbled out an explanation: "Casket – blood of Rasputin – stolen – witch – over there – stop her – please!"

"Sure thing," he told her, easily parting the crowd.

"Please, don't hurt her!" she called after him, remembering just how strong he had seemed.

"Oh, I don't hurt people," he called back, "I'm a vegetarian."

"But, Hitler was a vegetarian!" She paused. "I think."

"No," Bigfoot called back, "Hitler was a Nazi."

A few minutes later, Bigfoot was back, carrying the casket in one hand and the witch in the other.

"Here you go, one casket retrieved intact and one witch unharmed, more or less." He dropped the woman in a heap on the floor and handed the casket to Sally. "You know, if you wipe the green muck off her face, I think you'll discover this ersatz witch is, in fact, the famous media witch Juniper Sage."

"Juniper Sage?" exclaimed Sally, who recognised the name. "Doesn't she do tarot reading on some satellite channel?"

"Indeed, she does," Bigfoot nodded. "She is a leading figure in occult, oddball circles. Clearly, somehow, she heard about your vial of Rasputin's blood and came to steal it."

"And, I would've gotten away with it, too, if it wasn't for your pesky Sasquatch!"

"I prefer Bigfoot, personally."

"What's going on?" John called. Still being buttonholed by the joke reteller, he hadn't been able to tell what the rumpus was all about. His plea went unanswered as the man drone on, "– and then it said to the lemming –"

"Well, I'd better be going," said Bigfoot, "before any police or reporters show up. I absolutely detest getting my picture in the paper. Cheerio! Maybe I'll see you next Hallowe'en, eh?"

"Cheerio..." For some reason, Sally was beginning to wonder if she had had the genuine cryptozoological anomaly as a guest at her party.

"Because it's a Saturday!" finished the man retelling Bigfoot's joke, before collapsing in a fit of manic laughter.

"I feel very confused," said John, who'd failed to follow either the joke or whatever had just happened.

"Bye!" Bigfoot waved at him as he went past.

"Uh, bye," he replied. "Happy Hallowe'en."

"He's a real costumed hero," someone was saying as he wandered over towards Sally.

"A hero, definitely," said Sally, "and certainly real. But, I'm not too sure about the costume..."

DJ Tyrer is the person behind Atlantean Publishing and has been widely published in anthologies and magazines in the UK,

USA *and elsewhere, most recently in* Cosmic Horror *(Dark Hall Press) and* Serial Killers Quattuor *(JWK Fiction), as well as in* Sorcery & Sanctity: A Homage to Arthur Machen *(Hieroglyphics Press),* All Hallows' Evil *and* Undead of Winter *(both* Mystery & Horror LLC*) and* Fossil Lake *(Daverana Enterprises/Sabledrake Enterprises), as well as two novellas available on Kindle:* The Yellow House *(Dynatox Ministries) and* Acting Strangely *(Jazzclaw Publishing).*

DEAD PEOPLE, SERIOUSLY

By F. R. Michaels

I'm in Hoop's basement when he brings the dead rat back to life. Hoop draws the circle and says the words and then *pow*! The candle flames shake, an electric smell, and the rat jumps and squeals and kicks around – Hoop is trying to act all cool but he almost leaps out of his own skin. He's writing stuff down really fast, giggling like the devil.

"I told you, man," he says to me. "This is real. This is power, right here."

The rat's twisting on the table, screeching.

"I dunno, Hoop," I tell him. "This is some sick stuff we're playing with. This is like – evil, man."

"Of course it's evil," Hoop says, laughing. "That's the whole point, dumbass. Can't chicken out on me now, B-man. We got one month. Moon's gotta be full again, then we do this for real."

For real means Parkwood, the cemetery uptown. For real means a human being. All of a sudden, this stops being a game. We're suburban college kids, a couple of geeky frat-boys messing around with occult stuff we pulled off the Internet. Six months ago we took a road trip out to Westchester to buy some dusty old book from this dusty old dude who couldn't wait to get rid of it. I should have talked Hoop out of it then but I never was good at talk. Maybe I should have just hit him with a shovel.

"No turning back now, B-man," Hoop says.

He takes the big old book and slams it down, crushing

the writhing rat.

Tuesday night, it's like two a.m., and we're dumpster diving behind the campus hospital. We're looking for human bones; we need them crushed up for the "formula" as Hoop calls it. Hoop pulls out these big bolt cutters and cuts the padlock on the red medical waste bin. I'm smaller, so I'm going in, and I'm freaking out.

"What if I get stuck with a dirty needle?" I'm saying. "There's like, AIDS and Ebola in there..."

"There's no Ebola in Paumanok County," Hoop says.

He's crouched down, wrapping duct tape around my painter's pants, which are tucked into my old high-top Converse. I got an American flag bandanna over my nose and mouth, paintball goggles over my eyes, yellow dishwashing gloves over my hands, and a hair-net from when Hoop worked at Taco Bell. This is my hazmat suit as Hoop boosts me up. The bin's got mostly dirty bandages, stained rust-red and yellow. I'm breathing through my mouth and my goggles are fogging up.

"Hurry up, man!" Hoop says. He's got the flashlight, shining it into the bin.

Like I'm reaching into a bear-trap, I start feeling my way through the debris. It's nasty. I pull up a loose bag with a hard lump in it. We inspect it with the flashlight.

"What kind of bone is that?" Hoop asks.

"I dunno, I'm a Comp Sci major," I tell him.

"I think it's a cyst," he says, shaking the bag.

"Gross," I say. "Still, like, same stuff, right? Good enough?"

Hoop shines the light in my face. "B-man, we are attempting an incantation to reverse the process of death itself," he says. "We can't use a cyst."

"Well, sorry, but nobody's throwing out whole skeletons!"

Hoop throws the bag back in the bin and says, more to

himself than me, "The formula needs a circle sown with sea salt and bone powder, and it's got to be big. We need human bones. A lot of them..."

Flashing lights appear. I dive into the bin and Hoop hits the ground, but the lights roll past: an ambulance pulling up to the emergency room entrance around the corner. Hoop pops back up and reaches into the bin to pull me out.

"Plan B," he says.

Truth is, I liked hanging out with Sebastian Hooper. I'd spent my whole life safe, shuffling a path-of-least-resistance toward adulthood. Hoop lived on the edge, he'd do anything. I'd met him during a computer lab; he talked me into helping him out with something he wanted over the Internet, something totally illegal (no, I'm not telling what), and he started including me with his friends. He was an occult freak, into "magick" with a K. I didn't like that kind of stuff, but I liked being included. That was two semesters ago. And now it's Thursday, past midnight, and we're in a historical cemetery outside Port Adams wearing black and carrying shovels. Plan B.

"This is a bad idea, Hoop," I whisper, as we walk in a crouch between the headstones, choosing a victim. "Raiding a garbage bin is one thing; this is grave robbing. We could go to jail for this!"

"Only if we're caught," Hoop says. "You gotta understand one thing, B-man: the rules don't apply to men like you and me."

If you've been to Port Adams, you know the cemetery I'm talking about: the one on the hill overlooking the harbor, about fifty headstones going back to the 1700s, surrounded by a wrought-iron fence. We find a grave in a far corner that can't be seen from the road. Terence Gardner, born 1865, died 1902.

Picking the right grave was important, Hoop was explaining as we shoveled. Too old, they're dust. Too new, too much meat left. We're hoping for a body decayed proper-like, forget the whole skeleton, just grab some legs and arms, and we're done.

My shovel scrapes against wood. We're so close, and then I hear voices.

"Shh!" I whisper. "Someone's coming."

We duck down into the hole we've made and freeze. We hear footsteps crunching leaves, and people talking.

A female voice, loud and clear: "Is someone here with us tonight?"

I poke my head up. A fat middle-aged woman is wandering around the graveyard holding up a miniature tape recorder. Right behind her is a bald man with a goatee carrying a video camera.

"Are there any spirits that would like to contact us?" the man says.

Hoop bangs his head against the dirt. "You have got to be kidding me. . ." he growls.

"Did you hear that?" the fat woman whispers excitedly. "That was a man's voice!"

"Are you trying to communicate with us?" the man calls out.

"What do we do?" I whisper back in a panic.

"They want to communicate, I'm going to communicate," Hoop says. "You stay down."

He jumps up out of the hole and pulls his hood down over his face, then walks towards our paranormal investigators.

"Get out!" he says.

"Oh my gracious!" the woman says, even more excited now. They still don't see him, these numbnuts. "That was loud and clear!"

"Apparently not!" Hoop says, and this time he's practically on top of them. "Seriously: Get out!"

The fat woman lets out a short shriek when she spots him. Hoop reaches behind his back and pulls something out from under his black sweatshirt.

"Excuse me, but who—" the man with goatee starts.

"What part of 'get out' don't you dickheads understand?" Hoop says. He has something in his hand. I can't see it but I know what it is by the way he's holding it. Hoop has a gun.

There are two bright flashes and two loud *pokk*! *pokk*! sounds. My heart stops for a second, but he just fires two rounds at their feet. Our ghost hunters huff their way out at a run.

"You come back, you're gonna be ghosts!" Hoop calls out after them.

He runs back toward me.

"Come on, we gotta get done and get out, before they bring John Law," he says.

"You didn't tell me you were carrying a gun," I say, trying to make it sound like it's not that big a deal.

To Hoop, it isn't. "Sometimes I do. Glock nine millimeter, I bought it in Tennessee. You want I get you one?"

"Um, naw, I'm all right," I reply.

We clear the dirt and chop through the rotten wood with our shovels, our ears out for sirens. Hoop shines his red penlight. Bones. Hoop yanks the legs out and starts stuffing them into a plastic garbage bag. Arms, too. I hold the bag open; I'm not touching the dead guy. Sorry about all this, Mr. Gardner.

I fill in the hole and replace the grass, and Hoop runs out with his penlight and retrieves the two shells from the shots he fired, then pushes over a couple of random headstones.

"Let them think it was vandals," he says.

As we head back on Route 48 two police cruisers zoom past us going the other way, lights flashing: John Law, protecting the public, your tax dollars at work. I'm hyperventilating but Hoop's beaming.

"We did good, B-man," he says.

We lay low for a few days, which suits me because I got blisters from shoveling and my back's killing me. There's a blurb on the local news, some talk round campus, but John Law don't come pounding on our doors, so done is done. Only, I'm having a bad case of the guilts, and what's more, I have nightmares about Terence Gardner coming after me from the grave. I tell Hoop, but he laughs it off.

"Let him come," he says. "What's he gonna do? We got his arms and legs..."

The next step is crushing up the bones, which is really hard work. Hoop gets this idea to heat the bones first. One of his other friends (Alison: blue hair, lip ring) knows where we could use a really big oven. Hoop doesn't tell her what it's for, but that's how we spend the following night: Cooking dug-up corpse bones. Stunk the place up so bad we waited outside in the cold. But the idea works; crushing up the bones is still hard but at least we're getting powder. (By the way, whoever's reading this, don't eat pizza from Gianelli's on Wayburn Street ever again.)

The weeks crawl by. Hoop's buried in that old book, scribbling notes, preparing the "formula." Me, I can't eat, I don't sleep. The other night I woke up and thought I saw a figure in black standing at the foot of my bed, looking down at me.

"A ninja?" Hoop asked when I told him.

"No, not a ninja, I mean like the Devil!" I explained.

"Too bad," he replied. "Ninjas are cool."

I think this was about the time I started to wonder if Hoop really understood any of this shit we were doing.

Parkwood's a really nice cemetery: hills ringed by dense woods, gardens, fountains, and a sweet view of the village of Stony Hollow. You can do worse than be buried here when your candle goes out. Unless, of course, some asshole's going to bring you back from the dead. When I get there, Hoop's waiting. I've been rehearsing in my head what I'd say to him, how I'd talk him out of all this. There's the circle sown into the ground, made from sea-salt and the bones we smashed up. Incense is burning, and that horrible old book is propped open on a beat-up music stand. Hoop's decked out for the event: black pants, boots, and what looks like a cloak. He's got a skull ring on his finger and he's even wearing eyeliner. He sees me and blows out a breath.

"See, man, this is why you never win at anything," he says, plucking at my sweatshirt and looking down at my painter's pants (leftover duct tape still sticking to the cuffs). "You don't dress for success."

"I should dress like you?" I reply. "You look like a Transylvanian pimp. And what's with the guy-liner?"

"I am a necromancer," he says.

"You're a biology major."

"Not anymore," he says. "I am a master of the Arts of Magick, and you are my apprentice."

"I don't know, Hoop," I say. "This stuff is getting out of hand."

"B-man, you have been with me on this from the start," he says. "You're not losing your nerve now, are you?"

"I'm not losing my nerve. I'm just thinking maybe we ought to slow down a bit. I mean, look, what say we do bring some dead dude back to life – what are we gonna do with him? It's not like we need a zombie butler or anything..."

"Who says we're just raising one?" Hoop quips.

"Whoa, wait – Hoop, how many were you thinking of raising...?"

"All of them," he says quietly.

Suddenly I'm very cold. I say: "What?"

Hoop grabs my arm, and I feel my flesh crawl. "You and I, we are going to raise an army of the dead! The Zombie apocalypse, with us at the reins."

I'm ready to throw up. "Army of the dead? To do what?"

"To teach everyone who ever hurt us that they tangled

with the wrong people." Hoop's face was right up into mine. "Every man, woman, and mutant who ever crossed us, they're going to wish they'd never been born. We're not just going to be famous, B-man, we're going to be gods!"

I'm just staring at him at this point. Yeah, I thought this whole business was nuts, but I never knew it was *this* nuts.

"Hoop, seriously, take a deep breath, man," I tell him. "You're talking about murder!"

"I am talking about justice!" Hoop screams into my face. He backs up and runs his fingers through his hair, calms himself. When he speaks again, his voice almost breaks. "Aren't you tired of the bullshit, B-man? Aren't you tired of the disrespect? Like life is some sort of A-list party and the bouncer won't let you into the club, even though you're better than every one of those sorry-assed losers that are allowed in? C'mon, B-man, I thought you would be the one to understand."

"Dude, I understand." Ouch, do I understand. "But – and try to follow me here, because this part's kind of important – using black magic to murder people does not get us into the party!"

He doesn't say anything, so I continue.

"Hoop, I been left out my whole life, man. You just find people like yourself and make your own party. I thought - I thought that's what we were doing, you and me, you know? I mean, playing with this occult stuff is bad enough, but killing people? What's that's going to solve, man?"

He shakes his head again, and looks at me.

"Even you, B-man," he says sadly. "Even you. The one man I thought I could trust." He wipes tears out of his eyes, smearing his eye-makeup. "This sucks. I didn't want to have to do this, but you're either by my side, or you're in my way."

And I'm looking right into the barrel of his gun, the nine millimeter he bought in Tennessee. From this close it looks as big as a sewer pipe. I'm not brave. But I can't give in, no matter what, not even my life, because when this shit hits the

Internet tomorrow I'd rather be the guy that got killed trying to stop him than the stupid monkey-boy that tagged along.

"Put the gun away, Hoop," I say. My voice is a croak.

"I'm sorry, man, but if you're not with me, you're against me. You're a traitor."

He's crying. He squeezes his eyes shut, and uses the forearm of his gun hand to wipe the tears from his face.

I can't tackle him; he's stronger than me. If I turn and run, he'll shoot me in the back. I reach down to grab a handful of dirt and throw it in his eyes, but it's all leaves and grass. We watch it flutter to the ground between us, and then I've used up my little window of opportunity and I'm backpedaling as fast as I can. The backs of my legs hit a low hedge and I go over backwards just as the gun goes off. The bushes edge a steep hill and I'm sliding on my back through brambles and woods before everything goes dark.

Yeah, I fainted. Peed myself, too. Go ahead, make fun.

I wake up to the sound of Hoop's chanting. I'm at the bottom of a gully, lying on my back in an inch of freezing rainwater. The moon's full, but the canopy of trees is pitch black. Hoop must have thought he'd shot me when he saw me go down, or maybe he couldn't find me in the underbrush in the dark.

Moving slowly, I roll over on my stomach and inch my way toward the sound of Hoop's voice. He's going through with the rite and I'm the only one who can stop him. My hand comes down on a big rock and I bring it with me. If I can surprise him I can bash his head in and get the gun away from him, scuff out the circle, break the spell.

As I reach the top, I know I'm too late; I smell ozone and sulfur and I know he's finished the spell. There's a pressure wave shuddering through the ground, like a tremor. I stay on my belly and peer through the gap I plowed through the bushes when I fell.

Hoop's back is to me, his arms raised, chanting. The

ground is alive. The soil is moving, undulating, bubbling up around the graves. A decayed hand breaks the surface – then another, and another. He's done it. The asshole's actually done it. The dead are rising from their graves. Arms follow the hands, and the cemetery is alive with groping limbs, the sounds of scuffling and moaning and the smell of decay and holy shit it's horrific and the only reason I don't piss myself is because I already did. My mind is going as fast as it can, trying to think of a way to stop this...

And what the hell, I actually think of it.

In the book is a banishment rite, a counter-formula that reverses the necromancy spell. I know this because that stupid book was Hoop's only topic of conversation for half a year, and even when I had two wads of my own dirty laundry pressed over my ears so I wouldn't have to listen to it anymore, the information sunk in against my will. Hoop always kept the materials for the counter-formula ready and the page marked. This was our control rod, the emergency valve we were supposed to pull if everything went all meltdown-like. But I had to get to the book, and all I could do now was hang back and watch and wait for the opportunity to present itself.

The first zombie frees himself from his grave and stands, shaking the soil off his body. Another climbs out and stands; this one's an old woman. The rest are coming out also, and I notice three things: First, the spell did not come off perfectly. Not all the corpses are coming forth, maybe a random twenty or thirty, tops. Second, most of them were seriously old when they died. Third, all of the men are wearing suits and ties and the women are wearing gowns. Half of them are holding rosaries.

If this is the zombie apocalypse, it's going to look like an old-folks' church social.

I don't think Hoop notices any of this; even with his back to me, I can see him vibrating with excitement.

The last of the dead climbs free of his grave – whoa, I

know this guy: Doug Chelsey, we went to high school together, he was killed by a drunk driver; I went to the funeral. Hard to tell with the decomposition and all, but it looks like Doug's the only corpse here under seventy.

Hoop clears his throat and raises his arms. I know what he's going to say, I helped him write it.

"The dead of Parkwood Cemetery," Hoop proclaims. "Hearken to me! I, the Necromancer Sebastian, have summoned you from your graves! I command you!"

There is a pause. The nearest undead, standing near a headstone that I can read in the moonlight, Stephen George Jackson, 1928-2003, looks around briefly, then looks back at Hoop. Its voice, when it speaks, is a ragged hiss.

"What?" it says.

"I am the necromancer that summoned you," Hoop repeats, a little less ostentatiously this time. "From your graves. I command you."

There's another pause as the dead look at each other again.

"To do what?" the corpse of Stephen George Jackson asks.

"On this night," Hoop says, back in character, "you will descend upon the town of Stony Hollow, and kill and devour every living man, woman, and child, without mercy. This I command!"

The corpse of Stephen George Jackson blinks its dead eyes at Sebastian Hooper.

"I'm an accountant," it says.

"Excuse me?" Hoop says.

"I'm an accountant," the zombie says. "I don't kill people. Steve Jackson, CPA. Jackson, Bell, and Associates, on Main Street. Tax preparation and personal finance."

"No longer," Hoops says. "You walk this earth to satisfy your hunger for human flesh."

"Excuse me, young man," another zombie, Ellen Sanders-Mowbrey, 1906-1990, *May We Meet Again in Heaven,* says. Her voice is even worse than Jackson's. "Do you mean devour, as in eat? People? Raw?" She wrinkles the hole where her nose used to be. "That's disgusting."

"I don't have any hunger for human flesh," Stephen George Jackson says.

"No?" Hoop asks.

"No."

"Me neither," offers Ryan Dunston, 1927-2008, *May Angels Guide Thee to Eternal Peace*.

"I could go for a steak," says a voice from the back of the pack. There's a murmur of agreement.

Another zombie walks up to the front of the group. I can't see the headstone, but I recognize her as the old lady who used to play the organ in our church: Ruth Robinson, everyone called her "Miss Ruth". She's wearing choir robes and holding a Bible. She looks Hoop up and down.

"Is this the Resurrection?" she asks. "I'm asking because you don't look like the Lord Jesus."

"What?" Hoop says. "No, no, I'm not Jesus..."

"Then what in the Sam Hill are we doing out of our graves?" Miss Ruth demands. She taps her Bible with a bony finger. "We are promised at the Resurrection that we will be brought forth perfect in body and spirit and Lord Jesus will carry those who believe in Him to eternal paradise! Hallelujah!"

"Look, lady..." Hoop says.

"The Bible don't say anything about some fool wearing eye makeup waking you up from the grave, and then you have to dig your own self out!" Miss Ruth finishes.

The undead are nodding and murmuring agreement. This is starting to get weird. Um, weirder.

Two newcomers walk in through a gap in the fence, a man and a woman. He's wearing a yarmulke. Hoop's spell must have caught the corner of the Jewish cemetery next door.

"Hello? I know this is going to sound strange, but we've been summoned from our graves, and we're here," he says.

———

He looks pretty freshly dead, and his voice sounds almost normal. "We're from Beth Shalom cemetery. I'm Benjamin Moskowitz, this is my wife Ruby."

"Hello," Ruby says.

A chorus of helloes comes from the assembled dead.

"So, nu, this is the Resurrection?" Benjamin Moskowitz asks.

"No," Miss Ruth growls, "it ain't. It's some dumb-ass fool dressing up like Dracula and messing about!"

"I am not messing about!" Hoop protests.

"He wants us to kill everyone in Stony Hollow," Stephen George Jackson adds.

"What?" Ruby Moskowitz exclaims. "That's awful! My Benjamin wouldn't hurt a fly!"

"My grandchildren live in Stony Hollow," says Mrs. Agnes Emerson, *Beloved Mother and Grandmother*, 1914-1998. "And look, fresh flowers! Aw, they still think of me, how sweet..."

"Look, boy," says Frederick "Pappy" McGuiness, *WWI Vet*, 1898-1977, emphatically. "I ain't going nowheres, and I ain't killing nobody."

"By the dark covenants by which I resurrected you," Hoop insists, "you are bound to me, and you will obey!"

"Blow it out your ass!" Frederick "Pappy" McGuiness responds.

"You listen to me, young man," Miss Ruth says. "I played the organ at many a funeral in this here parish, and I can tell you the folk buried in this cemetery are fine, upstanding people. We didn't do the Devil's work when we was alive, and we ain't doing it now that we's dead. We are good, God-fearing Christians here!"

"And Jews," Ruby Moskowitz says.

"And Jews," Miss Ruth adds, with a gracious nod toward the Moskowitzes. "And if'n we had Buddhists and Muslims and Hindus and Atheists here too, they also would tell you to... to..."

"Blow it out your ass!" Frederick "Pappy" McGuiness repeats.

"What the man says," Miss Ruth finishes with a nod.

That makes me snort a laugh just loud enough for Hoop and the dead folks to glance in my direction, so I duck down behind the bushes with my rock. I know I came to stop him, but at this point I am just watching the show. Hoop's trying to hold it together but he's unraveling fast.

"Your protests are futile," Hoop says. He's trying to sound confident, but he's breathing heavily. "When the hunger comes, you will kill, and you will devour the flesh of the living!"

"Why all this talk of killing?" Benjamin Moskowitz asks. "Kill, devour, destroy – why you want we should do such awful things?"

Hoop is breathing hard. "So, you need to hear the story? You need to know of the pain? How growing up was a living hell, because I was different...?"

Et cetera, et cetera - I kind of tune out at this point, it's what he said before. Hell, I've lived it. Neglected at home, picked on at school, the oddball who never fit in. The pain is real, but I'm looking at the undead people here and thinking about what they lived through – this McGuiness guy fought in World War I – and none of what Hoop's saying seems all that important by comparison. And what's worse, I realize that Hoop doesn't want justice, he just wants to be the one who inflicts the pain for a change. He wants the power he felt he's never had. And now he's got it, and it ain't doing him a damn bit of good.

"They mocked me," Hoop finishes, "but they didn't know who the hell they were dealing with, what I'm capable of. The subhuman scum who let it happen are going to pay."

There's a pause. The dead are waiting for more, but that's all Hoop says.

"That's it?" Ryan Dunston says. "That's what this is about?"

"So you're telling us," Stephen George Jackson says slowly, "that you did this black magic mumbo jumbo, and brought us all back from the dead, just because some kids gave you wedgies in tenth grade?"

"Nancy-boy," McGuiness growls. "Grow a pair of balls and deal with your problems like a man."

Benjamin Moskowitz is shaking his head. "Justice is one thing, but this is just petty vengeance. Be a *mensch*."

"People can be cruel," Mrs. Agnes Emerson says, not unkindly. "But you'll never win by doing evil for evil, young man."

"Rise above," Miss Ruth sings out. "Like the Good Book says!"

"No! Wait!" Hoop yells. Even in the moonlight, I can see his ears are red. "My reasons are my own! For any reason, or for no reason, I command you, and you – *will* – obey!"

There was another pause.

"Or else what?" Ryan Dunston asks.

"Or else, I will return you to the oblivion from whence you came!" Hoop threatens.

"Oh, would you?" asks Mrs. Agnes Emerson. "I was resting quite peacefully, and to be honest, it's cold out here."

A murmur of agreement comes from the assembled dead.

"No, no, no!" Hoop shouts. "I have not come this far to be thwarted just because the living dead are a bunch of crotchety old farts with moral objections to my plans for vengeance! I will have my revenge! You will destroy Stony Hollow!"

"Kid, we built Stony Hollow!" Ryan Dunston says. "We fought wars, we raised families, started businesses, and when times were tough we banded together and helped each other out. What have you ever done, except piss and moan about how unfair your life is?"

"How dare you!" Hoop shrieks, his voice cracking. "I have broken the sacred seals of life and death! I am a necromancer!"

Doug Chelsey thinks this over and says, "Um, does that mean you want to have sex with dead people?"

In the ensuing silence, some the zombies take a discreet step back.

"What?" Hoop says. "No! No! that's a, um . . ."

"Necrophile," Ruby Moskowitz supplies.

"Thank you," Hoop says. "Necrophile. I am a necromancer, a sorcerer!"

"So how do you know that?" Ben Moskowitz asks his late wife.

"What? It was on Jeopardy," she explains.

"And by the dark covenants by which I have summoned you," Hoop plows on, talking over the Moskowitzes, "you will do as I command!"

There is a long silence, after which Peter Wm. Forrest, *In the Arms of the Angels*, 1936-2010, says: "I don't know about the rest of you, but I've had just about enough of this asshole."

"Me too," Stephen George Jackson agrees.

"Let's beat the shit out of him!" Frederick "Pappy" McGuiness suggests.

There's a growl of agreement from the crowd of undead corpses. They start lurching towards Hoop.

"Use the banishment rite, dumbass! Undo the spell!" I whisper desperately at him.

Hoop flips a few pages of the book, but he's rattled. He pulls out his gun instead.

"Stay back!" he warns.

"Or what?" Dunston says. "You'll kill us?"

Hoop levels the gun and fires a bullet. He shoots another at McGuiness, and one at Forrest. The zombies just look down at the holes, then back up at Hoop.

"Real tough guy, ain't you?" McGuiness says. "Hope you saved a bullet for yourself."

Hoop's watching him advance, watching all of them advance, lurching toward him.

"I did," he says quietly, and puts the gun in his mouth.

I jump up and yell "Don't!" but the gun goes off at the same time and no one hears me.

Sebastian Hooper falls to the ground like a puppet with its strings cut. The shock lasts a second, and then I feel only disgust. Hoop, man, you are such a dick.

No point in hiding any longer. I drop my rock and walk out to where Hoop's lying.

"Now who in blazes are you?" says Ryan Dunston.

Doug Chelsey is staring at me. "Byron?"

Yeah, that's my name. I hate it.

"Hey, Doug." He's hard to look at. The accident smashed his head in. The coffin was closed at the funeral.

"What are you doing here?" Doug asks. "Are you dead, too?"

"No, I'm in college," I say. "I came to stop him, really."

Stephen George Jackson looks around. "You're a bit late with the cavalry, you don't mind me saying."

"Yes, and I'm sorry about that. But I – I can reverse the spell. Send you all back to – to your rest."

Benjamin Moskowitz nods approvingly. "Finally, someone talking sense for a change."

I step over Hoop's body and go the book. The page is marked, the materials are in a pouch hanging from the music stand. The rite is six lines of ancient Sumerian or something, but Hoop wrote it all out phonetically on half a sheet of loose leaf that's taped to the page. I can do this.

"So what do we do?" Mrs. Agnes Emerson asks. "Should we dig ourselves back underground?"

"I wouldn't worry about it," I reply, sounding more confident than I feel. "The Parkwood staff will rebury you. Just stand by your headstones so they know who's who."

"Oh! Wait, we have to get back to Beth Shalom!" Moskowitz says. "Come on, Ruby!" He takes his wife's arm and they stump back through the gap in the fence.

I watch the rest of them sort themselves out by their

headstones; whole lives marked by a slabs of granite with two dates separated by a dash. I read somewhere that it was the dash that was the important part. Everything you ever did in your life – that was the dash. I thought about what Dunston said, Stephen George Jackson starting his own business, McGuinness fighting in World War I, Miss Ruth playing the organ in church, Mrs. Emerson raising her kids and grand-kids, and even Doug Chelsey. The dash, however long or short it is, the dash is what counts.

Flashing red lights are approaching from the distance; someone heard the shots and summoned the Law, but it'll take time to get here. The dead are waiting. And the man who summoned them is lying in a heap at my feet with a bullet in his brain. Retribution's a game for chumps. Dead people, seriously.

"So, um, how's college?" Doug Chelsey asks.

"Sucks," I tell him. "How's, uh, being dead?"

He shrugs. "Quiet. Just waiting for Judgment Day, I guess." He fidgets a bit, then says, "Listen, Byron – um, you see my Dad, tell him - tell him I said I'm sorry."

"No need, Doug," I reply. "I went to your funeral. Your dad was there. He said a lot of good things about you."

"Really? He did?" Doug smiles. I can't look at it. "Cool..."

"Look, I hate to interrupt, but are you doing this or what?" Peter Wm. Forrest, *In the Arms of the Angels*, 1936-2010, asks. He's scratching himself. "Decomposition itches like crazy."

"Yeah, just, uh, waiting for the Moskowitzes," I tell him.

"We're ready, young man!" Ruby's voice comes from past the fence.

The pouch is filled with palm ashes and coal dust; I cast it about like I saw Hoop do, and speak the words. With my foot, I scuff out a gap in the magic circle, and it's done.

There's a pause, then the good deceased people of Parkwood Cemetery sink to the ground. Doug's still smiling.

———

240

Pappy McGuiness even gives me a little nod of approval as he falls.

And I'm alone. Rest in peace, everybody. Even you, Hoop.

They'll find Sebastian Hooper, dead among the exhumed corpses, and wonder what the hell went on at Parkwood cemetery this night. They'll rebury the bodies. They won't find the book, I made sure of that. Everyone knows Hoop and I hung out; it won't be long before I'll have to answer a lot of questions... but that's the least of my problems.

I'm heading for the shower when I take off my shirt and I see for the first time that it's soaked with blood. There's a hole in it. I put my finger through. It's a bullet hole. There's a matching hole in my chest. I put my finger in that one, too.

I guess Hoop didn't miss.

I'm also guessing he wasn't thinking about his dead buddy lying in the gully when he chanted his stupid necromancer's spell. Thanks, Hoop, I suppose we're even. Only thing is, I broke the spell. The dead went back to their rest. Not me, though. Was it because I was inside the circle? I feel OK.

Maybe I shouldn't have thrown out that book.

Whatever. I'm hitting the shower and hitting the sack. I just saw the dead rise from their graves, watched my best friend kill himself, and midterms are in two weeks. I got enough to deal with right now; I'll sort the rest of it out tomorrow. Being dead was easy compared to this. I guess I'll just have to tough it out. I have my own dash to fill out, after all.

And if the figure in black shows up at the foot of my bed again, I'll kick his sorry ass straight back to Hell.

Frank Raymond Michaels (F. R. Michaels) is actually a very nice, normal person who happens to like weird stories and scary artwork. No, seriously. He lives on Long Island with his wife, daughter, several cats, a small dog, a big dog, and whoever happens to be in his basement at the time. He writes horror and dark fantasy.

His first short story, "Mrs. Edgecliff", appeared in Alfred Hitchcock's Mystery Magazine and received an honorable mention in The Year's Finest Fantasy and Horror Sixth Annual Collection by Ellen Datlow and Terri Windling. Another short story, "Fluf", appeared in Haunts magazine and was made into a short film that was shown at the Sundance film festival. He also does artwork and illustrations that have appeared in various fan publications and small press works.

He is currently working on several short horror fiction and artwork projects and a Swords and Sorcery novel.

VICTORY OF THE DARK LORD

By Jason Andrew

"Barring that natural expression of villainy which we all have, the man looked honest enough." -- Mark Twain

Zombies lumbered past the dais, schlepping thick rolled tapestries of red and black. They moaned and groaned softly to each other, discussing their favorite reality show. Mongrel slowly followed them, scratching at the gnats that occupied his ruddy fur. The henchman growled through his fangs, and then gestured wildly with his massive ape-arms while he barked orders at them to raise the banners of the Dark Lord over the colossal marble columns.

The Dark Lord noted that they completed the work swiftly. As long as zombies were supplied with a hearty amount of zesty unicorn brains, they were eager workers and actually quite useful for repetitive tasks. Their only real downside was the lack of motivation and independent thought, which required a good deal of supervision. Still, zombies were slightly more useful than the average teenager slaving away at the burger hut and they worked for considerably less than minimum wage.

The Great Hall was starting to look presentable for the battle scene this evening. The Dark Lord nodded once towards Mongrel as an affirmation. It was important to give positive feedback to your henchman to maximize results. "Excellent! Make sure the zombies are in the correct costumes for the Battle at Desolation Pass and ensure that they understand their instructions."

Mongrel growled and repeated the orders to the zombies. "Remember! No biting! No killing! Double rations to anyone that loses a limb." The thought of double rations left the zombies licking their putrid lips and groaning with hunger. The henchman shouted the orders a third time to burn it into their decaying heads. "No biting! No killing!"

The Brain-Spiders from the Crab Cluster skittered across down the colossal marble columns and chittered before the Dark Lord. His black robes billowed as he pointed to the corner behind the throne. "You can build your nest there. Remember to only bite Kaldar once to weaken him. Twice might kill him."

The chorus of chittered acknowledgements echoed in the chamber of the Great Hall. The flock of Brain-Spiders washed over the ceiling until they started to spin their crystalline silk webs in the corner as directed. Satisfied, he took his throne, sipped his bottled water, and then started reading through the script for next month's holiday battle. "Who wrote this script?" The Dark Lord threw down the water onto the stone floor. "Calliope!"

An elfin girl with dark curly hair and almond eyes meekly curtsied before the throne. "Yes, Lord."

Twin red eyes blared from the darkness under the hood of the Dark Lord. "Did you write this hackneyed dreck?"

Calliope shivered. Her beautiful lips trembled. "Yes, Lord."

He flipped through the pages of the script with a skeletal hand until he found the exact passage and read it aloud. "And then the Christmas Spirit envelops the Dark Lord and banishes him to the darkness for another year." Must we rehash that cliché every year? "Woe unto you, Kaldar?" Who says that? The Dark Lord persona should be the stuff of nightmares and the light of hope from an over-commercialized holiday kills me? If I am not terrifying, then my defeat means nothing!"

"You did approve the vacation time for a third of our

staff. We'll need to outsource for better menace. Do I have approval to extend the budget?" Calliope asked, nervous.

"Rewrite first. Then we'll discuss the budget."

"Lord, may I ask a question?" The Dark Lord grunted his approval. It was important for henchmen to ask questions rather than make errors. "I think the problem is with the meta-story. Kaldar has defeated the Dark Lord almost twenty-seven times without being hurt. If the Dark Lord is so powerful, why not kill Kaldar and get another hero? You have potent magic. You surely know all of his secrets by now. We could have killed him in his sleep a hundred times. Why not kill him and conquer the realm?"

"Fool! Did you know that Darmin the Dark Dragon once opened a portal to Hades and almost used the unlimited legions of Hell to conquer the world?" The Dark Lord shook his head. "With a little help, Keldar drove that overgrown iguana back to the dimension of Leng! All of those years meticulously planning would have been down the drain because of a giant lizard with an itchy trigger finger. I swear that mutant moron is like a dog chasing a car! What would he have done if he had conquered the world? Take their gold and sit on it in some dank cave for a hundred years?"

"Why not take over for yourself?" the script writer asked.

"Do you know how many villains there are in the world? Hundreds. A dozen of them are comparable in power only to myself; each with burning ambition, horrendous powers and insidious plans. Why would I want the competition to come after me?"

"Don't you want to rule the realms?" she asked confused.

"*Want* to rule the realms? Don't you get it, yet? I *rule* the realms. I set the weight and measure of coins across the land. The great civilizations rise and fall upon my command and Keldar is my great instrument."

Calliope scratched her head. "I know you're the power

behind the throne, boss! Why bother to have these fights at all? Why not kill Keldar and be done with it? You'd save a fortune on the budget alone."

"The threat of Keldar keeps those villains at bay! The idea of the eternal struggle between good and evil has been burned into our souls. We believe in the myths. That faith dictates actions. When there is a true threat from one of the dangerous ones, I send our weapon into the fold armed with insider knowledge."

"Think of the fear! The money! The women!"

The Dark Lord shrugged. "I have more money than God and many are the women frustrated by Keldar's lack of interest. I do not want for the lack of company."

"Wait? Keldar is gay?" Calliope asked, shocked.

"Do you think a straight man does that many crunches for his abs? Haven't you noticed the subtle homoerotic butt slaps that he gives Gordo? Or how short those mighty fur shorts are? Seriously? I know you are a partially imaginary creature, but that should be obvious."

"He is slower than an iceberg. How effective can he be against a dragon?" Calliope asked.

"He is the perfect draft horse with a sword that rewards his ignorance with strength. That's the true benefit of blind faith. He believes in the strength of his convictions and when Gordo offers the proper hint with perfectly timed comedy, the day is won."

Calliope put her hands on her hips exacerbated. "Seriously, though, he hasn't noticed that we kidnap Gordo ever third Thursday?"

"When you are the son of a god, each day is like the next," the Dark Lord explained. "Now remember we need the red mutagenic crystals next time. Those will repel the dragon's magic and keep the capital safe."

"Yes, sir."

Mongrel returned and knelt before the throne. "Keldar is almost through the pass. He merely needs to slay the Bear

---

Sisters."

"Yes, that should prove suitably frightening for him." The Dark Lord sighed once more and then drew away his hood. His greyish skin turned to a fine ivory. His black eyes lightened to sky blue and his ears sharpened. He blinked once more, despising the Gordo face. "Don't tie me too tight this time!"

"Yes, Sire."

"Wear the cloak as commanded, and you are going to have to let him kill you this time."

Mongrel moaned. "Again?"

"We could let him push you down the cliff."

"That takes forever to clean up," Calliope complained.

"Beheading it is." He coughed, getting used to his new face. "Remember to threaten my soul. Imply that you might have taken liberties with my bottom."

Mongrel blinked, knowing how jealous Kaldar raged over his beloved sidekick. "Sire?"

"I am trying to pass a new tax and I need Keldar to feel extra sympathy with me this week to support it."

"As you wish, Lord."

"He comes."

"Places everyone!"

The golden hilt of Tyrfing glittered in the moonlight as the mighty Kaldar Hervarar slashed and bashed the limbs of the limitless legion of soulless Draugr. The burning blade felled the undead as the hero split their skulls in twain one by one. He laughed at their rotting breath howling for revenge. They clawed at his armor and bit his flesh, but nay he would not surrender this night or any other. This quest was not for glory nor honor, but for the life of his friend Gordo.

The thrice-damned Dark Lord had stolen his squire once more and dragged him to the very heart of evil; the Caverns of Darkness. How dare they block his passage through Desolation Pass? Did they not know that he wielded the mighty Tyrfing forged by the dwarves, Dvalin and Durin?

This time he would slay of the minions of evil and place the Dark Lord's head upon a pike for all in the realm to witness. He raged against the Bear Sisters and battled through the Brain-Spiders until he reached the throne room. The monstrous ape-creature known as Mongrel wore the long black robes of the Dark Lord. Gordo was in chains, whipped, at his feet. "Gordo! Do not fear, Lad. I'll save you!"

Gordo groaned and then put on his best helpless face. It killed his soul, but he yelped his lines. "Help me, Keldar! Help me!"

Jason Andrew lives in Seattle, Washington with his wife Lisa. He is an Associate member of the Science Fiction and Fantasy Writers of America, Active Member of the Horror Writer's Association, and member of the International Association of Media Tie-In Writers.

By day, he works as a mild-mannered technical writer. By night, he writes stories of the fantastic and occasionally fights crime. As a child, Jason spent his Saturdays watching the Creature Feature classics and furiously scribbling down stories. His first short story, written at age six, titled "The Wolfman Eats Perry Mason" was severely rejected. It also caused his grandmother to watch him very closely for a few years.

His short fiction has appeared in markets such as Shine: An Anthology of Optimistic SF *(Harper Collins),* Frontier Cthulhu: Ancient Horrors in the New World *(Chaosium), and* Coins of Chaos *(Edge Science Fiction and Fantasy Publishing). In 2011, his story "Moonlight in Scarlet" received an honorable mention in Ellen Datlow's List for* Best Horror of the Year.

In addition, Jason has written for a number of role-playing games such as Call of Cthulhu, Shadowrun, *and* Vampire: The Masquerade. *His most recent projects include* Hunters Hunted 2 (The Onyx Path), Anarchs Unbound (The Onyx Path), *and* Atomic Age Cthulhu: Terrifying Tales of the Mythos Menace *(Chaosium). Recently, he served as Developer for* Mind's Eye Theatre: Vampire The Masquerade *for By Night Studios.*

DELIVER US

By Patrick Evans

I know it's rude to turn your nose up at everything when Someone welcomes you into His Kingdom Eternal.

But it's just all so derivative. Halos. Harps. Everyone in sandals. Everyone in long starchy white dresses, hopping from fluffy white cloud to fluffy white cloud.

Heaven is a lot like the band camp my parents sent me to when I was twelve and played the French horn. Especially the daily activities charts posted on bulletin boards. Up here the activities are hymn singing, harp recitals, and volleyball. Jesus can spin off as many manifestations of Himself as He wants, so each volleyball court has its very own whistle-blowing Christ calling fouls in a black and white striped referee's shirt.

Jesus is a little bit obsessed with volleyball.

And just like in band camp, you know these activities are really only keeping you busy so you don't have time to think about what's going on over at the girls' camp on the other side of the lake. If, for instance, they're doing something that's got them all sweaty. Maybe taking off their shirts. There actually is a giant lake up here that divides the women's souls from the men's. It's called *Lake God Is Great*. Jesus says we're too dead and immaterial to procreate, so there's no reason any of us should be sullied by 'propinquity' to the opposite sex. Meanwhile I'm going crazy up here with nothing but guys to look at day and night. All I can think about is the other side of that lake. About a naked pillow fight between Helen of Troy and Marilyn Monroe.

The only women allowed on the men's side are the female saints. Saints get the run of the place. But the female saints are a lot like the bag ladies in parks down on Earth. They just wander around looking kind of deranged and really needing a bath. Very occasionally we catch a glimpse of the Virgin Mary, who has offices on both sides of the lake. I met her on my first day. I held out my hand and said my name was Dean and told her that even though I was Protestant I was a huge fan. For someone who's supposed to be so damned nice she looked at me like I was a leper or a pervert. She didn't shake my hand, just kept on walking, faster now, saying she had to hurry back to her loom to make shrouds for martyrs. "But it's lovely to meet you, Bean."

She called me Bean.

The Pearly Gates were closed when I first arrived last Saturday afternoon. Saint Peter was guarding them, standing in a trim, cream-colored suit at a podium, looking like a maître d'. Without so much as glancing up from his clipboard he said to me, "Seems you kicked a woman's wheelchair in 2002."

"Oh," I said, looking down. "Right." Then I looked up again. "But it wasn't a wheelchair, sir. It was one of those electric scooters for fat people. She ran over my toe. Sir."

Peter tapped his pen in an ominous slow rhythm on the clipboard.

"My baby toe," I said pitifully.

He flipped the page. "You certainly didn't abstain from pre-marital sex, did you? Dear, dear me." He flipped another page. Finally he looked up at me with eyes dull as cardboard. "Well. At least you managed to avoid the really filthy stuff. No riding crops or handcuffs. Or role-plays where an intruder sneaks into your bedroom wearing nothing but a pink balaclava. And she aims an éclair at your face like it's a gun. And even though you're begging for mercy, she goes ahead and *squeezes* that pastry at you, just squeezes it till all the custard squirts out and *covers* your face. Absolutely *covers* it." He gasped, tugged at his tie, shivered, and finally stepped aside. The gates creaked open. "Get in before I change my mind."

The gates were still closing behind me when I saw Trevor, with wide-open arms, bounding my way across the clouds.

Before Trevor and I died we were in a punk band called Rancid Balls. I was the dangerously sexy singer-guitarist with washboard abs. Our buddy Ed was the skinny pale bass player who majorly upped our cool factor because he looked like a heroin addict. (He was really just a vegan.) And Trevor was our drummer. He was also the perfect fat dim-witted sidekick for me and all my adventures, which I probably would have published in a best-selling memoir if I hadn't died.

Sure, we were three civil servants in our thirties spiking our hair on Friday nights to relive our teenage punk glory days. But man, Rancid Balls rocked hard. And a guy never had better buddies than Trevor and Ed. We even got killed together. We were all leaving a rooftop gig in an elevator when the cables snapped.

Trevor died instantly. I died after five days in a coma.

Reunited in Heaven, I gave him a great big hug. "Hey, is Ed here?"

Trevor shook his head. "Either he survived, or he's still dying…or he's you-know-where."

"In Hell? No chance," I said. "Who'd send a great guy like Ed to Hell?"

Trevor nodded. "Sure. Sure, he's gotta be alive." His face brightened. "Okay, then. You ready for some awesome news?"

"Am I!"

"You're in my cabin, dude!"

"Cabin?"

Trevor led me to a vast cloud on which floated

thousands of rows of crude wooden shacks. We walked through row after row until finally he stopped at the weather-warped plywood door to Cabin 79,856. Trevor gave the door a gentle push and it flew open, smacking against the inside wall.

Whenever I pictured Heaven, I never saw myself sharing a cabin with forty other guys. Not only do we still need sleep—we're dead—but we sleep in bunk beds. *Bunk beds*. That night I met the guy who had the bunk above mine: Tchenguiz the Appalling from Attila the Hun's Mongol hordes. Super nice guy, but he snored and hollered battle-cries in his sleep and was so damn muscular, his mattress sank right down to my groin. We're immaterial beings, which means no gravity, but somehow I still had Mongol ass bouncing on my crotch all night.

The next morning I admitted to Trevor the whole set-up had me worried.

"Aw, it's not so bad," he said sunnily, stretching on his bunk. Then he burst into tears. He wailed that he was tone deaf on the harp, kept messing up the hymn lyrics, and was too out of shape for volleyball. "And why am I still fat in Heaven? Why am I still hungry all the time?" Trevor curled up into a ball and started sucking his thumb. "I need a woman," he sobbed. "And a burger."

Jesus was everywhere, but I never saw God the Father. Nobody below the rank of Saint was allowed to gaze upon His countenance. 'Countenance' was Heaven's ten-dollar word for 'face.' Apparently the rest of us would burst into flame if we caught so much as a glimpse of God's countenance. So He sat on His Throne all day, locked inside a big fancy cathedral, and only ever got up for His afternoon stroll in the rear garden from two to four o'clock. That's when the faithful were allowed to go in and worship His Throne.

Tchenguiz warned me that because this was God's throne I always had to capitalize 'Throne.' I said there didn't appear to be any paper or pens in Heaven, so what difference did it make?

"You must to capitalize it in your head, friend Dean," said Tchenguiz. "They'll see it if you don't."

On my second day in Heaven I lined up to check out this Throne for myself, figuring it'd be two hundred feet tall with all kinds of jewels and gold carvings of bearded guys and maybe a bunch of cherubs flapping around. But it was just a boxy, human-sized arm chair made of what appeared to be granite. It looked agonizingly uncomfortable.

God's omnipotent but He can't even conjure up a throw cushion for Himself.

At yesterday's singing practice, Jesus taught some of us boys a hymn that's been lost on earth since the Crusades. It was called, 'Lo, How the Infidel's Head Doth Bounce!' Jesus kept making us stop because, "Something sounds weird."

Turned out it was Trevor mistakenly singing 'bed' instead of 'head.'

Jesus said, "Gentleman, can we just once get through all ten verses without stopping?" He wore that tight little smile of His, but you could always tell when Christ was royally pissed because His beard would start to smoke.

There's no question Trevor was a moron, so I could sympathize with Jesus' frustration. But why was He getting all snippy over a stupid little sing-along? Thirty feet to my left there was another manifestation of Jesus blowing a whistle to call foul at the *Titanic Vs. Lusitania Victims Volleyball Smackdown*. And thirty feet to my right yet another manifestation of Him was on His hands and knees, peering over a cloud to spy on a lesbian wedding in Rockport so He could weep for all humanity. And I just—

Ngh.

Okay.

He was annoying. So very Incredibly Omnipotently Annoying.

253

There. I said it. I capitalized it in my head, too.

Seven days. Seven days in Heaven and I was going nuts.

Sunday afternoons, we were allowed to make one phone call to the women's camp on the other side of the lake. There was a row of 500 phones, and if you divide 500 by every man who ever got into Heaven over the last 250,000 years, you get a sense of how long the line-ups were. The phones were those 1980s-style wall units with the long curly cords. Only these weren't fastened to a wall. They just floated in a long line.

I called my Mom to tell her I was dead.

"Oh, that's all I need," she moaned. "Has anyone mentioned The Rancid Ball?"

"Rancid *Balls*, Mom. Balls plural."

"I don't care if it's one ball, two balls, or a thousand balls. If it ever gets out that I have a son in a pornographic rock band it'll *ruin* my social standing here. You have no idea what it's like sharing a cabin with gossips like Florence Nightingale and Mootga, Skull Queen of the Mastodon Clan."

"Mom, you're in Heaven. Everyone's equal here. You don't have to worry about your social standing anymore."

She laughed bitterly. "Dean, grow up. Do you really think Josephine Bonaparte sees herself on the same social footing as some soot-covered little illiterate who got herself tossed into a volcano when she was twelve?"

"Jesus, Mom."

"Don't you mention Jesus to me! Now that you're here I have to live in terror He'll get wind of your Rancid Balls and pack you off to Hell. I'll never live it down."

"Jesus already knows about the band, Mom. He knows everything."

"I suppose after I died your father took up with Ginny Gaynes."

"Well, no. Dad came out of the closet. He married Paolo, your gardener."

"My God! Paolo's gay?"

"Mom. Look, there's something I've waited a long time to tell you. When you choked to death on that canapé it really messed me up. Bad. Because all we ever did was fight. But what got me through was the belief that one day I'd see you in Heaven and all our old tensions would be gone and we—"

"How did you make that elevator crash?"

"What?"

"You and your Rancid Balls were drunk and jumping up and down in that elevator, weren't you?"

"Get a grip, Mom! We weren't drunk. And who the hell jumps up and down in an elevator?"

Strictly speaking, we were drunk. And jumping up and down.

The more this conversation frustrated me, the farther I wandered away from the phone base. By now the cord was dangling five feet across the cloud.

Just then Saint Lucy happened by. As always, she was carrying her eyeballs on a dinner plate, which she'd done ever since the Romans popped them out during a persecution. Supposedly she had some kind of Holy Second Sight to compensate, but at least once a week she got herself tangled in a volleyball net, and at Thursday's harp recital she was strumming a barbecue grill.

Sure enough, she tripped on my phone cord and stumbled forward screaming, "Yi! Yi!"

And just then Saint Agatha, the one who carries her severed breasts on a plate, was coming in the opposite direction. Bam! Both Saints collided, fell, disappeared into the wisps on the surface of the cloud, and then jumped to their feet again. Their plates were empty.

Saint Lucy yelled in Sicilian at Agatha. Agatha yelled back at her in Sicilian. Whatever she said must have been pretty bad because Lucy screamed and threw her plate at her. Naturally, having no eyes, she missed Agatha and the plate whizzed over my shoulder, shattering against the floating base of my phone.

And that's when things started getting weird.

The line got all crackly. At first I thought it was just Mom's post-nasal drip, but then an eerily familiar man's voice appeared over the phone: "Hello? Who's this?"

"It's Dean," I said uncertainly.

"Dean? Buddy! It's Ed!"

"Ed?"

"Yeah, man! How you doin'?"

"I'm dead. I was just on the phone to my mother."

"I guess the lines musta got crossed. What are the chances, huh? So you in Heaven, man?"

"Yeah. Where are you?"

"I'm in Hell!"

"Hell? Ed! Why'd they send you to Hell?"

"Well, it's kind of a funny story," he said. "Turns out when I was alive I was, like, just the teensiest bit on the serial killer end of the spectrum. But nobody you'd miss. Mostly crack whores."

"No!"

"Yeah. But hey, don't sweat it. It's actually kind of a sweet deal down here. They torment you by rotating you through each of the Seven Deadly Sins until you can't take it any more. So you eat burgers and fries and ice cream till you puke. Then you lie around on a comfy old couch watching satellite TV till all 10,000 channels get boring. Then," he snorted, "you have sex till your dick's practically ready to drop off."

"*What*?" I nearly dropped the receiver. "Shouldn't you be getting roasted on a spit? Jabbed with hot pokers? Needles in your eyes?"

"Oh, sure, sure, you can get all that in Hell. A lot of the girls here are kinky like that."

My head was spinning. "I don't believe this."

"And Satan! He's learning to cook, right? Turns out he's this really talented chef but just never believed in himself enough to pursue it. Buddy, he makes this chocolate cake that is to die for. If you weren't already dead you'd blow your brains out just to get a mouthful of—"

"Wait wait wait. Wait! You're a *killer*?"

"Technically. In a manner of speaking. Yes."

"Okay, so *technically* you're a total fucking psycho. And you're getting *chocolate cake. And kinky sex*!"

"How dare you speak to me like that!"

It was my mother, back on the line.

"I can assure you nobody here is giving me chocolate cake," she said. "And I can especially assure you I have never had *kinky sex*!" Then, under her breath: "What have you heard? Did Mootga phone you?"

General MacArthur had been behind me in the phone line-up. Now he was one of a dozen souls helping the two Saints look for their lost eyeballs and breasts in the cloud. He was trying to order Thog, a 19,000 year-old hunter-gatherer, to go ask Jesus for a chalkboard so he could map out a proper military search detail. Like everybody else around here, MacArthur seemed to be coming unglued. "Not a flint knife!" he said. "A chalkboard! Good God, man, I'll have you in irons for this!"

It was enough already.

"Mom. I love you, and goodbye forever."

I hung up the phone and ran to my cabin.

Trevor was there, napping.

"Buddy," I said, shaking him. "Wake up. We're getting out of here."

"A burger?" he mumbled.

"Trevor! Wake up! We're getting out of here!"

"I told you. I'm not going to the stupid Hymn-A-Thon." He rolled sulkily onto his belly.

"No, you're not," I said. "You and me are going to Hell."

Monday, 2 a.m.

While I kept a lookout, Trevor was trying to pick the lock on the door to Mary's office suite where she did all her looming. He was using a tuning pin broken off his harp. "I need my lock-picks," he grumbled.

"You had lock picks?" I said.

"Yeah. I used to burgle senior citizens to pay my pot dealer."

"You robbed senior citizens to buy drugs and you still got into Heaven?"

"Hey, I was a good person with a bad habit."

The door swung open.

"Still got the magic fingers," he said happily.

We crept into the lobby. Holy Roman Emperor Charlemagne, who in Heaven was Mary's administrative assistant, had his giant golden throne set up behind a cheap particle-board desk with a telephone and a stapler. Mary's office was in back. All the lights were off but as soon as we entered, we were bathed in the loom's holy golden glow.

"You sure about this?" Trevor said.

"Absolutely. We do it on three."

Trevor nodded queasily. We each grabbed hold of the loom and hauled it over our heads. On a count of three we threw it across the room, at the door—which opened an instant before the loom hit.

It was Charlemagne. He was in his dressing gown and slippers and carrying a golden scepter with a giant ruby head. He screamed and ducked just as the loom smashed to pieces against the doorframe and fell, tangling him in a net of warp threads and twisted gold.

We hurried over to free him.

"What are you wretches doing?" he yelled.

I was scared, but I put on all the attitude I could muster. "Pretty obvious what we're doing, ain't it? Charlie-boy?"

"And just as obvious you're twelve hours late, you cur!"

"Twelve hours—what?"

"You were supposed to do the job at 2 p.m. Not in the black of night!"

"The job?"

"The job, you whoreson! Clearing out the office!"

"Clearing out the office?"

Charlemagne turned to Trevor. "Does your associate have brain-fever? He parrots my every word."

"Does my associate have brain-fever?" Trevor said.

Turns out Mary had signed a book deal just one day earlier and quit the looming business. She'd gone into seclusion for the next two centuries to write a book on self-esteem and healthy eating for teenage girls. Charlemagne sighed gloomily. "And do you know where they've transferred me—Charlemagne, *Imperator Romanorum?*"

We shook our heads.

"Eucharist Quality Control!" he roared. "I ruled an Empire—and they sit me down beside a conveyor belt looking for Eucharists that are cut too thick! The penny-pinching fish-breathed sons of—oh, oh, if only I could say it!"

Trevor put his hand Charlemagne's shoulder. "Go on, let it out. You'll feel better."

Charlemagne bopped him in the nose with his scepter. "I know that, you oaf! If I say it they'll hear me and put me in charge of volleyballs."

"Volleyballs?" I said.

Charlemagne looked at Trevor. "Was that a question, or is he still parroting me?"

"It was a question," Trevor said, rubbing his nose, and mouthing the word 'asshole.'

"They'll make me the wretch," Charlemagne said, "whose job it is to haul out all those giant mesh bags that hold the volleyballs and then distribute a ball to each court."

"Oh, yeah, that'd be rough," Trevor said. "It's what, fifteen balls in a bag? One ball per court. Twelve guys to a court...."

"I know all this," Charlemagne growled.

"So if you take every guy who ever went to Heaven and divide that number by twelve—"

"Silence!" He bopped Trevor in the nose again. Then he

slid down the doorframe to the floor and buried his face in his hands. "Ay, me," he moaned. "I need a woman."

He looked up, despondently. At Trevor.

"Or even a man of ample bosoms...."

We were at the Pearly Gates. The sun wasn't up yet. There was still time before Peter began his shift.

Unlike Mary's offices, the Pearly Gates were impregnable, sealed with a thick pearly chain and a pearly combination lock. We were trying to scale the bars, but they were too pearly-smooth to allow a good sandal purchase.

"We're gonna break our necks," Trevor fretted.

"Trevor, we're dead. Our necks are immaterial."

"I still say this is crazy."

"Buddy, think. When God threw Satan out of Heaven, where'd he land?"

"In Hell."

"There you go. We get over these gates, flutter downwards for a little while, and then it's party time."

But it wasn't party time yet. We made several more attempts. It was hopeless. The gates were just too slippery.

I got an idea. I ran to the athletics equipment storage cathedral and came back with two of the stretchy mesh bags full of volleyballs that had struck such terror in Charlemagne.

"What are those for?" Trevor said.

Sitting down on one of the bags and pulling the handles up into my crotch, I started bouncing up and down, building a momentum that let me bounce higher each time.

Trevor laughed. He sat on the other bag and did the same. "Hey, this is fun!"

Higher and higher we bounced. We were almost high enough to clear the gates when a man's voice cried out: *"Gentlemen, release your balls this instant!"*

It was Saint Peter. We both let go and belly-flopped onto the cloud, the balls in our bags spilling out everywhere.

"What are you doing?" Peter said. He was wearing a red

kimono and a luminous green night cream.

I steeled my courage. "You wanna know what we were doing?" I got to my feet. My balance was off from all the bouncing, so I swayed with what looked like a drunken belligerence. "We were trying to plummet down to Hell to — to be with Gloriously Evil Wonderful Worshipful Satan whom we worship and adore. What do you think of that, eh? Pete? Petey? Buddy-boy!"

Peter smiled. "*Buddy-boy*. Oh, I like that. It sounds so — rugged."

"That's it? That's all you have to say?"

"That, and nobody falls into Hell. You have to be sent. If you'd gotten over that gate you'd have plummeted forty feet into the sandal repair shop." He yawned. "All right. Back to bed for me. God's planning a big nuclear reactor meltdown tomorrow. If I don't get my eight hours, this here buddy-boy is liable to fly into a nasty rage and just toss all the newcomers down to Hell."

As Peter sauntered off, Trevor looked at me. He was shaking with rage and terror.

"You're gonna get us put on volleyball duty!"

We went back to our cabin to get some rest, but I couldn't sleep.

If the only way to get to Hell was by getting sent there, we would have to do something unspeakably atrocious to deserve it. Something so bad that God would have no choice but to send us to Hell if He wanted to save countenance.

I wondered if there might be something in this reactor meltdown He was planning.

I poked Tchenguiz's ass through his mattress. "Yo. Tchenguiz. You awake?"

"I am now, friend Dean!" he said, turning onto his side. His giant smiling face appeared over the edge of his bunk.

Tchenguiz loved to gossip, and he was also in charge of refreshments for God's Disaster Planning Committee.

"I hear God's planning some big nuclear meltdown."

"Aye! Nuclear refractor! Big ka-boom! Many, many dead!"

"So how does that work, exactly?"

"Ka-boom," Tchenguiz said simply.

"Yeah. But how does God make ka-boom? Does He just kind of will it? Or wave a wand or something?"

"No, friend Dean. God fashions a mighty bolt of Heavenly Fire."

"And He throws it at the reactor?"

"No, God is far too merciful. He makes one of His Saints throw the bolt through the hole."

There was something I could use here. I could feel it.

"What hole?"

"The magical hole that opens onto anywhere in the world God chooses, friend Dean."

"And where is this hole?"

"Why, in the floor, friend Dean."

"What floor? Where?"

"In the Hole Room, friend Dean."

"And where's the Hole Room?"

"Down the hall, friend Dean."

"*Down what hall, Tchenguiz?*"

"The hall behind God's Throne, friend Dean."

Finally.

"And so what time is ka-boom?"

"3 p.m. today, friend Dean. I serve refreshments at 3:10."

And there it was, like a bolt of Heavenly Fire in my head—a plan that would damn me and Trevor like nobody had been damned before.

2 p.m. Trevor was lagging behind me on the steps of God's cathedral.

"They're gonna mess us up so bad for this," he muttered.

"Just chill, for God's sake," I snapped. "We gotta look like we have complete authority here."

Trevor looked at me with frightened puppy eyes. He followed me inside where the souls of men were queued up by the hundreds in a maze of rope barriers leading to the Throne. It looked like a bank at lunchtime.

"Coming through! Coming through!" I shouted, pushing aside the crowd. I strode brazenly up the steps of the dais where the Throne sat. "Sorry folks. Viewing's cancelled. God put in a work order re. a wobbly Throne leg. We need space to maneuver so that means everybody out. Let's go...."

No one dared question a Holy Work Order. The crowd shuffled out, most of the souls grumbling because Throne Worshipping once a week was considered a legitimate excuse for missing volleyball practice.

"Damn, that was easy!" I said laughing as I moved to the back of the Throne. Trevor stayed on the red carpet in front of the dais.

"Will you get up here already?"

He slowly climbed the steps. I gave the Throne a test push from the rear. The granite was back-breaking. I was definitely going to need Trevor's bulk, and was grateful his soul was as super-sized as his body had been.

Trevor reached out to touch the Throne and pulled back, shaking. "So there's slutty girls in Hell, right?"

"For the billionth time, yes!"

He nodded slowly, squatted, closed his eyes tight, and tilted the Throne onto its rear legs. With me pushing and Trevor pulling, we managed to bump the Throne down the stairs and onto the red carpet. Then the job got easier, but not much. We used the carpet to drag the Throne through the door behind the dais and into a lavish corridor with wood paneling and gold-leaf wallpaper. We came to a door with a sign that read Hole Room and pushed it open.

The room was empty except for a stone fireplace and a gory painting of a crucified Jesus hanging over the mantle. In the center of the room, cut into a beautiful Persian rug, was a big round hole.

The hole was the perfect size.

"This is too easy. It's all too easy," Trevor fretted as we dragged the Throne into the Hole Room. "It's a trap. God knows what we're doing. God knows everything."

"If God knew everything, the door on our cabin wouldn't slam against the wall every time some asshole came in."

We dragged the Throne right up to the edge of the hole.

All it needed now was a push.

We took a moment to kneel and look through the hole. Way down below was the reactor site. A large concrete containment building sat beside a steam-belching cooling tower, and both were nestled among the green parks and big backyards of some idyllic, bike-riding suburban community.

I stood up again. "Okay."

"Wait—Dean, wait," Trevor said, standing up too.

"Oh, *what?*"

"Think about it, man. We drop the Throne on a nuclear reactor—think of all the people we'll kill."

"They're gonna die anyway."

"But what if more people die from the falling Throne than from the God-bolt? I mean, which has more juice—one little bolt of Heavenly fire, or the Throne of God?" His chest started heaving. "We're murderers, man!"

"Trevor, why do I *always* have to spell everything out for you?" And just as I opened my mouth to start spelling I realized he was right. He was right! I wanted to go to Hell because I was horny and lazy. I was a civil-servant rock-star, not a mass murderer.

I dropped to my knees. "Oh, buddy. What's happened to me, man?"

Trevor dropped to his knees beside me and we both started to cry. Hard.

"This place," I sobbed. "This place has made me crazy!"

"There's probably innocent little kittens down there," Trevor wailed.

———

"They don't have kittens at nuclear reactors, you fuckwit."

As we blubbered, I spotted something leaning against the fireplace. It was a long, thin piece of wood carved in the shape of a lightning bolt. I went over and picked it up. It was painted gold and weighed about as much as a hockey stick.

"Trevor," I said. "I think this is the bolt of Heavenly fire."

Trevor shook his head. "That's a fire poker."

"It's wood, you amoeba."

A new idea struck me.

"Okay," I said. "Okay, we're back on the fast track to Hell. We're gonna break this thing."

"Break the God-bolt?"

"Yeah. It's just wood! I could totally snap this." My heart was racing with excitement. "Think about it, man! We can screw up this whole nuclear massacre of God's, save some lives, and piss Him off enough to get sent to Hell. How's that sound?"

Trevor wiped his eyes with his meaty hands. "Bad," he said.

"You got a better idea? You been practicing for tomorrow's Heavenly Harp Hoedown?"

Trevor winced, then nodded. "Okay. Do it."

I braced the bolt against my knee and pulled both ends back.

It snapped.

A moment of perfect stillness and silence followed. And then a series of strobing orange, silver and blue lights filled the room. Appearing out of nowhere, dozens of translucent cherubs began flying around, all of them screeching in agony. Wind crashed in from all directions and great tremors shook the cathedral floor, throwing both of us off our feet.

The Throne was moving. The tremors in the floor were vibrating it over the edge of the hole.

"The chair!" Trevor screamed.

We both dived for it, but we were too late. We held onto the rim of the hole while the Divine hurricane raged around us—and watched as the Throne of God plummeted Earthward, smaller and smaller on its missile course to the reactor.

"Oh, Trevor. Trevor," I cried. "I *begged* you not to break that stick!"

We sat cross-legged on a cloud, at Saint Peter's feet. His arms were crossed.

"One of the technicians was trying to rescue a litter of kittens from the roof of the reactor when the Throne landed," he said. "You missed the technician, but the kittens are just a furry red smear now. Still what's a few kittens, hm?" He spread his arms. "Why, you're heroes! This mysterious 'chair-shaped meteorite' landed directly inside the reactor and is expected to burn for two million years. Unlimited power. No more fossil fuels. No more global warming. Bravo, boys!"

I shrugged with all the insolence I could muster. Trevor stared guiltily into his lap.

"But here's the hitch," Peter hissed. "None of this was God's plan! You cannot *begin* to conceive of His wrath right now. He refuses to come out of His room. He won't even open the door for a tray."

I shrugged again.

"You guys wanted to go to Hell?" Peter thrust his index finger into the air. "You got it!"

Suddenly the cloud we were sitting on gave way. We were falling. Falling fast—through clouds, and then into clear blue sky. We saw the earth racing to meet us, a vast expanse of grassy rolling plains. And as we braced ourselves to splatter all over the ground, we passed through that too. Now we were falling through solid rock, through complete darkness. Down and down until the black of the earth's crust began to warm with a fiery glow.

Finally we landed with a soft bump in a vast

subterranean cavern. We could see clearly now because the cave walls glowed like red-hot coals.

A giant rust-encrusted iron gate loomed above us, and there it was—the sign!

Abandon hope all ye who enter here.

"You did it man," Trevor whispered in awe. "You did it."

"We did it, buddy," I said. Although for the record, it was all me.

I pushed open the gate. There was a long dark tunnel on the other side. Make no mistake, I was glad to be here, but that tunnel was pretty ominous. As we walked the fiery glow behind us gradually faded until we were groping in the dark with outstretched arms.

Finally we reached the tunnel's end. Blindly feeling around the cave wall, my fingers discovered the outline of a door. It was a simple wooden door with a rattly old doorknob.

I put my hand on the knob. "Ready to get this party started?" I said to Trevor, suppressing the tremor in my voice.

Trevor was so nervous he was barely audible. "Do it," he whispered.

I turned the knob and pushed open the door.

We were blinded by a great light.

It took a moment for my vision to recover but when it did my stomach seemed to fold in on itself. This light—it was sunshine.

We stepped through the door and onto a cloud. We were in the sky again!

Saint Peter was there, in front of the Pearly Gates, smiling brilliantly.

"Ta-daa!"

I gasped, tried to speak, and choked.

"Yes, God loves a good twist ending," Peter said. "This is His Big Surprise Revelation, the secret that's sealed on the lips of every soul up here who knows it." He lowered his voice for dramatic effect. "*Heaven's made for sinners.*"

I was able, at least, to stammer now.

"But—but wait—wait—Ed—Ed said—"

"Yes, yes, your friend Edward told you on the phone that he was in Hell and Hell was one big wonderful naughty party with women in balaclavas smearing custard on everyone."

"Well, no. There was no custard. Man, what is it with you and custard?"

"It was all a con," Peter said proudly. "Edward is still on Earth, still very much alive and expected to make a full recovery—though it is true he's a serial killer. Otherwise, this entire Hell business was a set-up designed to torment you sinners with hope. Lovely hopeless hope! We planned it down to the smallest detail. Except the bit with the Throne. Oh, brother. The last time God was this angry, He made all of Heaven spend an entire summer listening to Joan of Arc's Christmas Album on repeat."

"So if sinners go to Heaven," Trevor said dazedly, "where do all the innocent folks go?"

"Oh, they come here too. Nobody likes a goody two-shoes."

Trevor glared hatefully at me.

Screw him. He robbed senior citizens to buy weed.

"Why am I such a sinner?" I yelled. "What'd I ever do that was so goddamn bad?"

"Like you have to ask!" Saint Peter threw his head back indignantly. "*Rancid Balls*? Lord, love us!"

Behind the Pearly Gates we could hear several thousand manifestations of Christ blowing their referee's whistles in unison to mark the end of volleyball practice.

"You two. Volleyball duty. Chop chop," Peter said, snapping his fingers. The Pearly Gates opened. Peter stood aside for us to enter. "Go grab your *ball sacks*, buddy-boys!" He laughed uproariously. "Oh, I do love a bit of innuendo."

Patrick Evans used to write dreary, arty, slice-of-life stories in which nothing ever happened. He finally embraced his innate weirdness, turned to speculative fiction, and has published works in the anthologies Age of Certainty *and* Fresh Blood. *Having lived his entire life in Toronto, Canada, he recently moved to Brighton, UK, to celebrate his mid-life crisis on a British beach.*